Someone was looking at the place next door

Ben swore under his breath. The house had been empty for a long time, and he'd hoped things would stay that way.

A woman was coming out of the house. Sunlight caught fiery sparks in her hair. Behind her—good God!—were two kids. Now she was shaking the real estate guy's hand—not a good sign. And the kids were trotting down the lane toward Ben.

Then the woman was hurrying after the two kids, almost breaking into a run. Ben pulled his Stetson lower over his forehead and waited. The kids' father, if there was one, was nowhere to be seen.

The boy was skinny and freckled, hair a dark auburn. The little girl was a flat-out redhead, like her mother.

Mom arrived just then, hand outstretched. "Hi, I'm Judith Kane. We're going to be neighbors."

Reluctantly he took her hand, which proved to be small, slender, soft. She wasn't a country woman. "Ben McKinsey."

Judith Kane might be a beautiful woman, but she also had children. And he couldn't handle children. Why did she have to choose *this* house? Why not one of the half dozen rental places in town? Was God paying him back for some sin?

Some sin, he thought ironically. If God was getting him, he knew what for.

ABOUT THE AUTHOR

Janice Kay Johnson is the highly acclaimed author of thirty-four published or upcoming books. She has written for adults, children and young adults—and one of her Superromance novels, *Home Again,* was a RITA Award finalist. When not researching or writing her books, Janice quilts, grows antique roses, chauffeurs her two daughters to soccer and play rehearsals, takes care of her dogs and cats (too many to itemize!) and volunteers at a no-kill cat shelter.

Also available this month is Janice's story "Mother Knows Best" in the anthology *For My Daughter.* And in 1999 watch for an exciting Superromance trilogy from this outstanding author.

Books by Janice Kay Johnson

HARLEQUIN SUPERROMANCE

Don't miss any of our special offers. Write to us at the following address for information on our newest releases.

Harlequin Reader Service
U.S.: 3010 Walden Ave., P.O. Box 1325, Buffalo, NY 14269
Canadian: P.O. Box 609, Fort Erie, Ont. L2A 5X3

THE FAMILY NEXT DOOR
Janice Kay Johnson

Harlequin Books

TORONTO · NEW YORK · LONDON
AMSTERDAM · PARIS · SYDNEY · HAMBURG
STOCKHOLM · ATHENS · TOKYO · MILAN
MADRID · WARSAW · BUDAPEST · AUCKLAND

ISBN 0-373-70789-4

THE FAMILY NEXT DOOR

THE FAMILY
NEXT DOOR

PROLOGUE

JUDITH KANE STARED at the television screen. Amid a wash of golden light and romantic music, a mother embraced her fair-haired daughter. Credits rolled down the increasingly misty picture.

With the suddenness of a blow, anguish gripped Judith, cramping her stomach, stealing her breath, momentarily paralyzing her. Oh, God, would it never get any easier?

She swallowed. Movement returned and she used the remote control to turn off the television set.

"Hey, I was watching!" her nine-year-old son complained.

"Tough," Judith said, her tone astonishingly normal, unsympathetic, motherly. He couldn't know how she suffered. At least she had him; she didn't want him ever to believe that he wasn't enough. "Time for you to do your homework."

Zach turned beseeching brown eyes on her. "All I have is spelling. Can't I do it tonight?"

"Nope," she said firmly. "Tonight we may decide we want to play a game or read for longer than usual. But we won't be able to if you have to do homework."

"Oh, okay," he agreed, disgruntled. When he

thought she wasn't looking, he scrunched his freckled nose at her.

She pretended not to see. As he got out his notebook at the kitchen table and she opened the dishwasher to unload it, Judith ran an internal check. The anguish had subsided, ebbing like a tide, leaving only a salty trace of its presence.

Would the time ever come when she could think of Sophie without that heavy, heart-wrenching pain? When she might go for days without a sudden reminder catching her unaware with the force of a blow and all but immobilizing her?

Did she *want* the image of Sophie's sweet face to leave her, even for a few minutes? The idea was terrifying. Nothing, she thought fiercely, would ever make her forget her small daughter.

Drawing a deep breath, she glanced toward Zach, to see that he was watching her anxiously. Judith managed to produce a reassuring smile for his benefit. After a moment, seeming satisfied, he bent his head over his work and began laboriously copying spelling words.

The dishwasher was empty; Judith scanned the kitchen, but counters, sink and floor were spotless. She hadn't always been such a compulsive housekeeper. Now she was constantly searching for something—anything—to keep her mind occupied.

When the telephone rang, her heart lurched. After two years, she still reacted the same every time. As if *this* call were the one, as if a voice would say, "Mrs. Kane, we have Sophie right here."

"Hello?" she said.

"Mrs. Kane?"

She knew the caller instantly, and her pulse leaped. Hope drained her strength and she sagged against the tiled edge of the counter. "Yes?" she said, with both eagerness and dread.

"This is Detective Edgekoski." The police officer didn't immediately go on.

In his hesitation she read bad news, the worst, and she stood frozen with her back to her son, her fingers squeezing the hard plastic of the phone until it creaked. She couldn't say a word. *Please, God,* she prayed, as she had prayed countless times these last two years. Always fruitlessly. But this time her prayer was different.... *Not dead. Please. Let her be alive. Healthy. Still my Sophie.*

"Mrs. Kane—" the policeman's voice was gentle "—we've found your daughter and your ex-husband."

A sobbing breath escaped her. "Is she...?"

"She's fine. She's in a receiving home waiting for you to come and get her. They were in Kansas City, Missouri. A mother at your daughter's preschool recognized Sophie from a photograph on the back of a local mailer. She called the police."

Judith couldn't think, could only feel. "Oh, thank God! I need to get a flight." Her mind jumped. "She's really waiting for me? Is she...is she anxious to come home?"

"I'm sorry, Mrs. Kane," he replied patiently, "they didn't say. She's undoubtedly scared. Why don't you let me know when you have a flight reservation, and then I'll alert the Kansas City police that you're coming."

"Yes. Fine." She scribbled his phone number down, as if she hadn't called him weekly for years, begging, pleading, nagging, bullying. A moment later, she hung up the receiver and turned to her son.

He was staring at her. "You're crying."

She touched her wet cheek in vague surprise. "They've found Sophie."

Zach's mouth worked, but he said nothing for the longest time. At last, he swallowed. "And...and Dad, too?"

"Yes." *May he burn in hell.* "Yes, the police found both of them."

"Are you sad?" he whispered, eyes saucer wide.

"No." Through her tears, a smile trembled, widened, blazed with joy and trepidation. "No, I'm gloriously happy!" She laughed and held out her arms. "Let me hug you. Then we have to get ready to go pick up your sister."

CHAPTER ONE

JUDITH PARKED at the curb behind the real estate agent's car and got out. The interior of her van was stifling but shadowy; now the direct heat of the sun struck her with a physical shock.

Zach had wanted to look at all the other houses, but the hundred-degree temperature had apparently ener vated him, too, because this time he didn't say anything or make any move to follow her. In her booster seat in back, Sophie sat sucking her thumb, staring vacantly ahead. She was five years old and due to start kindergarten this fall, but either she was immature or she had regressed because of the trauma of losing her father. Was she ready for school? The psychologist she'd seen since her return thought she was, that kindergarten would be good for her. Judith wasn't so sure. Another worry to add to her list. She suppressed a sigh.

Lyle Strother, cool from his late-model air-conditioned Ford, stepped out and hoisted his pants. His belly immediately settled back over the waistband.

"Nice four-bedroom ranch," the real estate agent said. "Two and a half baths—something you'll appreciate with the kids there. Walking distance to the elementary school."

She turned to face the house. The lawn was patched with brown; the leaves on twin apple trees hung limp. The house itself was well cared for, clapboards painted white, black shutters, a big picture window in front.

"Air-conditioned," he added.

Longing seized her. Rylan *was* behind bars, after all, at least for the moment. Surely they were safe here, in such a small town. This was a good neighborhood. Zach would like being able to walk to school, to the town swimming pool, maybe to friends' houses eventually. She could walk to work. The house was empty, the agent had said; they could move right in.

And it was air-conditioned.

But what if a judge let Rylan go? She'd been warned he would probably be released on bail. And even after he came to trial... She'd heard so many horror stories about noncustodial fathers who'd stolen their children and barely been slapped on the wrist after they were caught. A policewoman in Kansas City had privately told her that when Sophie was torn from him, Judith's ex-husband had sworn he'd be back for her. "Tell that to your mother, the bitch!" he'd bellowed as they shoved him into a police car.

"I don't know," she said. "I'm used to living on acreage." That was a flat lie—she'd spent her entire life in Boston and never even had a real yard, much less a pasture. "Do you have anything farther out of town?"

Lyle looked at her as if she were crazy. Maybe he was right. "A single woman with kids, you're better off in town."

She gritted her teeth but figured she didn't dare

alienate him. Besides, hadn't she chosen a small community like this precisely because she knew people would stick their noses into each other's business? Now was no time to start resenting it!

When she said nothing, he hooked his thumbs in his belt and hoisted again, just as uselessly. Why did he bother? Judith wondered.

Sounding exasperated, he offered, "Now, I do have some places for sale...."

She wouldn't buy until she knew they were going to stay. Until she knew they were safe, that this could be home.

"I need to rent at first."

"You don't even want to look inside?" He jerked his head toward the house.

"Maybe I'll come back to this one."

He gave a noisy sigh. "I do know of a little place that's available out of town. Nothing near as nice as this. No air-conditioning. I don't even know if it has a dishwasher."

Judith pulled her shirt away from her sticky skin. "It's almost September. Surely it won't stay this hot much longer."

Lyle shrugged. "Don't know how good the furnace is, either."

Wonderful. Judith knew winters were cold here in Mad River, just on the east side of the Cascade Mountains in Washington State. Before she'd accepted the job here, teaching a fifth-grade class, she had gone to the library and read everything she could find about it, including temperature extremes.

She felt the sweat trickling down her back. Those

temperature readings had been pretty abstract when she was sitting in the cool, dimly lit Boston Public Library.

"May I see this other place?" she asked, struggling to stay pleasant. "If it doesn't suit, we can come back here."

The agent gave his balding head a disgusted shake. "Your decision. Just stick right behind me."

As if there were any traffic to make trailing him a challenge.

The town was so small they reached its outskirts in minutes. Judith didn't know whether they were still in the city limits or not when he turned off the paved road onto a dirt one. In his wake, a cloud of dust enveloped her car.

Zach roused from his trance. "Where are we going?"

"To look at another house."

"But nobody lives out here."

He was right, she thought uneasily. Woods that looked awfully dry to her New England eye clambered up a rocky ridge to one side of the lane; on the other, a bare trickle in an otherwise parched streambed meandered through the scant grass of a pasture bordered by a split-rail fence.

Living in town had its dangers, but she didn't want to be too isolated, either. There had to be neighbors nearby, somebody who would notice a stranger lurking around or trying to pull one of her children into a car.

The reluctant thought came: Sophie wouldn't need pulling; she'd go willingly. That was part of what terrified Judith. Rylan could take her back so easily.

"Well, if we don't like it..." she began.

"Horses."

At the one single word, Judith jerked her head up. "What?"

Glancing in the rearview mirror, she saw that Sophie had momentarily taken her thumb from her mouth and was—miracle of miracles—focusing on something outside the car. "Horses," she said again, almost eagerly.

It was true. A palomino and a brown horse stood motionless, heads hanging, in the meager shade of a dry pine tree.

"That's right," Judith said in that fake cheery voice she hated. "Maybe they'll be our neighbors."

Predictably, Zach piped up, "Can *we* have a horse?"

"Well, probably not for now."

"Why not?"

The car jolted into a rut and Judith's head struck the roof. She slowed still further and blinked grit from her eyes. "I wouldn't know how to take care of one," she admitted. And what if they had to move again? Would they haul a horse trailer with them? But she didn't want to tell the children that living here might not be permanent.

What good would it do to flee, anyway? her logical side demanded. It wasn't as if she were in hiding here; she'd taken a job under her own name, and her father and mother and Rylan's parents knew where she and the children were. A private investigator could find them with no trouble. To go into hiding, she would have to steal the children from their grandparents as

Rylan had with Sophie, and she couldn't do that to either of them. And how would she make a living if she couldn't use her teaching certificate? Waitressing wouldn't support the three of them very well.

But if Rylan came here, he'd stand out. She was counting on getting to know people and letting their neighborly eyes help keep her children safe.

Maybe he wouldn't even try, once he found she'd sold her town house and they had vanished. She was convinced he'd taken Sophie because he knew it was the best way to hurt her, Judith, not because he really wanted to be a single parent. He hadn't been such a good father back when she'd asked him to spend more time with their children.

The blue Ford ahead passed a two-story white farm-house on the right, with a red barn behind it. Some-body did live here. They wouldn't be entirely alone. The lane narrowed further, and a few hundred yards beyond, it ended in the yard of a ramshackle house not old enough to have character but too old for air-conditioning.

It wasn't as bad as she'd imagined, Judith thought optimistically. Maybe it would do. It felt…safe here, so far off the main road. And the only way in and out required going by the other house first.

She put the van in park and turned off the engine. In the silence, she said, "You guys want to get out and look at this one?"

She braced herself for sullenness from Zach. To her surprise, he said, "Yeah, okay," and unbuckled his seat belt.

Cheeks flushed, Sophie stuck out her lower lip. "Can I go look at the horses?"

Feeling helpless, Judith said in that same false tone, "I'm afraid not, kiddo. What if they bite or kick or something? But if we rent this house, maybe their owner will let you pet them some time."

The five-year-old's mouth trembled. "I want to pet them now."

Oh, God. To make Sophie happy, wasn't it worth traipsing over to that split-rail fence to have a look at those poor hot horses, which were unlikely in this heat to do more than twitch an ear?

"Well...maybe after we've looked at the house," she said weakly.

Sophie gave her a measuring stare from gray eyes rather like Judith's own. "Okay," she said, and didn't protest when Judith climbed into the back and unfastened her seat belt.

Lyle was running a finger over the dusty hood of his formerly shiny blue car. The toothy smile that had greeted her at each of the previous houses was markedly absent. His gaze went past her to the drab, single-story house. "Not much to look at."

Beige paint was starting to peel, and the varying colors of roof shingles showed where patching had been done. The windows looked blank, covered only by cheap blinds, but the frames appeared solid and were made of wood.

"Well...it could use some work."

"Hasn't been anyone in it for eight months or so."

Which undoubtedly meant that gritty dirt had penetrated cupboards and closets, and spiderwebs would adorn corners. Well, she could clean, and school didn't start for two weeks.

"Is it owned by the people who live back in that farmhouse?" she asked, starting up the steps. The house did have an old-fashioned porch, at least, which she liked. And two big old lilac bushes, one on either side of the steps.

"Nah." Lyle was searching his heavy ring of keys for the right one. "Police chief lives there. Ben McKinsey. Not real sociable. He'd probably let this place fall to ruin if it was his."

"The police chief?" Judith turned to gaze consideringly back at the farmhouse. Sophie and Zach, sitting on the porch steps, did the same.

"Folks who own this place live over t'other side of the mountains. Issaquah. Bought this figuring they could keep it rented." His tone suggested they were fools. "There was talk about a ski area up here. Came to nothing."

She didn't care about ski areas or her future landlord, only her new neighbor. A policeman. How lucky could they get?

"Ah." The real estate agent had found the right key and inserted it into the lock.

The door gave way, and Judith, holding her breath, stepped across the threshold. Unless the interior was really, really terrible, this would be their new home.

The moment she saw the large living room and the neat brick fireplace, she let out a sigh of relief. Yes!

Zach was already thundering down the hall toward the bedrooms. Sophie, as usual, hung back. When Judith held out a hand, she shrank away. Though Judith knew she should be used to it, she still hurt every time her daughter rejected her.

She looked up to meet the agent's eyes. She'd seen him watching her with Sophie before, and by now puzzlement bordered closely on suspicion.

"She's tired," Judith said, forcing a smile. "We drove across the country in just five days, you know."

Only after a pointed pause did he nod and say expressionlessly, "Hadn't you better take a look at the kitchen?"

She bit her lip. "Yes. Of course."

Was there hardwood under the worn brown carpet? Judith was already making plans, mentally scrubbing the narrow sash windows until they shone, putting up new blinds, setting out her furniture once it arrived. If the rent was as low as she hoped, she wouldn't have to dip into the money she would use to buy a house once they were permanently settled.

Maybe here in Mad River; she didn't know. The name of the town reflected its oddity, or maybe her state of mind. This was an alien land, nothing like their old home, but for now it felt safe. Shielding her children from their father was all that counted.

THE POLICE RADIO crackled. Frowning, Ben McKinsey ignored it. Ahead of him, a kid who couldn't have been more than five or six years old was walking alongside the highway. The dirt shoulder wasn't very wide, and he flinched when a car whizzed by. Ben put on his flashers, slowed his squad car and eased to a stop behind him.

The boy gave a frightened look over his shoulder

but stopped walking when he saw the police officer get out of the car.

Ben didn't much like kids, but he'd look damned silly calling in backup to deal with this one. He headed toward the boy, hearing how forced his bantering tone sounded. "Hi, young man. You going somewhere special?"

Well, hell. A kid wouldn't recognize insincerity.

A short haircut didn't keep a cowlick from standing straight up on the crown of the boy's head. Skinny legs stuck out of blue soccer shorts. Dirty toes poked out of leather sandals.

Ben wondered if he had underestimated the kid. His eyes narrowed and he thought long and hard about whether he should answer any questions, but finally he said with dignity, "My mom's waiting for me. She works at the AM-PM."

The convenience store-gas station was another half mile away and across a busy intersecting road. What in tarnation was the kid doing out here alone?

Frowning, Ben asked, "Don't you have a baby-sitter who could have driven you or at least walked with you?"

"Lisa and her boyfriend were smooching." The boy made a horrible face. "I *told* her I wanted my mom, but she didn't listen. So I just left."

"Ah." If his mom didn't take care of the baby-sitter, Ben would. Hoping to be persuasive, he went with the favorite-uncle tone again. "Well, you just hop on in my car, and I'll take you to find your mom."

A semi thundered by, and the kid almost stumbled into the ditch. But still he hesitated, scuffing the dirt with one foot. "I'm not supposed to get in cars unless it's Mom's friend Janet or maybe my uncle John. I don't know you."

Why "maybe" Uncle John? Ben wondered. Okay, forget uncles, favorite or otherwise. "Has your mom ever talked to you about what to do if you get in trouble or you're lost? Who you should go to for help?"

His forehead puckered. "Yes. She said I should look for a policeman." His face cleared. "That's what you are, isn't it?"

"That's me." Ben raised an eyebrow. "I'd say you're in trouble right now. A highway is no place for a boy your age to be walking."

A pickup pulling a horse trailer passed next, the trailer swaying. The boy darted a scared look after it, then directed one at Ben. The frying pan and the fire. Smart kid.

"Okay," he finally decided. When Ben held open the passenger-side door, he scrambled in, looking curiously miniature inside the police car.

Once behind the wheel, Ben said, "I'm Chief McKinsey. What's your name?"

"I'm a muk, too."

In the act of pulling out onto the highway, he shot the kid a glance. "A muk?"

"My name," the little boy said precisely, "is Jonathan McDaniel. You know. *Mc.*"

Ben might not like kids, but he had to smile. "Gotcha."

He parked out front of the store, and he and Jonathan went in. Ben prayed that Mom really did work here and this was her shift. He didn't know what in hell he'd do with this kid if he couldn't find his mother. He sure wasn't going to leave him with the baby-sitter, but taking him to a receiving home seemed a little extreme. He was decently dressed and looked healthy enough. Dirty, but Ben seemed to remember that boys his age were always dirty.

The heavy gray-haired woman behind the cash register couldn't be the kid's mother. Jonathan glanced dismissively at her and rotated in place, scanning the store.

"Mommy!" he cried suddenly, and a young woman coming out of a back room hurried toward them.

"Jon! What are you doing here?" Crouching, she hugged her son protectively and looked up at Ben. "Is...is something wrong?"

He explained the circumstances; she chewed the kid out, but her eyes glittered dangerously when he told her about the baby-sitter being too busy smooching to notice Jonathan leaving.

"It'll have to be back to the day-care center, then," she said helplessly. "They charge so much, but I have to know Jon is safe."

The kid didn't look distressed by his mother's exasperation. Jonathan was bound to get in trouble again down the road, Ben suspected, but thank God he wasn't his problem anymore. With a tip of his hat, Ben uttered a terse goodbye and got back in his squad car. He fastidiously brushed dirt from the passenger seat where Jonathan's small rump had rested. Personally, he'd rather have a drunk in his car than a kid.

Back at the station, he dealt with some paperwork. His phone stayed silent, and according to the dispatcher, all was quiet in the little town of Mad River. Hell, the only crime he could imagine anyone committing in this heat was breaking into the grocery store freezer.

Ben wasn't in a half-bad mood when he turned onto his own road. He'd change to shorts, switch on the fans, indulge in a cold beer, maybe watch the Mariners game on TV.

Sherlock and Travis stood in the shade, using their tails to whisk away the flies. They didn't even lift their heads at the sound of his car, although normally they'd canter on over to the barn to demand alfalfa or oats. He'd wait until it cooled down some to feed them.

Movement caught Ben's eye and he swore under his breath. Someone was looking at the Weller place. He recognized Lyle Strother's blue Ford Taurus.

The last renter had been a reclusive fellow who hadn't bothered Ben much. He'd turned out to be a damned nuisance, though, when someone at the public utility noticed his excessive—and illicit—use of power. Hundreds of thousands of dollars' worth of marijuana plants had been reaching maturity in the bedrooms and living room. The guy had balls to set up business next door to a cop. Ben had kept to himself his regret at losing such an inoffensive neighbor.

The house wasn't exactly a desirable property, and lately real estate had been depressed around here. Nobody had even looked at the place for a long time. He'd hoped things would stay that way.

A woman was coming out of the house. Sunlight caught fiery sparks in her hair. Behind her—good God!—were two kids. They'd probably all climb in that red van and go back to town, find a rental near the school. But no, she was shaking Lyle's hand—not a good sign. And the kids were trotting down the lane toward Ben.

He debated whether or not to hide in the house, but he never had been a coward. He might as well find out the worst.

Now the woman was hurrying after the two kids, almost breaking into a run. They were probably hellions, and she didn't want them making a bad impression on him. Ben pulled his Stetson lower over his forehead and waited, arms crossed, focusing more on the kids than the mother. The father, if there was one, was nowhere to be seen.

The boy was skinny and freckled, hair a dark auburn. The little girl was a flat-out redhead, like her mother.

It was the boy who called, "Are those horses yours?"

"They're mine."

He stopped in front of Ben. "Can we pet 'em?" he asked eagerly. His sister, wearing shortalls and sandals, hid behind her brother.

"No." He didn't smile or make any apologies. "They're not children's ponies. You might get hurt."

"But we could just give 'em a carrot or something," the boy said mulishly.

His mother arrived, hand outstretched. "Hi, we've just rented the house next door. We'll be neighbors. I'm Judith Kane."

At the sight of her close up, he had the strangest reaction. Just a zap, as if he'd scuffed his feet on carpet and then touched something metal. Before he could analyze it further, her words penetrated. He thought an obscenity he didn't utter.

Reluctantly he took her hand, which proved to be small, slender, soft. She wasn't a countrywoman. "Ben McKinsey."

"My children seem to be enchanted with your horses." She said it apologetically, but with underlying teasing, as if she assumed he'd humor them just because they were children.

"I was just telling them to stay out of the pasture." He let go of her hand and flexed his fingers. "They might get kicked."

"Oh." She hesitated, as though expecting him to say more, maybe soften his refusal. When he didn't, her small chin went up a notch. "Certainly," she said crisply. "I'll make sure they don't go near them. Sophie, honey…" She reached out a hand, but the little girl edged away, keeping the brother between her and her mother.

"I want to pet the horsies."

"I'm sorry, sweetie…" Judith Kane sounded remarkably ineffectual. "This man will be our neighbor, but he says the horses aren't safe for you."

The kid howled, "But you *said* we could pet them!"

"I said maybe." Mom circled the boy to reach her daughter, grimly determined despite the half affronted, half apologetic glances she darted at Ben. "We have to go back to town now."

"I don't wanna!"

God almighty. Was he going to have to listen to

them screaming from here on out? Why did they have to choose this house? Why not one of the half-dozen places for rent in town? Was God paying him back for some sin?

Some sin, he thought ironically. If God was getting him, he knew what for.

Judith Kane chased the kid around and finally scooped her up. She carried her off kicking and screaming as if her toenails were being pulled out. Spoiled little brat.

Ben transferred his gaze to the boy, who hadn't moved.

"Hadn't you better go? You don't want your mom to leave you behind."

Something flickered in those dark eyes. "My mom wouldn't leave me."

The cop in Ben noticed two oddities about this simple statement. The first was the emphasis on "mom." So Dad *had* left them. The second was the uncertainty beneath his outward bravado. So maybe the kid was scared that Mom would desert him, too.

Ben gave an internal shrug. Divorce did ugly things to kids. Not that it was his problem, thank God.

"It wouldn't have hurt you to let her pet them," the boy said, and turned and ran off.

Ben didn't even flinch. If he humored them, they'd be over here all the time. If he'd wanted kids, by God he'd have had them.

Too bad Judith Kane came with such a burden, though, he reflected as he watched her stuff the little brat in the van and presumably buckle her in a car seat. She was a beauty despite the carrottop. He guessed that's why he'd felt that peculiar shock; he didn't often meet a woman he wanted on first sight.

Well, this one might have nice breasts, a cute butt and green-gray eyes with a hint of desperation in them, but she also had children.

What a waste.

CHAPTER TWO

ZACH HOVERED over Judith. Sophie peeked from behind him. "Mom," he said, "can't we just go *look* at the horses? We won't go inside the fence or anything."

Judith wiped a smudge of paint from the bare wood floor. She'd painted the living-room walls pale peach and now was doing the woodwork in white. The floor, stripped of the carpet, could have used refinishing, but after all, this was a rental.

"No," she repeated with eroding patience, "you may not. Chief McKinsey made it clear he wanted you guys to stay away from his horses." *And from him.*

"But I'm bored," Zach whined.

Sinking back on her heels, Judith sighed. "I know, hon. I wish you could help me with this part of the painting, but it takes practice. Besides—" she smiled encouragement at her daughter "—Sophie would be bored without you to keep her company."

"But she doesn't want to do anything." He paused, then added sulkily, "Not like there's anything to do anyway. It's too hot to run around, and our board games are boring. Besides, all she can play are dumb little kid ones."

Sophie's eyes widened and tears sparkled in them. "I'm good at games!"

His lip curled. "Yeah, right."

"Am!" she cried, and whirled and fled the living room.

"Zach, for Pete's sake..." Judith gritted her teeth. It wasn't his fault that his sister cried so easily. "She *is* a little kid. Now, go check to be sure she hasn't run out of the house."

"Gol," he mumbled, and shuffled off.

She couldn't blame him for being bored and impatient with having to watch his sister. He wasn't used to having a little sister. The one-hundred-plus degrees outside added to the misery. Judith could only pray it didn't stay this hot for the next month. From Zach's point of view, the worst part was that she was busy making the house livable and had no time to spend at the town swimming pool or playing games or making cookies with them. She had only a few days before it was time to report to Lincoln Elementary School and begin getting her classroom ready for the fifth graders who would arrive eagerly—and not so eagerly—on September 4.

Starting Monday, Zach and Sophie would be enrolled in a YWCA program for children that continued until the first day of school. Judith had been reluctant to put them in it sooner; the move was a big change, and Sophie already felt as if she had been wrenched from the familiar to live with strangers.

Pain tightened Judith's throat, and she briefly closed her eyes. She'd been so sure nothing would ever upset her again if only she had her child back. What she hadn't anticipated was that her own daughter would have forgotten her.

"Zach?" she called.

"She's in bed," he called back. "I think she's falling asleep."

It was naptime. Judith took advantage of the lull to paint as quickly as she could without being sloppy. Maybe Zach would find something to keep himself busy for a few minutes. Maybe he'd fall asleep, too.

If only there were kids next door....

My fault, she thought. She could have rented that house in town. Judith paused to wipe the sweat from her forehead and made a face. That *air-conditioned* house in town. The one that hadn't needed weeks of work to make it livable. Undoubtedly Zach would have found other boys to play with. Probably half the kids in town were at the local pool splashing one another and roughhousing.

But she couldn't afford the time to watch him. And even if he were willing to try to meet other boys on his own if she just dropped him off, she felt uncomfortable with the idea. She couldn't let him get in the habit of riding a bike to friends' houses or hanging out at the school. She had to keep him close. Besides, she needed him to help take care of Sophie.

Maybe that wasn't fair to him, but what alternative did she have? As she painted her way around the corner toward the fireplace, Judith's thoughts circled relentlessly in a rut already well-worn. Why not put Sophie in day care if she didn't have time to spend with her anyway? Zach would be happier—

"Mom."

Zach spoke from so close behind her Judith jumped. "Oh! You scared me."

"How come you're frowning?"

She managed to smile for his benefit—she'd had plenty of practice coming up with those smiles, no matter the turmoil she felt inside. "I was just wishing—" She stopped. "Oh, pooh. Let me finish the woodwork in here, and when Sophie wakes from her nap, we'll go swimming. How's that grab you?"

"Cool!" he said. "I thought you were going to paint the kitchen cabinets, too."

"Tomorrow," she decided. "Or maybe tonight, after it cools down and Sophie goes to bed. Want to help?"

"Do I have to be really, really careful?"

"Nah." Judith nudged him with her shoulder. "We'll lay newspapers on the floor and take the handles off. Just as long as you don't paint the hinges, you can slap it on." And she could go along behind him, smoothing out drips and wiping up messes. The job would undoubtedly be slower than if she did it herself, but the payoff was worth it.

"Cool," he said again. "I wish my Nintendo was here."

"Read," she said firmly.

Zach made a face but turned and left the living room. If he picked up a book at all, it would probably be horror, but reading was reading. Right?

She started on the fireplace surround and mantel, from which she'd earlier sanded flakes of olive green paint. Underneath might be beautiful wood, but she hadn't the time to strip it. Besides…this wasn't her house.

Her thoughts jumped back into the rut. If only the guy next door weren't such a jerk. She'd seen the thinly veiled irritation on his face. Either he didn't like kids, or hers had pushed the wrong button. If she hadn't already signed the papers, she might have changed her mind about renting this house, once she'd met Chief Ben McKinsey.

She could tell Lyle Strother didn't like him, either. What was it he'd said? *Not real sociable.* She snorted. If that wasn't the understatement of the year. Their new neighbor had been in his yard a couple of times when she passed, and his squad car had met her van in the long lane on one of her trips to town. She'd made herself smile and wave, even if she'd rather have snubbed him. The best he'd done in return was tip his hat or incline his head with cool civility.

Jerk. Judith still burned when she thought of the way he'd stood there, a monolith, not saying a single friendly word, not expressing the slightest regret to the kids about the horses, although he must have seen their disappointment. What had really gotten her was the assessing way he'd looked her over. He'd been summing her up as a woman even as he was stony cold to her children. A word for him leaped to mind that was more profane than *jerk* but expressed the same idea.

She had to keep reminding herself that she didn't need a best friend next door. She needed a guard, and she had a suspicion he'd be a dependable one. He'd struck her as a man who would do his duty, whatever his personal feelings for the victims. For her children. He'd looked competent enough: big and solid and intelligent, with a craggy face that missed handsome but would still flutter female hearts if his expression wasn't so grim.

Grim was good, Judith told herself, dipping the brush into the can of paint and ignoring the ache of little-used muscles in her upper arm and shoulder. Grim was an eight-foot-high stone wall around her children. Friendly might be sucked in by Rylan's charm. She pictured Ben McKinsey's square-jawed, expressionless face. No, he and Rylan were as dissimilar as they could be. They wouldn't like each other.

If Chief McKinsey didn't give pony rides to Zach and Sophie, so be it.

She finished the last stroke across the mantel and stepped back to admire her work. The effect was bright, clean, warm, even elegant. The kitchen could wait. She'd soak the brush, find her own bathing suit and spend some time with her children.

As if in response to her thoughts, Zach bounded into the living room. ''Sophie's awake!''

Judith slapped the cover on the paint can. ''Then let's get this show on the road.''

''YOUR ROOM LOOKS terrific.'' Carol Galindez, the principal, leaned comfortably against Judith's desk. ''I like the dinosaur posters and mobile.''

Judith, too, gazed with satisfaction around her classroom, which had gone from bare and impersonal to comfortable and cheerful in record time. ''I've always been interested in dinosaurs myself, and I've found that fifth graders are the perfect age to get excited about the subject. I've got some great books—I'll bring in some fossils...." She smiled. "Then I'll ask the kids to do projects and write reports. With luck, they'll still be enthusiastic."

"We're very fortunate to have found you with such short notice." The words hung in the air, not quite a question, but inquiring nonetheless.

Judith hesitated. The school district had been desperate for a teacher when the one she'd replaced resigned long after most of those looking for jobs had already signed contracts elsewhere. The relative isolation of the school kept down the number of applicants, the superintendent admitted. Instead of asking her to fly out, he, Carol Galindez and someone from personnel had interviewed Judith in a lengthy conference call. She knew they'd checked her references, and then they had promptly offered her the job. In the interview, she'd simply said that she needed a change. Now, she decided, the time had come for honesty.

"I'm the lucky one to find a position in a place that suited us so well, considering most jobs were filled by the time I decided I had to move," she admitted. "I felt we'd be better off in a small town. My ex-husband is currently awaiting trial for having taken our daughter and fled the state with her. I have no idea what kind of prison term he'll get. I'm afraid he'll try again. I want to live in the kind of community where people would notice a strange man talking to the kids or...oh, trying to take them from school." She let out a gusty sigh.

Carol Galindez was in her mid to late forties, a

plump but stylish woman with dark eyes, wavy bru-
nette hair worn in a French roll and a taste for bright
colors. She'd straightened as Judith spoke, her expression aghast.

"He stole your daughter? Judith, how dreadful! Did
the police get her back right away?"

"It took two years," she admitted, those simple
bald words failing to disguise the agony they repre-
sented. "Sophie was only three. She's forgotten me.
It's...it's been very difficult."

The principal surprised her by saying fiercely,
"We'll guard her with our lives—I promise you that!"
She reached out and squeezed Judith's hand, her
brown eyes compassionate. "I take it your son isn't
his? I'm sure Zachary was your only comfort."

"Actually—" Judith's throat felt thick "—Rylan is
Zach's father, too. I've...only been married the once.
But Zach happened to have gone to a friend's instead
of to the day-care center after school the afternoon Ry
picked Sophie up. We assume he'd intended to take
Zach, too. I have no idea why he didn't wait and do
it another time. Part of me was grateful, and the other
part..." This was still hard to talk about. "I hated to
think of Sophie alone," Judith said starkly. "Zach was
so proud to be a big brother. He'd always...shielded
her."

"Oh, Judith," Carol said again. "I'm so sorry.
You've lived every mother's nightmare."

"Except that I'm lucky. I have Sophie back."

"We'll help in any way we can," the principal
promised.

"Thank you." Judith felt her smile twist. "I didn't

mean to get off on personal stuff. I just thought you ought to know.''

"Yes." Now Carol looked thoughtful. "We'll have to let the kids' teachers know the situation. In the staff meeting, I'll remind the aides that we have children in this school involved in custodial disputes. That way they can stay on their toes when they're supervising recess.''

"Thank you," Judith said again. She strove to make her tone professional. "Was there anything else we should discuss about the start of school?''

Carol blinked, shifting gears. "Did I tell you about the DARE program?''

"DARE?''

"Drug Abuse Resistance Education." The principal went on to explain about the program, in which a police officer came into the schools weekly for a semester to talk to kids about drugs, smoking, alcohol and peer pressure. "The DARE program has had great results, and I encourage you to support Chief McKinsey in any way you can.''

"Chief McKinsey?" Judith repeated, unable to hide her astonishment.

"Yes, he's teaching it this year." Carol's perfectly plucked eyebrows rose. "You've met him?''

"We're...neighbors." She deliberately evaded the principal's gaze.

Carol asked bluntly, "Did you have a problem with him?''

"Heavens, no!" Judith lied. Well, half lied. "I just had the impression he wasn't crazy about kids. Maybe I hit him on a bad day.''

Carol was silent for a moment. Then she leaned forward and lowered her voice. "Just between you and me and the blackboard, I hear from the high-school principal that he can be pretty short with the teenagers. Which may not be a bad thing. He's probably trying to scare the kids when he's called out there for a fight or because drugs have been found in a locker." She grimaced. "I assume he wouldn't be planning to teach the DARE classes if he hated everybody under five feet tall."

Judith automatically straightened a transparency under the glass on the overhead projector. "Hasn't he done it before?"

"No. A young female officer has taught it the past several years. I hear she's having a difficult pregnancy and has taken some time off."

"Well..." What could she say? Maybe he'd turn out to be a wonder with children. Everyone's children but hers. "I'm sure it'll go fine. Does he start this first week?"

"Yes. We try to get the specialty schedule going immediately."

They talked a little more about the first few days of school before Judith locked her room and walked the principal back to her office.

It was stifling in the building, and through the windows ahead she could see the heat radiating off the pavement. "Do you send kids out to recess if it's still this hot?" she asked.

"I don't know if we've ever had to decide. This never lasts long," Carol assured her. "Days are getting shorter already—you've noticed, haven't you?—

and the thermometer ought to start dropping at night. By November, the sun beating down will be a pleasant dream.''

''Pleasant?'' she echoed dubiously.

''Well, you're from Massachusetts, so you know what cold weather is like.'' Carol grinned as she turned into the school office. ''Scared you yet?''

Judith laughed and headed out to the van, which was parked in the staff lot behind one wing of the L-shaped building. The school housed four classrooms at each grade level through sixth, and the middle school, right next door, encompassed seventh and eighth grades. The sports fields and playgrounds didn't abut each other, which she thought was just as well. Fifth and sixth graders already spent enough time thinking and talking about the opposite sex, makeup, popular music and how to look cool, without mixing with the older kids.

Sophie and Zach were safely ensconced in the YWCA program. Today the whole lot, brown-bag lunches in hand, had been loaded onto a rented school bus for a field trip to a lake where they could swim. Judith could go home for her own lunch and have several blissfully uninterrupted hours to continue unpacking her kitchen stuff now that she'd painted the cupboards.

The anticipation she felt at having some time without her children gave her a twinge of guilt, but she wouldn't let herself wallow in it. Everyone needed to be alone occasionally, and she couldn't remember the last time she'd been on her own. Sophie had alternately pushed her away and clung desperately these past two weeks, and probably she herself had needed to cling to her newfound daughter. But maybe now life would start getting back to normal. In the frantic haste of packing, selling their town house and moving, "normal" was the one thing she hadn't been able to give her small, frightened child. It could be that the familiarity of routine was what Sophie needed the most.

She liked the familiar, too, Judith realized as she drove a route she was already getting to know well. She idly noticed progress on a house being remodeled, how the river had dropped even further and the last of the grass had turned brown. She wasn't an adventurer by nature; she would be perfectly happy to live her entire life in a small town where she knew everyone.

Maybe Mad River. If only it would cool down. Rain. Clouds *were* gathering above the mountains. So far, distant thunderstorms hadn't brought the coveted rain, but maybe tonight.

As she rounded a curve, she suddenly realized how hard it was to hold on to the wheel. The van was pulling sharply to the left. It wasn't riding right, either. She braked carefully. As the van slowed, she felt and heard the bump, bump, bump of a flat tire. *Oh, hell,* she thought. Nobody got flat tires anymore!

She parked on the dusty verge of the road and watched a pickup roar past without stopping. She looked longingly after it. She'd never changed a tire in her life. No other cars appeared, and to each side were dry open woods. The nearest house was probably a quarter of a mile—and her own wasn't much farther. A mere stroll, were it not for the heat.

She was an intelligent woman, Judith told herself. She ought to be able to figure this out. She groped in the glove compartment for the driver's manual. At least in her old car she'd known where the spare was, but she'd traded in the trusty Toyota for this van, which had seemed more practical for the trip out here and their new life-style.

Per instructions, she opened the back hatch and leaned in. The floor panel lifted up, and sure enough, there was the tire. She hauled it out, letting it bounce onto the ground. In alarm, she noticed that there was something squishy about the way it landed. Judith leaned her weight onto it. The tire gave.

It was flat. She had a flat tire and a flat spare. Judith uttered a word she'd learned from one of her fifth graders.

She stared down the road and listened closely. Complete silence greeted her. Not a pine needle stirred. The heat was her only companion, pressing her down, singeing her skin.

Well, it wasn't that far home. She'd just have to walk. She could call a tow truck from there, then come back to meet it. A half mile more or less wouldn't kill her.

She'd gone about two hundred yards, the pavement burning the soles of her feet through her sandals with each step, when she heard the crunch of tires behind her. She glanced back to see a police car pulling onto the shoulder of the road. Surely not...

But yes, of course. She recognized him through the windshield. It had to be her new neighbor—Mr. Personality himself. Would he be grimly polite? She wondered if he knew he would be teaching in her class-room.

His car door slammed and he came toward her, even larger and more solid than she recalled. He touched the brim of his hat. "Ms. Kane."

Well, he remembered her name, at least. "Chief McKinsey," she said, inclining her head.

"Car break down?"

"Flat tire," Judith replied in the same tone, not let-ting herself crack a smile.

Under the shadow of the hat brim, his eyes swept over her. "Why don't I give you a hand changing it." His voice didn't rise to make it a question.

This expressionless stuff was killing her. She made a face. "The spare is flat, too."

"Ah. Well, I'll tell you what. I have a canister of that stuff we can use to inflate your tire. With luck, it'll hold until you get to the gas station."

She'd never heard of such a thing. She nodded knowledgeably and accepted his raised eyebrows as an invitation to return to her vehicle. But when she started to walk past his patrol car, Chief McKinsey said, "Why don't you get in. You look flushed. It's air-conditioned."

Oh, God, what she'd do for air-conditioning. He could lock her in the back behind that grille, just so long as it was cool.

"Thank you." Judith opened the door and sank into the blissful chill.

Ben McKinsey got in next to her and started the car. He turned toward her—uncomfortably close—to look over his shoulder as he backed his car up to hers, which was listing forlornly on the side of the road. She took the opportunity to snatch a good look at his face.

Heavy dark brows and spiky eyelashes surrounded his brown eyes, and deep lines were carved in his forehead and beside his mouth. There was a sprinkling of gray in his short dark hair, and his chin was stronger than it needed to be and just a little off center. He held his mouth so tightly she couldn't tell what it might look like relaxed into a smile.

He caught her gaze, but she whipped her head around before a staring match developed. And before he might conclude she was interested.

"Why don't you stay here," he suggested.

She blinked, realizing they'd come to a stop and he was already opening his door.

"Can I help...?"

"No." *Slam.*

Judith sighed. Did the man ever really and truly ask what someone wanted? Or did he use the question format only to issue orders?

Well, to heck with him. If he wanted to be dictatorial, let him. Her conscience niggled at that; after all, maybe he was trying to be chivalrous. Either way, she decided, she'd take him up on the offer.

She swiveled in the seat so that she could track him with the side mirror. He'd taken something out of the trunk that looked like a can of hair spray. No, whipping cream, she decided frivolously. Beside her right rear wheel, he sank to his haunches and began fiddling with her tire. She found herself fixated on the way his pants pulled tight over powerful thighs.

Catching herself, she lifted her shirt a few inches so cold air could find its way beneath. Jeez, what was wrong with her? This was not her kind of man, assuming she ever decided she wanted another man.

But somehow her eyes didn't stray from the mirror. He did have a nice body, she had to admit when he rose fluidly to his feet and strode toward her. Shoulders that could make a woman feel safe. Narrow hips. Long legs.

He stopped on her side of the squad car, and it took her a second to realize he was waiting for her to get out. The heat seemed even worse when she did.

"It's still a little low on air," McKinsey said, "but it ought to hold you long enough to get back to town. I'll follow you."

She shut his car door and made herself hold out a hand. "Thank you," she said.

His gaze touched her outstretched hand, and there was a discernible pause before he lifted his own and took hers. The grip was quick and hard; she felt the strength there, and an uneasy little quiver shinnied up her spine.

She scuttled toward her car like a mouse for its hole. Oh, yes, this man could more than stand up to Rylan.

All the way to town, she was aware of the police car right behind her, filling her rearview mirror. As she turned into the first full-service gas station, he sped up and passed her, lifting his hand in a choppy wave. She gave her horn a toot. He didn't even look back.

By the time they'd found the nail in her tire and fixed it, Judith was starved. At home, she was surprised to realize she'd only lost an hour, thanks to

Chief McKinsey—who had merely been doing his duty, not being neighborly, she reminded herself.

Judith unpacked and arranged a good part of her dishes and kitchen utensils before it was time to pick up the kids at the middle-school gymnasium where the YWCA camp was held. By then the air had a heavy, muggy feel to it, different from the usual dry heat. Black clouds climbed the ridges and peaks above town, making dusk seem closer. On the drive home, Zach chattered about his day and some boy named Chad who did a really great cannonball and could hold his breath underwater for three minutes.

Judith smiled over her shoulder. "Did you have fun, Sophie?"

Her thumb was firmly planted in her mouth, but after a moment she gave a shy nod. Her cheeks were flushed pink, but she didn't look sunburned. The leaders must be replenishing her sunblock frequently. Unlike Zach, whose skin had taken on a golden tan, Sophie would easily burn.

"Hey, it's raining!" Zach exclaimed.

Sure enough, scattered drops plopped on the windshield and kicked up puffs of dust on the roadside. Through Judith's open window came an odd metallic smell, as if the rain were creating a chemical reaction. "Let's hope it really pours," Judith said.

Thunder crawled overhead. Zach jumped, and Sophie shrank in her booster seat.

"It's okay," Judith said. "I didn't even see the lightning. I think it was miles away. Besides, we're safe in the car. We'll run into the house and watch the rain out the windows."

The horses were nowhere to be seen. They must have gone into the barn.

The light was eerie now, purplish and yellow at the same time. Judith felt the hair stand up on her arms. She parked as close to the front porch as she could, and after rolling up their windows, they all hurried inside.

It was dusky enough that she turned on every light switch she passed. After hurrying around to shut the kitchen and bedroom windows, she joined the children in the living room, where they stood in front of the picture window, which looked northwest at the mountains. Judith tentatively touched the top of Sophie's head, waiting for her to flinch or scoot to the other side of Zach, but instead her small hand crept into her mother's. Judith's heart gave a funny bump of pleasure. Progress.

Or perhaps any adult would do when Sophie was scared enough, Judith wryly admitted to herself. She laid her free hand on Zach's shoulder.

Lightning forked above, a shocking explosion of white light that imprinted itself on the inside of Judith's eyelids.

Sophie shivered. "I want Daddy."

It hurt every time. And what could Judith say? *If I can help it, you'll never see him again?*

"One thousand one," Judith counted, "one thousand two, one thousand three, one thousand four, one thousand—"

Thunder rumbled.

"Cool!" Zach exclaimed.

"A mile away. Did you know you can count to tell

how far away the lightning is?'' she asked Sophie. ''Five seconds for every mile. Next time, let's all count together.''

Lightning flared, and she and Zach recited aloud, ''One thousand one, one thousand two, one thousand—''

This time the thunder boomed and the windowpanes rattled. Sophie latched onto Judith, trembling so hard her leg vibrated. But when she suggested they read a story, the five-year-old shook her head hard.

Judith crouched down and wrapped Sophie securely in an embrace, which for once she accepted.

''You're right,'' she murmured, sitting down with her on the couch. ''It's less scary to watch the storm than it is to pretend it's not happening.''

Sophie nodded emphatically. Judith wondered if she was relating this fear to all she must feel about losing her father.

Still the lightning flung jagged rivers of cold white fury across the sky, which seemed to crack open from the force of the thunderclaps. The raindrops appeared weirdly large as they struck the window.

They quit counting; there wasn't time. The storm must be directly overhead. It was almost completely dark outside, although it couldn't be much past six. None of them said a word. They held one another on the couch and watched nature demonstrate her power.

Judith began counting again. Was the storm passing? A quarter of a mile. Half a mile. The windows no longer shook. The rain fell harder.

''Well,'' she said, feeling tension leaching out of her body, ''maybe we should think about dinner.''

White light flooded the sky again, thunder cracked—and the house was plunged into darkness.

Sophie shrieked, and even Zach pressed his body against his mother's. She took a breath, willing her voice not to betray her with a tremor. "Oh, darn. We lost our electricity. Cold sandwiches for us!"

"Will it…will it stay off long?" her son whispered.

"I have no idea," she admitted. "Let's find flashlights."

They only had three, and none was great. No candles; it hadn't occurred to her to buy any. Maybe she could start a fire in the fireplace—if she could find some matches.

Still holding Sophie's hand, Zach trailing her, Judith made her way to her bedroom. It wasn't completely dark, now that their eyes had adjusted; a glance at her watch told her it was seven o'clock. Thank goodness her flashlight was in the drawer in her bedside table. She was absurdly grateful for the small golden pool of light it cast on the wall.

She switched it off again. For now, they would save the battery.

"Let's go find yours," she said, and they trooped into Zach's room, which he was currently sharing with his sister, who didn't like to sleep alone.

The batteries on Zach's flashlight were dead. He probably read at night under his covers after she tucked him in. Sophie's was feeble. Judith briefly considered a quick trip to town—she could buy batteries and maybe hamburgers and French fries for dinner. But the electricity might well be off there, too, and with the way it was pouring… No. The house felt safe, snug. They'd manage. Sophie's flashlight would be adequate for the kids to make their way to the bathroom, assuming the electricity stayed off into the night.

"Do we have any more batteries?" Zach asked.

Another thing she'd meant to buy. All the staples she could have reached unhesitatingly for back home in Boston hadn't been worth shipping out here. She'd intended to stock up on necessities like lightbulbs and batteries. She would have. Eventually.

"Afraid not." She smiled cheerily. "Hungry?"

"Not really," her son said. "Can we...can you read a story or something?"

Sophie's head bobbed.

"Well, it's kind of dark for me to read, and I think we ought to save the flashlights for later. But how about if we play a game?"

They ended up snuggling on the couch, she and Zach playing a word game while Sophie clung to her, sucking her thumb. Rain continued to patter on the roof and window; the murkiness of a storm-clouded dusk settled into the darkness of night. At some point, Judith turned on her flashlight, knowing the children needed that comforting beacon.

"Mom." Zach squeezed more tightly against her. "Did you hear that?"

"Hear what?" It was ridiculous to whisper, but she did anyway.

"A...a bang."

This time she did hear it: a knock on the front door. "Someone's here," Judith said. How calm she sounded, considering her heart was drumming! "Remember, the doorbell doesn't work when the electricity's out.''

Judith lifted Sophie onto her hip. Her son stuck close to her as she went to the front door.

''Who's there?'' she called.

The deep voice was muffled. ''Ben McKinsey. Your neighbor.''

''Oh.'' As quickly as she could with one hand, she unlocked the dead bolt and flung open the heavy door.

The large bulk of a man stood on their porch. For a moment, she couldn't make him out above the beam of his powerful flashlight, which he'd aimed at his feet. She directed her light toward his chest. The police chief had changed out of his uniform. The shoulders of his denim shirt were wet and he held his Stetson in one hand. Shadowed above the beam of her light, his face looked even grimmer.

''Just wanted to be sure you have everything you need to sit out the storm.''

Pride made her want to claim they were fine. Which they were. Cold food and a little darkness never hurt anyone. But the children would be happier with some light, if he had candles or a lantern to spare.

''No,'' she admitted. ''I...wasn't really prepared for this.''

He grunted and shone his flashlight in the cardboard box he held in one arm. ''Brought some things. Just in case.''

Wonderingly, she looked. The beam picked out a camping lantern, candles and... Was that a pizza box in the bottom?

When she lifted her head, he shrugged. "Figured I could share my dinner."

It seemed he was neighborly after all. She had totally misjudged him.

On a rush of relief, Judith stepped back. "Please. Come in."

CHAPTER THREE

BEN FOLLOWED Judith Kane into her dark house, aware of the girl clinging to her like a limpet and the boy edging back just beyond the beam of the flashlight.

What the hell had gotten into him? He could have handed over the pizza, claimed he'd already eaten. Anything but come in.

He could excuse the impulse that had brought him over here; he liked to think he was a decent man. He'd grown up in a town where neighbors helped one another out. And he'd known for damn sure a city woman like her wouldn't be ready for power outages.

Ben remembered how terrified his little sister, Nora, had been when the electricity went out. Their mom had always been at work at night—she'd held down two jobs just to pay the rent and put food on the table. It had been left to Ben, the eldest, to comfort Nora. No matter how often he pointed out that once they went to bed, it would be dark anyway, she was still scared. She wanted to know she could turn on a light if she had to get up in the night. He guessed the little redheaded girl would feel the same.

"This is so kind of you," the children's mother was babbling. She was still wearing the shorts but had added a long-sleeved denim shirt over the sleeveless one. "I keep thinking of all the things we left behind when we moved—like candles and batteries. We didn't have anything like that camp lantern, though. The closest I ever came to camping was a picnic in the park. We're from Boston, you see."

He'd heard that New England accent in her voice. Why had a woman like her, with two children, moved all the way out from Boston, Massachusetts, to Mad River, the ass back of nowhere? And why rent a crappy little place like this when she was able to afford a top-of-the-line moving company to haul her stuff for her? That part he'd been wondering about ever since he'd seen that huge glossy moving van backed up to the house.

"Please, sit down."

Even in the shadows, he could tell that the living room had changed. His flashlight beam found a sofa— smooth, creamy leather. He settled on one end and lifted the lantern from the box. The boy perched on a chair.

"This is Sophie and Zach," she rattled on. "Did I already introduce them?" She laughed nervously. "I guess I did. Why don't you sit down, Chief McKinsey, and I'll just go get us some drinks from the refrigerator. What would you like? We have all kinds of pop and, um…"

"Beer?" He felt like a fool the minute the word left his mouth. Of course she wouldn't have beer. Not unless a man visited—which might be one reason she'd moved out here. He hadn't seen any other cars coming down the lane, though.

"I'm sorry. How about wine? What do you think, a good Cabernet Sauvignon with—what is it, pepperoni? Sausage? Everything but the kitchen sink?"

"Everything but the kitchen sink. That's okay. I'll take a cola." He turned the knob on the camp lantern one notch, waited two seconds and turned it the rest of the way. *Whoosh!* Bright white light filled the room.

"Cool!" the boy breathed.

Judith offered a smile as radiant as the lantern's glow. "Bless you. Here." She plopped Sophie on the couch next to him. "Honey, you stay with the police chief. I can't carry you and drinks and plates, too." She retreated through a dark doorway.

For an instant, all Ben could think about was how her bare leg, unnaturally pale in this light, had almost bumped him. He'd gotten a good look at those long, slim legs today when she'd walked ahead of him alongside the road. She had a hell of a body. And he must be desperate, he admitted, to get excited about a woman in shorts coming within a foot of him.

Then he stiffened, remembering the little girl. She sat so still beside him she might not have been breathing. Hell. She was scared of him. Or the darkness. Or maybe both.

"Mom doesn't have any matches," the boy piped up. "How come you didn't need one?"

Candles Ben could understand. But no matches?

"Modern technology. It's electronically sparked." He set the lantern safely in the middle of the table and leaned back slowly enough not to frighten the girl any further.

Out of the corner of his eye, Ben saw that her knees

were drawn up to her chest, her thumb was shoved in her mouth and she was staring unblinkingly at the lantern. Strange kid.

Cupboard doors banged somewhere in the house. Ben raised his voice. "You know you can't run water when the power is off."

She appeared like a shot, plates tucked under one arm, cans of pop under the other, that pitiful little flashlight gripped in her hand. "What?"

"Don't run the faucet. The well pump doesn't work without power," he said succinctly.

"Well?" she repeated, expression incredulous.

"Yeah. A big hole in the ground? We share a well. I maintain it. You pay me for water."

She digested that information. "Is the power off very often?"

"Fair amount." He lifted the pizza box out of the carton and set it on the coffee table, then saw the gleam of fine cherry wood and lifted it up. "What can I put this on?"

"Zach, will you help me?"

The kid took the plates from her, then helped her hand out the cans of pop without dropping any. She produced a magazine—some fancy one about decorating and architecture—and he put the pizza box back down on top of it.

"Oh, I forgot a knife," Judith Kane said suddenly.

"Who needs a knife?" Zach asked.

"And napkins."

"I can get 'em, Mom." The boy sprang to his feet.

"Take my flashlight." Ben handed it over.

The kid scooted off, the bright beam playing over

the walls—pink?—and an arrangement of pictures hung in the hall.

His mother came around and sat down on the other end of the couch. "This lantern is wonderful."

"You might want to buy yourself one." Surreptitiously, Ben watched the little girl, waiting for her to reattach herself to her mother. She didn't move.

"You've rescued me twice in one day."

"I wouldn't call this a rescue," he said dryly, opening the lid of the pizza box and starting to dish it out. The pizza wasn't as hot as it could be, but what the heck.

The girl—Sophie—took a plate from him but just stared at it.

"It's okay, honey," Judith Kane said gently. "If you don't like something, you can pick it off."

If you don't like something? Should he translate that as "I know you don't like anything on it"?

"What's that?" Sophie whispered.

Ben cocked his head. Beyond the circle of light came a hollow *thump, thump, thump,* followed by a clanking sound. *Thump, thump, thump, rattle.* It was getting closer. "Ooooh," said a ghostly voice from the darkness.

Judith snapped, "Zachary!" at the same moment the little girl scooted under Ben's arm and plastered herself to his side. He froze. What the hell—?

Laughing hysterically, the boy flung himself into his chair. "Did I scare you?"

Judith swiveled toward her daughter. "Sophie, honey..." Her voice sharpened as she turned back to her son. "Only your sister. That wasn't very nice. You tell her you're sorry."

"It was a joke!"

"You know she frightens easily. I've asked you to take special care of her." She sounded mad as hell, but her voice softened again when she leaned forward and held out her hands to her daughter. "Sweetie, come here."

Please, Ben thought. *Go to Mom.*

The little girl shook her head. Hard.

Ben's shoulder muscles were beginning to feel the strain from holding his arm away from her.

Judith stood, bringing a faint flowery scent with her, and started to pick up the kid anyway.

"No! I don't want to go with you!" Sophie screamed, and wrenched away, grabbing tighter hold of Ben. He automatically wrapped his arm around her.

Pain flashed across Judith Kane's face as she straightened. "Sweetheart, I was just trying to hold you. Chief McKinsey isn't used to having little girls on his lap."

The kid was frightened of her own mother? Against his side, he felt her little heart racing as quickly as a bird's. God. Was he going to have to report his new neighbor to Child Protective Services?

Her eyes met his, and he saw the desperation in them. "It's...she misses her father. I...I guess you've been elected as a substitute. I'm sorry."

"It's okay," he said, not meaning it, but the world wouldn't end if he had to cuddle a kindergartner for five minutes.

"Are you sure?"

"Yeah. I'm sure."

Looking tense, she settled back on the couch and picked up her plate. That was the moment the boy chose to turn on the flashlight. The beam skittered across the wall and then hit Ben straight in the eyes. He squeezed them shut for an instant, and when he opened them, the beam was drawing figure eights on the ceiling. Sophie had buried her face in his side.

"Can I use this to go to the bathroom?" Zach asked, too loudly. "It's better than mine. All Mom's bought me is a dumb kid one."

Ben was still seeing stars. He'd have given the kid hell except that he recognized the boy's general obnoxiousness as a bid for attention. Damned if he'd give it to him. "Yeah," Ben said shortly, "but don't flush."

The boy made a face. "Don't *flush?*"

At the same moment, Judith said, "Don't flush?"

Only the girl, slowly relaxing at his side, didn't seem to find the concept stunning. Ben felt as if he were dealing with travelers from the future who couldn't believe how primitive twentieth-century plumbing was. "You flush," he said, "water runs."

"But...but what if someone—"

Zach stopped dead. Thank God for small favors.

"I mean, I don't hafta... Not right now."

"Zachary," Judith said crisply, "we are eating."

Flushing—hey, a pun—the boy headed for the bathroom. An unpleasant thought struck Ben.

"How old is your son?"

"Nine. He's going into fourth grade." Her voice

gentled. "Sophie turned five in April, and she's starting kindergarten this year."

Ben made a noncommittal sound. Maybe he'd be
sorry he *wasn't* teaching drug abuse education to kids
the age of Zach Kane; he remembered his younger
brothers turning into snotty little jackasses at some
point. He hoped to God that wasn't at ten or eleven.
He should have kept a diary.

"Do you have children?" Judith asked.

He barely stopped himself from coming out with a
profane equivalent of "Are you kidding?" The little
one attached to him was a fresh reminder of how children trapped you. But he didn't have to be rude. "No"
was an adequate reply.

"We'll be working together, you know," she chattered on. "I'm a teacher. Fifth grade. Carol Galindez
tells me you're handling the DARE program this
year."

His worst nightmare. If he could have stuck it on
anyone else in the department, he would have. But not
a damned one of them was capable except for Julie
Robinson, busy breeding her own future fifth grader.
Ben didn't mind women cops; he just wished they
wouldn't get pregnant.

"You're a teacher," he said. Brilliant.

She glanced at her son, who had returned and
dropped to his knees, helping himself to pizza.
"Mmm-hmm. That's why we moved here. I got offered the job at Lincoln. I'm excited to get started."
She hesitated and set down her plate. "Sophie, honey,
would you like to eat some pizza now? Or...or sit on
my lap?"

The little girl shook her head.

"She's okay," Ben said again, meaning it more this time. It wasn't as if the kid were demanding anything from him. Her little body was warm and relaxed against his, bringing back some memories that weren't all unpleasant. "This your first teaching job?" he asked, to distract the child's mother.

Maybe she'd gone back to school after having kids. Despite her creamy skin and a pert nose that was cute as hell, his new neighbor had to be over thirty with a son in fourth grade.

"Heavens, no!" she exclaimed. "I've taught for seven years now. Fifth grade, sixth... The last couple of years I taught English to seventh and eighth graders. Now, there's an age to keep you on your toes!"

He had to agree with that assessment. The mini-criminals he considered middle schoolers. Pulling out their cigarettes before they'd cleared the school parking lot. Breaking windows with rocks. Lighting up joints behind the gym. Stealing a candy bar at the 7-Eleven. Taking Daddy's car for a joyride. Seemed like they all flirted with breaking the law, though he supposed that wasn't true. Maybe pretty Judith Kane had been so desperate to get back to teaching younger kids that she'd taken the first job she was offered.

"Why Mad River?" he asked.

"Oh... I wanted a small town." She studied the slice of pizza in her hand as though it held great fascination. "We needed a change. There was an opening here."

He'd been a cop too long not to notice the forced casualness in her tone, the way her body language had altered. Maybe she hadn't lied, but she was definitely being evasive.

None of his business, he told himself, as long as she didn't break the law. Her daughter's fear was enough to provoke him to run her through the computer, but hell, the school district must have done that. These days even volunteers got checked out by the state patrol. If it wasn't for the way the kid acted, he'd figure these folks were entitled to their privacy.

He just hoped a single mother and two kids allowed him his.

"Have you always lived here?" she asked.

"Last six years. Came from Seattle." After breaking up with Kelly, there was no way he could stay. And the kind of crime he'd seen as a detective in the Seattle PD was enough to make Mad River sound like heaven on earth. But he wasn't going to say any of that. He, too, could be evasive. "I grew up in a small town, though."

Up to this point, the boy had eaten in silence—pouting, Ben figured, after getting chewed out for scaring his sister. Hadn't seemed like much of an offense to Ben; he'd have thought it was funny when he was Zach's age, and his brothers had pulled that kind of stunt all the time. But clearly something unusual was going on here.

Now the nine-year-old piped up, "You ever shoot anybody?"

Yeah, he'd shot somebody, and still had nightmares about it. "No," he lied.

"Zach, what a thing to ask!" Judith said.

The boy ignored his mother's disapproval. "I wish *I* knew how to shoot a gun. Would you teach me?"

"Zach!"

"When you're a little older, the NRA offers classes in gun safety," Ben told him. "Around here, most everybody hunts."

"My father used to hunt." He gave his mother a sulky look. "Mom didn't like him to have a gun in the house."

"I'm with her on that. If you've got 'em in the house, they should be locked up. Too many accidents, otherwise."

"Mom's just scared of everything."

Ben watched Judith's spine stiffen. "That's enough, young man!" she reprimanded.

"I gotta go to the bafroom," said a little voice.

Ben lifted his arm from Sophie's shoulders. If she needed help, it wasn't coming from him.

"Do you want me to go with you, honey?" Judith asked gently.

Hesitation, then a small nod. The little girl wriggled to the edge of the couch and reached for her mother's hand, showing no sign of fear. They took Ben's flashlight and disappeared down the dark hall.

Conscious of a chill along his side where her warm body had been, Ben watched them go, frowning. Maybe the kid had just been looking for a substitute for the father she'd lost. He guessed he'd been that for his brothers and sister. They wouldn't have noticed any more than this girl had if they'd hurt their mother's feelings by turning to him first.

Still, Ben took the opportunity of being alone with

the boy to ask casually, "Your sister scared of your mom?"

His surprise looked legitimate. "Why would she be scared?"

"I don't know," Ben said truthfully. "You tell me."

The boy shrugged. "She misses our dad. That's all."

Ben opened his mouth to ask if his parents had just gotten a divorce, but he closed it again. Judith and Sophie were already coming back down the hall. The girl separated herself from her mother.

"Didn't hafta go," Sophie announced, and headed purposefully toward Ben.

He shot to his feet. "Listen, I'd better be off. I didn't let anyone at the station know where I was, and I should check in."

"Oh." For just an instant, Judith Kane sounded disappointed, even bereft. Then she produced a smile. "This was so nice of you. Let me get my flashlight and you can turn the lantern off."

"No, I'll leave it. I have another one. I'll trade you flashlights, too." He reached for hers. "I have some fresh batteries at home. We can exchange them tomorrow."

"Are you sure?"

"Yeah," he said roughly. "I'm sure." He crouched beside the lantern. "Zach, let me show you how to turn this off."

The boy listened solemnly to his explanation. "These are really cool," he declared. "We can get one, right, Mom?"

"Sounds like we'll have to, Zach," she agreed, "since Chief McKinsey says the power's often out."

"Why don't you make it 'Ben'?" he heard himself saying. He liked the way her kids' names came so softly and lovingly from her—except when she was annoyed at her son.

"Ben it is," she agreed with a quick smile. "Are you Benjamin?"

"Bennett."

He half expected to be ambushed by Sophie wanting a good-night kiss, but to his relief she clambered back onto the couch and stuck her thumb into her mouth again. Her whole body language was that of a child a hell of a lot younger than five, if Ben's memory served him right. Maybe she was mentally slow. That might explain the outburst and why her mother said the child frightened easily. He felt better with this explanation. Of course Judith wouldn't be anxious to tell every Tom, Dick or Harry that something was wrong with her kid.

"Good night," he said, nodding toward the little girl and then the boy. Only Zach responded.

Judith Kane thanked him six more times during the ten feet to the minuscule front entry. There was one awkward moment after he'd opened the door when they both hesitated, as if this had been a date and they weren't quite sure how to end it. The pale beam of the flashlight he held was aimed at the floor. A partial wall blocked the lantern and children from their view. He could just make out the pale oval of her face tilted up to him, and he remembered the one time they'd touched. Would he have the same strong reaction if he shook her hand again? Or—the thought came out of left field—what if he kissed her?

A woman with two young children? Was he nuts? Besides, she'd probably slug him. And with good reason.

Get the hell out of here, he ordered himself. Obeying the voice of wisdom, he nodded and settled his hat back on his head. "Good night."

"Good night," she echoed, so sweetly he almost raised the flashlight so he could see her face better, tell if she was wanting...

Oh, yeah, he jeered. She was hardly about to throw herself into the arms of a man just because he had fixed her flat tire and come bearing the gift of a camp lantern. The woman had a nice voice, just as she had nice legs. She made him think about things he hadn't thought about for a long time. It was a pretty good bet she wasn't thinking the same things.

Feeling like a fool, he nodded again and went down the porch steps into the rain, the inadequate beam of her light barely showing the way. Behind him, the door closed, shutting in any secrets the Kanes might have.

JUDITH DIDN'T ACTUALLY see her neighbor the next day; she heard the doorbell and the murmur of voices, and a moment later Zach reappeared in the kitchen with her flashlight in his hand.

"I gave him his," he said. "Look. Ours is really bright now." To demonstrate, he flicked it on and off, on and off.

Judith poured hot water over the tea bag in her mug. The warm glow of the stove burner had never looked so good. "Did you thank Chief McKinsey?"

"Sure." He frowned. "I guess."

She would have pursued the subject of his manners, but Sophie knocked over her glass of milk right then and began to cry. "I don't like milk!" she wailed. "Daddy didn't make me drink it!"

Daddy, it appeared, hadn't made her do anything she didn't want to do. Which might be true, Judith conceded; Rylan always had taken the easy road. On the other hand, she was beginning to suspect Sophie was using Daddy's name whenever it suited her purposes. Her stories about what Daddy had and hadn't let her do vacillated from day to day.

"But milk is good for you," Judith said gently, soaking up the spill with a sponge. "It makes your bones strong. And your teeth." She showed hers in a silly face and was rewarded by a tiny smile. "You want big shiny white teeth, don't you?"

"The better to eat you with!" Zach roared, and snapped his teeth shut just short of his sister's neck.

Sophie screamed, and tears flowed again. "I don't want big teeth! I want Daddy!"

Judith wheeled on her son in anger. "Zachary Kane, you go to your room this instant! What has gotten into you?"

She knew, of course. Several days later, she was still thinking about that incident and a couple of similar ones. Judith sat at her desk, facing an empty classroom. Guilt wouldn't let her concentrate on lesson plans.

She had overreacted. Zach wasn't doing anything any other boy his age wouldn't have done. But couldn't he understand that Sophie needed coddling? Judith had assumed that he would eagerly take over his role as protective big brother. But lately he seemed to be trying his hardest to upset Sophie with stunts like the one at the breakfast table.

Obviously he wanted Judith's undivided attention. She understood that he'd gotten used to having her to himself. But he wasn't an only child, and no matter how much extra attention she gave him, he acted as if it weren't enough.

He'd adjust, she told herself, sighing as she tried to turn her thoughts back to the American history unit she would be starting in only a few days. But thinking about school opening didn't distract her from her concerns about her children.

Once school started, Zach would be busier and away from Sophie all day. Before Judith knew it, their life would be back to the way it was before that terrible afternoon when she had gone to pick up Sophie at the day-care center, only to be told that she was already gone.

Panic shivered up Judith's spine, and she gave a little shudder. No! She wouldn't let herself relive the horror. She had Sophie back. She'd never lose her again.

Well... Judith smiled. Maybe she'd let Sophie go

off to college someday—when she was about thirty. But she'd have to come home summers.

"What are you smiling about?" Linda Mayfield, another fifth-grade teacher, appeared in the doorway.

"Oh..." Judith produced the only excuse that came to mind. "I was picturing our police chief teaching ten-year-olds how to handle peer pressure."

"Boggles the mind," Linda agreed. A thin, energetic woman with graying hair cut in a sleek cap, she smiled crookedly. "He almost arrested my son one time. Scared the pants off him." At Judith's look of inquiry, she grimaced. "Just the usual teenage pranks. But Ron was really toying with trouble that year, so I didn't mind. Still..."

The image of Ben McKinsey sitting on her couch, Sophie glued to his side, his arm held rigidly above her as though a hug would contaminate him, flashed before Judith's eyes. "Should be interesting," she said.

She might have actually been excited about having him in her classroom if he'd been friendlier since that night. She kept remembering the way he'd looked at her for a moment that had seemed to go on forever before he muttered a rough good-night. He hadn't once smiled that evening, yet she'd wanted him to kiss her. No, not wanted, exactly. Wondered what it would be like. Dreamed a little.

Oh, she'd been an idiot. Her kids had been right there in the dark house behind her. And she hardly even knew Ben McKinsey—and didn't like much of what she did know.

She'd baked banana bread the next day and taken it over to his house, but he hadn't been there, so she'd left the wrapped loaf propped inside his screen door with a note that said only "Thanks" and was signed with her name.

Any girlish dreams had withered the day after that, when their vehicles met in the lane and he barely tipped his hat at her as they passed. She'd seen him half a dozen times since then, and it was always the same thing. They were back to square one. Civil and incredibly distant. Not even neighborly.

Well, she would have enjoyed getting to know him, but so be it. She ought to tell him about her situation— about Rylan. The evening of the storm, she'd been thinking she would, as soon as she saw him without the kids. But now she couldn't bring herself to do it. Besides, Ry would be a stranger to him, and he wouldn't let a stranger take one of her children. Ben McKinsey might not be a friend, but he'd demonstrated that she could depend on him if she needed him. That was all that really mattered.

The weather had changed the past week, the air taking on a nip that spoke of autumn, the temperature dipping at night. The dry August had caused the leaves to turn color already, and vivid reds and yellows cloaked the foothills and tree-lined streets. Her coworkers hoped for rain and worried aloud about forest fires, a subject Judith was careful to keep from Sophie's ears.

The Sunday before school started, Judith called her parents and then Rylan's. Having the kids continue to feel close to their grandparents was important to her. Zach talked to Rylan's mother first; Sophie said a shy "Hi" and then thrust the phone at Judith.

"Sophie doesn't believe in long chats," Judith said lightly. "Maybe kindergarten will open her up a little."

If her mother-in-law responded, Judith didn't hear it over Zach's cackle.

"Yeah, like a clamshell! School will pry her open!" He drew out the word *pry,* pretending his hands were locked together and he was wrenching them apart.

Sophie's mouth trembled and she raced out of the kitchen. Still cackling, her brother chased after her.

Judith sighed into the receiver. "Zach *needs* school *I* need him to go."

"I remember that feeling," Mary Kane agreed, but not in her usual easy way. The constraint in her voice had Judith tensing even before she heard her mother-in-law's heavy sigh. "Rylan is out on bail," Mary told her. "The judge called to let us know. Apparently he had a girlfriend in Kansas City who put up the money. You know we never would have."

Rylan was no longer behind bars. "Yes," Judith said slowly. "Yes, I know."

They talked a while more, but the only thing of importance had been said: Ry was free. He could show up here anytime.

Judith felt curiously numb. And why not? She'd expected this, prepared for it. The news wasn't a bolt out of the blue. Tonight, when she ought to be falling asleep, was when the fear would come. She would think then about how gladly Sophie would run to her father. She would worry about Zach's ambivalence and the fact that she couldn't watch them every minute.

But there was nothing more she could do. And she didn't dare tell the children their father was out of jail. The last thing she wanted was for them to be watching for him.

No, she could only wait.

CHAPTER FOUR

JUDITH WOULD HAVE thought it was her own stress level affecting Zach that first day of school, had he not been so obnoxious lately anyway. He was so wild during breakfast that she had to send him to his room. During the drive to school he was sulky, instead, which actually felt like an improvement.

For Judith, this first day of school was what opening night must be like for an actor—exciting, yet fraught with the possibility for disaster. What if the kids hated her? What if teachers out here did things differently than they did back East? This new anxiety almost— but never completely—overrode her worry about Rylan.

She'd made arrangements for Zach and Sophie to go to their new classrooms a little early. Both their teachers had been updated about the situation with Rylan. Judith walked each of them to the door and then stood back as they hesitantly entered. Zach's expression was defiant. Sophie for once didn't want Daddy; it was Mommy to whom she clung.

"I don't wanna..." she whispered, huge gray eyes pleading.

But Sandra Craig, the pretty young kindergarten teacher, was already holding out a hand to her and smiling. "Sophie Kane, thank goodness you're early! Could you possibly help me by passing out some construction paper and yarn for an art project? I don't think I'm going to have time before the bell rings."

With only a few anxious backward glances, Sophie went with her new teacher. Feeling reassured, Judith continued on to her own classroom.

She sat behind her desk and looked over her quiet, peaceful domain. She was ready. Her stomach was calm until the bell rang, and she suddenly felt as if she might throw up her breakfast.

The hall thundered as hundreds of children stampeded toward their rooms. Seas of them poured through her open door, and she smiled and rose to greet them. "Good morning," she said, over and over, as if she were composed and confident.

Laughing, talking, roughhousing, they hung or dropped their coats and lunches in the closet, found their names on the desks and sat down. A second bell rang. The room fell silent, and twenty-six pairs of eyes gazed expectantly at her.

She drew a deep breath, smiled again and began her performance. "Hello. I'm Mrs. Kane. I'm new to your school, but I have taught fifth grade before, as well as sixth and seventh." Just so they'd know she wasn't a rookie. "Let's spend this morning going over the rules—" she laughed at their groans "—most of which I'm sure you know already and always obey. But first we'll get to know each other. Let's start with the roll call." She moved unhurriedly behind her desk and picked up the list of names. "Erica Adams," she began, and a blond girl tentatively raised her hand.

Twenty minutes into the day, Judith had discovered that fifth graders in the great American West weren't any different from those in Boston. She'd already known that three of the boys in her classroom read at second-grade level or below. One of them was the class clown, one hid in the back and the other watched everything with such sharp eyes she suspected he would pick up most of what the other kids did even without the required reading skills. Of the girls, two wore more makeup than Judith did. A few were getting breasts; the rest were still sticklike or plump. Half a dozen of her twenty-six students were exceptionally bright; they would be pulled out for an enrichment program twice a week. Most of the rest could be good students, too, with some encouragement. She could hardly wait to begin coaxing the best from each one of them.

By the end of the day, she was awash in a glow of contentment that she knew wouldn't last for the entire school year. But it reminded her of how much she loved her job.

Grateful that the school district offered full-day kindergarten, she hurried to Sophie's classroom first, just in time to see her teacher hug Sophie goodbye. The little girl stood stiff in the embrace, but her cheeks turned pink. Judith wanted to hold out her arms and sweep her daughter up. Instead, she held out a hand. "Hi, sweetie. Good day?"

Sophie came readily to her and slipped her hand into her mother's. She nodded, eyes bright. "I made a big purple cat with yellow whiskers. Mrs. Craig hung it on the wall. I wanted to make a horse, but I don't know how to draw one." She looked up eagerly. "Do you?"

She was talking. Really talking. Judith felt tears prick the backs of her eyes. "I'm not an artist, but I can try. Shall we draw when we get home?"

They'd arrived in front of Zach's classroom. He came out when he saw them. Boys were walking away in pairs and groups, laughing and shoving one another. He was alone.

"How was your day?" Judith asked.

He shrugged and looked down. "Okay," he said flatly.

Her bubble of joy popped. Of course this would be hard for him. Everyone else already had friends.

She squeezed his shoulder. "First day is scary, isn't it?"

He pulled away from her. "It's just boring."

Judith didn't argue. Instead, she chatted about her own day and rejoiced when Sophie joined in. Zach would come around, Judith told herself. Moving was harder on a child his age. But the other boys would soon accept him. In a couple of weeks, she'd be dragging him away from his gang and worrying that she couldn't keep him close to her.

Speed bumps required her to inch out of the parking lot. She turned left, past the middle school. Ahead of them, a police car was parked at the curb.

"There's Chief McKinsey," Zach said, displaying the first sign of animation since school let out. "I bet he's going to arrest someone. Maybe a kid." He sounded pleased at the prospect.

Ben McKinsey was coming down the steps of the

middle school, but he was alone. No thirteen-year-old was being dragged off to juvenile detention. In the dark-blue uniform, the police chief looked even more forbidding. As she began to speed up, he turned his head, frowning, and looked directly at the van. He gave a short, sharp nod, frowned more fiercely and strode toward his squad car.

Judith resisted the temptation to stick out her tongue. Zach slumped back in his seat. She hoped he wasn't building their neighbor up to be some kind of father figure. Chief Ben McKinsey wasn't volunteering. She glanced in her rearview mirror to see that Sophie, too, had turned her head to look at him, but in contrast to her earlier eagerness, she had stuck her thumb in her mouth again, and her eyes were wide with alarm.

Oh, Lord, did he remind her of the deputies who'd torn her father away from her? But if that was the case, why had Sophie wanted to hold on to him the other night? He'd been out of uniform then; had she forgotten he was a policeman?

Judith's mouth tightened. If Ben McKinsey upset her children in any way, even if it was inadvertent, she'd break the lease and find another rental. One with neighbors who smiled.

PAPERWORK WAS STREWN over Ben's battered metal desk, but instead of concentrating on it, he scowled at the tall bookcase across from him, which was stuffed with law books and overflowing binders—and was damned ugly. He ought to do something to make his office more livable.

The bookcase wasn't any worse than the black metal filing cabinets below an interior window shuttered with venetian blinds that were bent and snapped off in places. If he hadn't hung any pretty pictures in the six years he'd occupied this office, he wasn't likely to start now.

And if he was going to distract himself, it ought to be with the report he was supposed to be writing, not the state of his office. But he kept frowning into space.

It wasn't as if he'd never talked to school classes before, although he shunted the task onto one of his deputies whenever he could manage it. Other adults told him that stepping into a classroom with its familiar smell of chalk and polished linoleum and lunchboxes with three-day-old leftovers made them feel like kids again, anxious because they'd forgotten to study for a test twenty years in the past. When Ben stepped inside that door, it wasn't his own school days he remembered so much as his brothers' and sister's. All those times he'd had to drop off brown-bag lunches forgotten on the kitchen counter, or pick up Nora or Eddie or John when they threw up at recess, or even attend parent-teacher conferences when his mother couldn't get off work. Once he himself had graduated from high school he'd even chaperoned a couple of field trips.

A muscle in his jaw jerked. He didn't let himself think about those days very often, and with good reason. How he'd resented playing Daddy when he could have been partying with his friends or playing football! Later, when those same buddies went off to college without him, he'd felt even worse. He'd made the sacrifices he had to, but not gladly.

Water under the bridge, he told himself impatiently. Ben rotated his shoulders a few times and bent his head to each side to loosen the stiffness. Then he forced himself to read what he'd already written on the form in front of him.

Complainant says that the vehicle blocking an alley on the five-hundred block of Maple Street was left there during the night. Officer was unable to locate anyone in the immediate area who claimed knowledge of the vehicle. Registration checked. Officer attempted to contact owner.

He'd had to impound the station wagon just because that busybody Ruby Santoya took offense at anything slightly amiss within a ten-block radius of her home. Her browbeaten husband kept their lawn as beautiful as the greens at Pebble Beach Golf Course. The edges were razor sharp, the texture like velvet. Their car rarely sat in the driveway, never mind on the street. Windows sparkled, white paint shone. Ruby's roses won ribbons every year at the county fair, but as far as Ben was concerned, the bushes were ugly, perfectly spaced and pruned until they looked unnatural. Ruby used the excuse of walking her cocker spaniel to patrol the neighborhood for irregularities. Nobody even drove down the damn alley except the garbage truck, and pickup had been Monday. But what could Ben say? The car shouldn't have been left there.

He took up his pen again and wrote: ''Failed to

locate owner. Vehicle impounded.'' Sometimes he wondered what he was doing in a place like Mad River, where every crime committed could be summed up in a short weekly column in the local paper. This week's offenses consisted of a chain-link fence cut by unknown vandals; a stolen purse—the woman had left it in plain sight in an unlocked car, which in his book meant somebody had accepted an invitation; two tires swiped from behind an auto body shop; and now this—an impounded vehicle. Hot damn.

On the other hand, there was something to be said for a community where the worst crime was some wire cutters taken to a chain-link fence. People kept an eye out for one another. That made a difference. In an era of budget cuts, the council still managed to find the funds to support the DARE program in the school. That was the kind of attitude that kept this town peaceful.

Ben grunted. He wished like hell the program had been cut as decisively as that chain-link fence now that he had to do it.

One of his officers rapped on the glass square of his door. His grin was just this side of malicious. ''Hey, Boss! It's almost two o'clock!''

As if Ben didn't know.

Ten minutes later, carrying an armload of workbooks, he stood in front of the elementary school. Lincoln was a hodgepodge of buildings from different eras. The fifth-grade classroom where he was headed occupied a one-story, plain brick building typical of school architecture in the 1970s. Nothing fancy, but functional.

He didn't want to go in.

He wished like hell Judith Kane's class wasn't the first on his schedule for the week. He'd have liked to get a little practice in before he had to do his thing in front of his pretty neighbor.

He snorted. What was it that his mother used to say? *If wishes were dollar bills, who'd ever do a lick of work?*

Ben squared his shoulders and strode up the walkway and into the building. After detouring into the office to greet the secretary and the principal, he marched down the hall, hardly aware of the occasional kid who shied out of his way. He scanned the room numbers as he passed the doors. L9 was what he wanted.

He found it. Ms. Kane had put the name of each child in the class on a cat-shaped cutout of bright construction paper. They pounced and lounged their way along the hall. On the door itself was a cheerful, enormous lemon yellow mouse that said, "Mrs. Kane."

Ben felt more like a small, helpless mouse being offered as lunch to a boa constrictor.

Firming his jaw, he opened the door and stepped inside. A book in hand, Ms. Kane sat on her desk, slim legs crossed, her posture perfectly ladylike. Her straight skirt might have looked prim, had it not outlined her shape so well. Her head wasn't the only one that turned at the sound of the door. The students all looked up at the same time from open notebooks. A few appeared grateful that his existence would rescue them from the dreaded task of putting words on paper;

others gaped stupidly, as if he were as out of place in their classroom as a Hereford steer.

Judith set down her book and smiled even as she scooted off the desk. Her back stayed elegantly straight, and his gaze lingered on the long, graceful line of her neck, where wisps of coppery hair softened her crisp teacher bun.

"Class, you may put away your journals now. Chief McKinsey is here to begin the fifth-grade DARE program. Why don't we welcome him?"

A ragged chorus of greetings rewarded her prodding.

"'Afternoon," he responded, nodding. Crunch time.

"They're all yours, Chief McKinsey," Judith said, gesturing toward the rows of students. Then she strolled off to the side of the classroom, where she stood with her back to the windows.

Ben couldn't decide if she was smiling encouragement at him or enjoying his discomfiture. The bright light formed a kind of halo behind her, hurting his eyes. After a microscopic pause, he went to the front of the room.

"Some of you have probably already heard about the DARE program from older brothers and sisters," he began. The ones who were lighting cigarettes by the time they hit the sidewalk in front of the middle school. Keeping the sardonic thought to himself, he went on to give a brief outline of the material they would be covering. He tried to scare them with a few stories about the effects of drugs: the violence that came in their wake, the damage to the heart, the hurt to parents.

He handed out the workbooks they'd be using over the next couple of months and then talked about the rules. They were to raise their hands so that only one person spoke at a time. They should be positive and respectful and answer only questions that were comfortable to them. When sharing a story about drug or alcohol use, they were to use the words *someone I know* instead of a name. That last one he regretted; he might have learned some interesting things if he'd been able to pick their brains.

By the time he'd covered some of the vocabulary that would be important—words like *assertiveness, consequences* and *abuse*—Ben could feel he was losing his audience. He talked briefly about self-esteem, while his own sank. The kids were thumbing through the workbooks and whispering. Damn it, this was how the instructions told him to start! He spoke more loudly, earning a few renewed glances, which quickly drifted away.

How the hell did he keep their attention, short of coming down hard on them? That was his usual technique with kids, but a big part of the idea behind the DARE program was to make police officers seem friendly and accessible. He was supposed to become their buddy.

His mouth refused to stretch into an ingratiating smile.

He fell silent. One by one, the kids did the same. Puzzled glances replaced vacant ones.

Now what? Ben refused to turn to their teacher for help. Instead, he tried desperately to remember suggested ways to engage his audience but came up blank.

Very casually, as if a deafening silence were normal in a fifth-grade class, Judith strolled back to the front of the room. He would have had to draw a gun to evoke their instant attention the way her gentle voice did, Ben thought. What did she have that he didn't?

"Chief McKinsey told me that after he went over the basics, he wanted you guys to do some role playing. Why don't we have a couple of volunteers. Let's see." She surveyed the forest of waving hands. "Jennifer and...Tony."

Role playing. Yeah. He grabbed the idea like a flashlight in a dark warehouse. They'd done some of that at the police academy, and the DARE teacher's manual had suggested it. He'd figured on doing it later...but he'd forgotten that kids weren't so good at waiting for later.

"All right," he said, trying to pretend the whole idea had been his. "Jennifer, Tony has just reached over and taken the best part of your lunch. Some cookies your mom made. He takes stuff from you all the time. Your pencil, a bookmark you really like, part of your lunch money. He just laughs when you say, 'Hey, that's mine.' You've decided to confront him. What are you going to say?"

"Um..." Jennifer, a cute dark-haired girl in denim overalls and a tight little shirt that looked like the ones the teenagers wore, turned to Tony. She squeezed her hands in front of her, which had the effect of hunching her shoulders. "I really don't like it when you take stuff like that. It's mean. I'm going to tell the teacher if you don't give those cookies back."

Ben's mouth twitched. She'd come through, illustrating his point perfectly. "Okay, class," he said, facing them. "What do you think? Is he going to give them back?"

He got a shouted response that, taken as a sum, added up to a big *no*.

"Why not?"

She didn't sound tough enough, they decided. She hung her head; she didn't look him in the eye; she didn't act as if she'd really go to the teacher.

"All right. Switch places," Ben said to the two kids.

Tony came through right on cue. He snatched an invisible object from her, leaned toward her with comic-book viciousness and snapped, "Don't touch my stuff again! I know where you live!"

Ben had to suppress a grin. With some coaxing, the class conceded that while Tony's approach might work, it had problems, too. Tony was making an enemy, both through verbal threats and body language. They tried out some scenarios in which the wronged party calmly declared his—and her—rights and intentions by using eye contact, good posture and a tone that was neither aggressive nor wishy-washy.

At least he had the students looking thoughtful. Ben put them to work on a page in the workbook and then turned to Judith.

"Thanks," he said quietly. "I'm no teacher."

"You did fine," she assured him, also in a low voice. Her smile was as soft as he remembered it. "It'll get easier once you know the kids."

Oh, yeah. The fulfillment of a dream. He'd become intimately acquainted with a hundred ten-year-olds.

He frowned, thinking about the anger behind Tony's role-playing. Ben located him in the classroom and noticed that he was concentrating fiercely, although there was something clumsy about the way he held his pencil.

Ben's frown deepened. Maybe down the line he might find knowing these kids useful. If he had an idea of Tony's background, how his parents would react to a visit from the police, if required, whether the boy was a show-off or a bully, he might be able to head off trouble.

"Yeah," he said thoughtfully. The pupils' heads were all bent studiously over the open workbooks. Some of the kids chewed on their pencils or scribbled away in their books. Others sat frozen, pencil points poised above the ruled sheets. If he watched them long enough, even silently at work, he'd learn a fair amount about each one of them.

"That was a good exercise."

His attention snapped back. "Was it?"

"Mmm-hmm." Damn, that smile did something to his blood pressure. Her lips were pale, not pouty like a model's, but sweetly feminine. "I wish we could do more in the schools about relationships. Kids seem so blissfully unaware of how they come across to their peers. They trample on one another's feelings without even noticing."

Maybe they'd soak some grace up from her, Ben thought. "I'll bet you never have to raise your voice."

Her eyes, a clear gray-green, widened. "What?"

"Do you have any discipline problems?" He nodded toward the class, still hard at work.

"Well...not really." Her puzzlement showed.

"And I'll bet you don't accomplish it by yelling or threatening."

"No..."

He explained himself. "They'll learn from you."

She thought about it. "Maybe. Of course, every teacher hopes..." Then a hundred-watt smile blinked on. "Why, thank you."

Thank you? Understanding dawned. She'd taken it as a compliment. Well, he supposed it had been one. From what little he'd seen, Ben would be willing to bet she was a great teacher. He'd had one of those in sixth grade. Mrs. Lee. Sweet, strong willed, demanding, funny. He could still see her face clearly when those of other teachers had long since faded from his memory.

"Just an observation," he said uncomfortably. "By the way, uh, thanks for the banana bread. You didn't have to do that."

"You didn't have to come over when the electricity went off, either."

Her hand touched his, just a flutter of contact like a butterfly pausing between flowers. He felt it to the soles of his feet.

"I hadn't welcomed you." He looked toward the class, not her. "Figured your little girl might be scared."

What was wrong with him? He was *apologizing* because he didn't bake a casserole for every new resident of the crummy rental that happened to be down the lane from him? He'd be inviting her to tea next.

"She was."

He turned his head to see that hers was bowed, and her fingers were twisting together. The curiosity he'd tamped down sharpened again. Why did her five-year-old daughter make Judith Kane so anxious? He almost asked, "Is something wrong with her?" But that was a little blunt even for him. Besides, he didn't get a chance.

His pretty redheaded neighbor glanced up at the clock and straightened. "Class, time to put away your materials. But first, let's thank Chief McKinsey for coming."

The applause was more enthusiastic than he deserved, probably prompted by the kids' desire to please their teacher.

"See you next week," Ben told them, and nodded at Judith.

A wispy blond girl was already waving her hand for attention. "Mrs. Kane. Mrs. Kane!"

"Yes, Glenna?" Turning her head, Judith gave Ben an apologetic smile. "Thank you," she mouthed.

He nodded again and left. Students were already pouring out of classrooms, racing for the bus lines or, in the case of those who walked home, heading for the front doors. Twenty feet from Judith Kane's fifth-grade classroom, an alcove led to the gymnasium. Ben stepped around the corner before he got run down by the stampede.

"Ben! Crime broken out in our schools?" The stocky man who edged out of the flow of traffic was already completely gray although only in his midthirties. A plumbing contractor, Clay was a friend of Ben's. They did some cattle penning together.

"Just the rush hour," he said, nodding at the short bodies packing the hall. "What are you doing here?"

"Shari bulldozed me into picking up Sean for an orthodontist appointment. Braces," he added. "Four thousand bucks' worth of 'em."

Ben shook his head in sympathy. "I'm teaching the DARE program this year."

Over Clay's shoulder, he could just see Judith's door at an angle. He liked the way she said goodbye to each student individually, touching a shoulder here, smiling there, whispering a few words to earn a shy smile in return. He could tell when the last kid was gone, because she vanished. Probably she'd grade papers, or whatever else teachers did, while she waited for her own children.

But seconds later, she popped back out, purse over her shoulder. She came straight down the hall toward him, but she was hurrying too much to look to the right or left. Her anxiety was invisible, but he felt it coming from her like the stink from a skunk.

Curiosity nudged him. "Excuse me," he said to Clay, and stepped into the press of bodies to trail her. He hardly knew what was driving him; for God's sake, the woman probably had a dentist appointment! But something odd was going on with that small family, and he found he couldn't ignore the hints the way he had with the last renter.

Judith turned briskly into another wing of the school. Here the artwork on the walls got cruder and the elbows jabbing Ben were lower to the ground and sharper. Halfway down the hall, she stopped at a classroom door. The teacher there seemed to be waiting for her; Sophie must have been the last student out, because the moment she handed Judith's daughter over, the younger teacher waved goodbye and turned out her classroom lights. Holding her little girl's hand tightly, Judith rushed back the way she'd come.

Ben faded into a recessed area leading to the girl's bathroom. He almost fell over as the door opened behind him.

"Excuse me, mister," a small voice said. It belonged to a pink-cheeked, ponytailed cherub in green corduroy overalls.

"Sorry," he said, moving aside. Judith, towing her daughter and still oblivious to his presence, had already gone by him.

"It's Chief Muck!" another small voice cried in delight.

Ben turned his head. He had no trouble recognizing the boy, who carried a backpack big enough to topple him over. "Jonathan," Ben acknowledged. "Did your mom fire your baby-sitter?"

He nodded. "And Mom called her mother. Lisa was in big, fat trouble." He clearly relished the idea.

"She deserved it." Out of the corner of his eye, Ben saw Judith disappear around the corner. "Ah, excuse me," he said to the boy. Ben got his feet trampled on, but he made it to the corner in time to see her stop at another classroom door. In a replay of the scene with her daughter, her son was handed into her care.

Both kids with her, Judith slowed her pace. He guessed they were heading for the parking lot and decided to drop the tail.

Watching them go, Ben shook his head. It was the

strangest damn thing. He had the distinct impression that both teachers had waited for her, holding her kids until she came. Why didn't Sophie and Zach just make their way to her classroom? Why did she go collect them as if they weren't capable of finding her?

Something was wrong. Part of him didn't want to know what it was. But he was a cop, and he knew his duty.

No matter how pretty Judith Kane was, no matter how soft her smile, he had to find out what was going on with her and her kids.

CHAPTER FIVE

ONLY FOUR DAYS BACK at work, and Judith was already grateful for the weekend! She'd forgotten how hectic working and parenting and running a household could be.

If only she didn't have to live with uneasiness about Rylan prickling her nerves like the tension in the air before a storm. She and the kids had already done the grocery shopping this morning, she'd mowed the pitiful excuse for a lawn using the worthless piece of junk the real estate agent had called a mower and after lunch, while Sophie napped, she and Zach had tried phoning both sets of grandparents. Judith's parents had announced their intention of flying out here for Christmas, which had Zach excited. Ry's parents weren't home, which added to Judith's worries; she'd counted on them to give her updates. When, oh, when, would he finally stand trial? How had he managed all the continuances they'd reported? Why had the judge let him out on bail, when he'd threatened her the way he had during the arrest?

She straightened from scrubbing the bathtub. *Don't think about him,* she told herself. He wouldn't dare come after the kids now, not when he had to see his lawyer and make regular appearances in court. Rylan would be cocky; he'd be sure that he was going to get off, that the judge would sympathize with him, see how much he claimed to love his daughter and agree that his ex-wife should be blamed for making him unhappy. Rylan had always slid out from under every serious consequence in his life; he'd figure this one wouldn't be any exception.

He would bide his time.

She didn't have to worry. Not yet.

Somehow Judith failed to reassure herself.

She did succeed, however, in pulling herself back to the here and now. Thanks to her efforts, the old white porcelain bathtub gleamed everywhere it wasn't chipped. Satisfied, she turned to tackle the sink next, then she'd mop the bathroom and kitchen floors.

The bathroom door stood open, and she could hear canned laughter from the television in the living room. When she stopped cleaning to put dinner on, she'd suggest the kids dream up something more worthwhile to do, but for now, having them so easily occupied was a blessing.

She hummed as she washed the bathroom sink and counter and replaced the cap on Sophie's toothpaste. Sophie liked a different flavor from the one Judith and Zach used. Good thing, too. Sophie squished the tube in the middle and let the toothpaste overflow and then harden. Maybe it was genetic; Rylan had been a slob, also.

Sometimes it was hard for Judith to remember why she had thought she was in love with him at one time. Drying the faucet so it shone, she made a face in the shiny chrome. She'd been young and impressionable.

No, check that. Dumb and hormone ruled. Rylan Kane
was dark haired, blue eyed, wiry and lithe. And that
smile! His eyes would glow like the licks of blue deep
in a hot fire. A dimple would form in one lean cheek
when his white teeth flashed. Oh, yes, Ry was sexy.
And he could make her laugh, even years later when
she should have known better.

Judith sighed. Her own father was so…so *nice*. He
wasn't a complicated man. What you saw was what
you got: integrity, reliability, kindness. Not witty conversation or a wicked laugh or hints of devilment. Dad
had been balding for as long as she could remember,
and softening around the middle, too.

Maybe it was the contrast that had made Rylan so
irresistible to Judith, who was fresh out of college and
ready for a man who quickened her pulse and stole
her breath away.

Well, she'd found him, all right. She'd just been too
stupid to realize that he was also selfish, a little cruel
and completely faithless. Or that he was capable of
going to such lengths to hurt her, just because she'd
grown up enough to see him for what he was.

There she went again. Why was she wasting time
thinking about him? she asked herself, frowning. If she
must picture Ry, it ought to be behind bars, where he
would eventually end up. She hoped they made in-
mates at the county jail work. At least Rylan would
get a taste of real life. She liked the idea of him with
his hands deep in hot sudsy water, or dishing up two
hundred plates of some sloppy casserole.

It was petty of her, but she took pleasure in fanta-
sizing about Rylan suffering in small ways as well as

large. But she didn't forget what was most important: he'd lost his children forever.

After hanging up fresh towels, Judith put away the cleaning supplies and headed toward the kitchen. On the way, she glanced into the living room. Slumped low on the couch, Zach stared unblinking at the screen, even though he'd seen the video playing a hundred times. Cable wasn't available this far out of town, and with the antenna, only two networks came in clearly.

Judith half smiled and shook her head. *Batman* was unlikely to have been Sophie's first choice. She leaned over the back of the big, overstuffed chair. "Honey, do you want to come cook dinner with—"

Sophie's most precious possession, a faded flannel crib blanket she'd somehow managed to cling to during all the moves with her father, was balled into one corner of the chair. Sophie herself was nowhere to be seen.

Judith looked up. Zach was still staring at the TV as if he hadn't even noticed his sister's presence, never mind her absence.

Bathroom... No, of course not. She'd just been cleaning it. A flutter of anxiety tickled in her chest. The kids' bedroom. Sophie had gotten bored with the movie and was playing with her doll or a puzzle. Judith had only half formed the thought before she was hurrying down the hall.

The bedroom door stood ajar. The light was off. No toys littered the floor. The bedcovers were still smooth from this morning's change of sheets.

"Sophie?"

Silence.

Judith whirled and opened the door to the spare bedroom that would be her daughter's when she felt brave enough to sleep alone. Maybe...

No. Furnished only with a bookshelf and an unused child's desk, this room was dim and empty.

Now the anxiety was mutating into panic. Sophie wouldn't have willingly gone far without her blanket. Besides, since they'd been here several weeks, she hadn't left the front porch on her own.

The kitchen. Would she have tried to get herself something to eat?

Deserted.

Judith rushed from window to window, searching desperately for her daughter's small figure. She could be crouched in the grass, watching a bug, or picking the purple asters in the weedy flower beds.

She wasn't doing either.

"Zach!" Judith punched the power button on the television set, turning it off.

"Hey!" He scowled. "I was watching!"

"Where is Sophie?"

"She's right..." His gaze failed to find his sister in the big chair. "She was there a minute ago."

"A minute?" Judith breathed deeply before she let herself say, "Zachary, think. When was the last time you saw your sister?"

He shrank back into the chair, his brown eyes not wanting to meet hers. "Not very long ago. I mean, it couldn't have been more than five or ten minutes."

"Or half an hour?"

"I wasn't paying attention!" he burst out. "Why

do I have to watch her all the time, anyway? It's not like Dad would want her back! He'd probably take me, instead.''

''What a horrible thing to say!'' Judith's throat hurt. ''We'll discuss it later. Now, get up and help me find Sophie. I've looked in the bedrooms already. You search more carefully in case she's hiding for fun. I'll go outside.''

On the porch, she shaded her eyes against the setting sun. The lane was still, tan against the yellow brown of the dry grass.

''Sophie!'' Rushing down the steps, Judith stumbled. ''Honey,'' she called, ''we're not playing hide-and-seek. Please come out!''

No sign of the five year-old. Judith circled the house, panic winging into terror. Once she caught sight of Zach in the window; when he saw her, he shook his head. The flutter in her chest had grown into huge wings beating in fright, leaving her gasping for breath and screaming her daughter's name over and over.

She began running down the lane toward the police chief's house. Dear God, let him be home. He'd help her. If Rylan had taken Sophie...

''Sophie!'' she screamed. Again and again.

Uniformed and hatless, Ben came running to meet her halfway between their houses. He gripped her arms and gave her a shake. ''Calm down!'' he snapped. ''Tell me what's wrong.''

He was right. She would be of no use if she was hysterical. Oh, God, she was shaking. *Please, please, please,* she prayed wordlessly.

"It's Sophie." Her voice broke. "She's...she's missing." Judith reached out and gripped his shirtfront. "I should have told you about my ex-husband. He might have taken her. He did before. Please. You've got to find her."

HE MIGHT HAVE ROOM for doubts later; he'd once been involved in an ugly case where a mother had sold her newborn baby and pretended he'd been kidnapped. She'd sobbed and clutched at him, also.

Judith Kane was hiding out from her ex-husband, afraid he'd steal the kids. No wonder she was so protective! In her spot, he'd have chosen a town like Mad River, too.

Ben gave her another shake, just enough to jolt her from the hysteria. "Was he arrested?"

Her wide, terror-filled eyes latched onto his. "Yes, but he's out on bail. He could have found us." Every word was ragged. "He...Sophie didn't even take her blanket. She never goes anywhere..." Her breath hitched on a sob.

Ben broke his own rules and hugged her—hard. "Maybe that just means she didn't go very far. Where have you looked?"

She quivered against him like a glass house in an earthquake. Right before it broke. Pulling away, she cried, "Everywhere!" Her eyes closed as she visibly tried to collect herself. When she opened them again, they were shimmering. "No. In the house. Zach's searching under beds and in closets right now in case..." She swallowed.

"In case she's hiding."

"Yes."

"All right." He released her and frowned, turning to survey the wooded hillside beyond and the field that separated their houses. "Is she brave enough to set off exploring?"

"I don't know!" Judith balled her hand against her mouth, holding back a sob. "I've only had her back three months. She was gone a long time. Years."

Another question answered. So that was why she didn't know her own daughter. If admitting the truth was such a torment, what must those empty years have been like?

He didn't let himself acknowledge the parallel that wasn't one, because unlike her he'd chosen the empty years. He hadn't wanted to be a father. Not then. Not now.

Ben's mind cleared and he began thinking like a cop. That bastard wasn't going to get away with stealing the little girl who had hugged Ben's side for reassurance in the dark. But chances were, the ex hadn't even tried. Ninety-nine times out of a hundred, missing children had wandered away or gone to friends' houses without telling their parents, or else they were sleeping somewhere nobody had thought to look.

"She wanted to meet my horses," he said.

Her sharp intake of breath told him the possibility was one she hadn't considered. "She *is* crazy about horses. Oh, no! You said they'd hurt her."

"Probably not," he admitted grudgingly. "If she doesn't spook them."

Judith whirled and hurried down the lane at a speed

his long strides barely matched. ''If she went all that way by herself without asking me...''

''You'll wring her neck?''

''Yes!'' She stepped in a pothole and would have gone down if Ben hadn't grabbed her arm. ''No. Of course not. Oh, please. If only it's that simple. I won't even be mad. I promise. Oh, please.''

She wasn't addressing him anymore. She was bargaining with God. He'd done that before himself, with mixed results.

His two-story house blocked their view of the pasture. He and Judith circled the back porch. She was running now, and only the fence stopped her. She gripped the top rail so hard her knuckles showed white, and she lifted herself on tiptoe, as if that would help.

''I don't see her!'' She looked around frantically. ''She's not there!''

His heart drummed. If the little girl wasn't here, he'd have no choice but to call up a manhunt.

''I don't see the horses, either,'' Ben said.

''No.'' With a sob, she flung herself away from the fence and raced for the barn.

He was at her heels. Barely inside the wide double doors, Ben heard singing.

Judith froze. ''Sophie?'' she whispered.

'''Twinkle, twinkle, little star, how I wonder what you are!''' The high voice was a tiny thread, almost lost in the cavernous interior of a barn built for fifty animals, not two.

''Sophie?'' Judith moved forward again. ''Sophie, honey! Where are you?''

The singing stopped abruptly. "I don't wanna go home."

Around the corner, past stacked bales of hay, were the two stalls open to the pasture. Sherlock, a sorrel, snoozed lazily on his side of the four-foot divider; Travis McGee, the palomino gelding, lipped hay from the girl's hand.

Her little butt was planted on the hard-packed dirt floor just outside the enclosure. One forearm and her chin rested on the lowest rail; with the other hand she tugged a few more strands of alfalfa from the nearest bale and offered them to Travis. The damn horse would probably have eaten himself into a major stomachache if Sophie had discovered the molasses-coated oats in the nearby barrel.

"Sophie." Judith crouched just behind her. "I was worried."

"The horses are nice."

"But look how big their feet are. And their teeth. They could hurt you by accident. That's why Ben asked you not to come over here."

The little girl still didn't turn her head. "His lips are really soft." She giggled. "See? He wouldn't bite me."

Judith's jaw firmed. "Sophie, stand up. We're going home now."

"Don't wanna." The kid grabbed the rail.

Ben felt stirrings of amusement. *Yeah, Mom,* he thought, *what are you going to do now?*

She must be really steamed, because all traces of her frantic worry were gone.

"Sophie Kane, you are in trouble. You know better

than to leave without telling me. Now, we *are* going home.'' She lifted her daughter, breaking her grip on the rail, and held her tight when she began drumming her heels, sobbing and trying to throw herself backward.

Judith raised her voice over the din. ''Thank you for your help. I'm sorry Sophie trespassed.''

''I'll walk you home.''

Over the kid's screaming, Judith asked, ''Are you sure?''

Who was she kidding? Did she think he'd quietly go away without finding out more about this ex-husband who was likely to come around looking to steal her kids? Maybe she regretted telling him as much as she had.

Good God. Maybe the ex-husband had legal custody and *she* was the one on the lam.

No, he reflected, if that was the case, she wouldn't be able to hold a job as a teacher, where school officials would scrutinize her credentials and run a background check. Unless, Ben amended, the superintendent had hired her in such a hurry he hadn't done a proper investigation. Or unless she'd come up with a whole new identity.

''I'm sure. Want me to carry her?''

''No. I've got her.''

They walked side by side, not even trying to talk over the kid's unceasing screams. She had the lungs to grow up and be an opera singer. Her mother looked increasingly grim. Poor strategy on little Sophie's part. Pitiful whimpers would have gotten her further.

He should have been irritated. All that hysteria over

a five-year-old sneaking off to the barn to visit the horses. And now the caterwauling. Ben couldn't quite figure out why his sense of humor had kicked in, instead. That and his curiosity. He wanted to know more about these neighbors. He sure as hell wanted to know enough to keep the ex from snatching the kids.

Judith marched right in the house, past the boy, who held the screen door open. As he watched his mother take Sophie through the living room and turn out of sight, he had the oddest damn expression on his face. Maybe wistful. Maybe resentful. Or even a little of both.

Ben hoped the bedroom doors had a lock; if not, that obstinate little brat was going to shoot right back out of there the minute Judith put her down. Might be a good idea for him to stay here, blocking the front door.

Ben laid his hand on the boy's shoulder. "Were you worried about her?"

Zach started, as though he'd forgotten anyone else was there. "I…" His face closed. "Nah. I thought she was hiding or something. She does stuff like that."

Definitely resentment.

"Your mom has to watch her pretty carefully, huh?"

"*I* have to watch her, you mean. It's like I have this job." Zach let the screen door slam then went over to an Adirondack chair and slumped down in it. "Other guys don't have to take care of their little sister all the time." His voice held heartfelt loathing.

"I had to." The words just slipped out, shocking Ben.

The boy turned to look at him in surprise. "Really?"

"Yeah." Ben half sat on the porch railing, legs stretched out before him, and gazed at his booted feet. "Two little brothers and a sister. Our mom was always working."

"What was your dad doing?"

"He'd died."

"After...after he was gone, was it hard not having a father? I mean, did you mind it just being you guys and your mom?"

Had he minded? Ben searched back twenty-five years to when he was this boy's age.

"Yeah. Probably. Guess I didn't have time to dwell on it. He was killed when his tractor rolled onto him. I was nine then. Our mother didn't have any real job skills. She couldn't go to work as a teacher, like your mom, and make a decent living. We moved into town and she got a job as a clerk at the five-and-dime store daytimes, and when that didn't bring in enough to support us, she became a waitress, too, five nights a week. From then on, I had to take care of my brothers and sister."

"Jeez," Zach breathed. "You were my age."

"Yep."

The kid digested that. "Did you *like* your little brothers and sister?"

"Like 'em?" As if it would have made any difference. Ben thought about how to answer. "I got along better with them before Dad died. Afterward, even though I wasn't very old, I was supposed to boss them around. All of a sudden, Mom was ordering them to do what I told them to. That didn't go over very well."

"But you could just, like, laze around and make them do everything, couldn't you?"

Ben grunted with amusement. "I was ten when Mom started working. My brothers were six and eight, my sister five. They weren't big enough to do 'everything.' I was the one who had to wait on them. The way your mom does on you. I made school lunches, cooked dinner, did the laundry...." He shook his head. "I even helped with homework and science projects."

"Jeez. And you didn't have just one little sister!"

"Nope." He hadn't been old enough to be a parent, not by any stretch. He'd hated tying shoelaces, slapping peanut butter and jam on bread, shoving little arms into coat sleeves, listening to spelling words and times tables. In comparison, this kid had it good. Ben hoped he realized that. "Your mom can't do everything," he said.

"I guess not," Zach agreed unhappily. He frowned at the screen door. "I liked it better with just Mom and me."

Ben shrugged. "Most older kids do. Learning to share your parents is part of growing up."

"I don't have a dad to share." His sullenness returned.

"Neither did I," Ben said with a decided lack of sympathy. "Neither do a lot of kids. You're luckier than some—you've got a great mother. Live with it."

His curtness earned him a scowl. "Like you know everything," the boy said rudely. "At least your dad died."

"And I did what I had to." Ben gave him a flat stare. "You're old enough to do the same."

"Why?" Zach's lip curled. "So I can be just like you?"

Ben would have been angrier but for the shock he felt. Was that what he sounded like? As if he thought he'd been noble?

He knew better. True nobility required generosity, a willing heart. Oh, he'd done what he had to do, all right, but he'd done it with the acid of resentment corroding what heart he had. And the scars it left had shaped his life, driven away the woman he thought he loved, left him an empty shell of a man living alone, policing a town where there wasn't enough passion to fuel real crime.

Noble? Oh, yeah. That was him. Sir Galahad himself.

"No," he said. "You don't want to be like me."

The boy started to say something, but he didn't have a chance. The screen door squeaked open and Judith stood framed in the doorway. Ben realized that only silence came from the house; he hadn't even noticed when Sophie quit screaming.

Judith's face was pale and set; dried tear tracks stained her cheeks. "Zach, please go in the house. You may watch your movie again for now, but we need to talk later."

"It's not my fault—"

"Later."

The boy's whole body quivered with outrage, but his mother won. After a moment, he stomped inside, letting the screen door slam so hard it bounced twice.

Judith closed her eyes and her shoulders sagged. Ben could see the effort it took her not to crumple into a chair and cry. She awakened his admiration by doing one better: she straightened her shoulders, opened her eyes and said forthrightly, "I'm sorry I made such a scene. I should have thought of the horses. I'm embarrassed that I didn't. I let my fears overwhelm me."

He didn't move from his comfortable perch on the porch rail. "Sounds like you have a good excuse for being afraid."

"Yes, but…"

"No buts. You have no reason to be embarrassed." Ben meant every word. "You did the right thing coming to me. If he'd had your daughter, it would have been important for us to act fast."

Her eyes filled with tears between one blink and the next, shimmering clear green and silver, like stones on the bottom of a mountain brook. "What am I going to do?" she whispered.

His hands itched to grasp her slender shoulders, squeeze comfortingly, maybe draw her into his arms. Instead, he rubbed his palms over his thighs. "Haven't you already done everything you can?"

"Yes. No." She bit her trembling lower lip. "I don't know! I thought I had, but he was in jail then." Her gaze clung to Ben's, beseeching. "I was so sure I could watch them every minute, but I can't, can I?"

"No," he said quietly, "and you shouldn't feel inadequate because you can't."

"The other teachers have been so good about this. And Carol—my principal—has been wonderful, but…" Judith crossed her arms tightly. "Basically,

I'm alone here. I should have stayed where I was. At least my parents were nearby.''

"Should you?"

For an instant, her eyes closed again and she hugged herself. "No. No, it's easier here. I just wish I had someone else to rely on. Maybe my parents would come out for a while. At least until Rylan's trial.''

"If they can, it might not be a bad idea," Ben agreed.

Her thoughts were running as frantically as a trapped rat; he could see it in her eyes.

"No," she said. "Or...maybe they would, but I can't ask them. They had this trip planned, you see. They're meeting some old friends in Belize. Mom and Dad haven't seen them in ten years.''

"What's more important?"

She didn't answer directly. "They didn't want me to marry Rylan. They didn't like him.''

Ben understood. She felt guilty because they'd been right. The choice had been hers, and now she was determined to bear the consequences alone.

"I'll make a few phone calls," he said. "Find out where he is, whether anybody has a leash on him.''

"A leash?"

"Whether they're checking on him. Whether anyone will notice if he vanishes.''

"Oh." Now those beautiful eyes were great pools of hope. "Would you really do that?"

He would have checked out her story anyway, so it bothered him some for her to look at him as a savior. Why couldn't she see through him as easily as her kid had?

"Tomorrow." Ben pulled a notebook from his back pocket and had her give names and dates. The details he needed. "You know, chances are he's too worried about the prison term he faces to even think about hunting you down."

Her fingers twisted together. "When they caught up with him, he made threats."

"We've all made threats we never intend to carry out."

"That's true." She tried to smile, her lips curving wanly. "Thank you. You've been so nice."

Noble.

"Just doing my job," Ben said brusquely. Time to get out of here. He pushed himself away from the railing, wishing to God she didn't look so much like a woman who needed to be held.

Her fingers squeezed her upper arms. "I'm sorry," she said again. "I'm sure you're right. He won't come. We'll be fine."

"Don't apologize!"

She flinched, and he cursed himself.

"He's the bastard. You have no reason to take the blame."

His neighbor gave a jerky nod.

"I'll stop by tomorrow," Ben told her, "after I've made those phone calls. Let me give you my phone number, if you need me before then."

"I'm sure I won't…"

His expression stopped her. "Go write it down before you forget." He recited the numbers twice and made her repeat them. He left her then, although with every step he felt the pull to go back.

But he didn't dare. He'd end up taking her in his arms. She'd cry on his shoulder, wet his shirtfront. He'd make foolish promises to keep her and the kids safe. And then he'd kiss her, and he especially didn't dare do that.

Judith Kane and her two troubled children were a danger he might not be able to escape.

CHAPTER SIX

"Do you really dislike Sophie so much?" Sitting on the foot of her son's bed, Judith tried not to sound angry or judgmental.

Yesterday Zach had shocked her a little with his lack of concern when Sophie went missing, not to mention his sneering insistence that their father wouldn't want her anyway. But maybe, Judith had decided, she was overreacting. What kid didn't think his younger sister was a pain in the neck? And she *had* been expecting a lot of him since their move.

Zach's only response was to shrug and refuse to look up. No surprise, considering he was already mad at her.

Judith stifled a sigh. "Just remember, if you play your cards right, Sophie will be your number-one fan. Little sisters are famous for adoring their big brothers."

He turned his face away.

Let it go, she thought. They'd always been close as mother and son; once he got over his anger at being chewed out for not watching Sophie better, they could have a real talk.

"I know it's a drag, having to keep an eye on her all the time," she said. "But I need your help."

He didn't move.

Judith sighed again and walked out of his room. She peeked in her bedroom to see that Sophie was sound asleep, round cheek flushed and her thumb slipping from her mouth. Tiny coppery wisps of hair curled around her face and, damp from perspiration, stuck to her forehead and temple. Judith stood looking at her for the longest time, fear and a painful kind of love and awe squeezed together in her chest. All those empty years, and now she could watch her daughter sleep.

Her fingernails bit into her palms. Rylan would not get Sophie again. Whatever it took to ensure that, Judith would do it.

The doorbell chimed, and she left Sophie napping. Judith hurried through the living room to the front door, eagerness supplanting the bittersweet emotions she felt for her daughter. It must be Ben; he'd promised to make those phone calls today and let her know what he had found out.

He was half-turned away, head tilted back, when she opened the door. Above, a tiny bird harried a hawk that floated lazily on an air draft. The small drama in the sky didn't explain why Judith's heart gave a funny little lurch.

How could she not notice the breadth of Ben's shoulders beneath a gray T-shirt that molded to the long muscles of his upper arms and the planes of his chest? The faded, dusty jeans showed off lean hips and long, tautly muscled legs. In profile, his straight nose and square chin made his face seem less harsh than she thought of it, but still uncompromisingly male.

The faint sheen of gray threading through his dark hair suited him, somehow reflecting the inner grimness she sensed but didn't understand.

He was a sexy man. And she had to tear her gaze from his strong brown throat and hope she wasn't blushing when he faced her.

"I...hello. Will you come in?"

One dark brow lifted, but his voice gave away nothing. "Why don't we stay out here. I was just unloading hay. I might track in dirt."

Judith nodded and stepped outside, easing the screen door closed so that it didn't wake Sophie. A new tension made her forget her self-consciousness. "Did you...did you find out anything?"

"I talked to the detective in Boston who handled your daughter's disappearance. Edgekoski. You know him?"

"We must have talked a hundred times."

"Ah. Well, Edgekoski put a call in to Kane while I was waiting on the other line." Ben stood close enough to touch, big, solid and reassuring. "Your ex answered. He was in his motel room, right where he was supposed to be."

"Motel," Judith echoed. Brilliant. He was giving her the best possible news, and she sounded like a parrot. After yesterday's idiotic behavior, he must wonder about her.

She was more worried about the foolishness of her reaction to Ben McKinsey. She needed him to make her feel safe. Yet when she was aware of him as a man, he became a threat to her on some level she hardly understood.

"Yeah," he said patiently. "One of those places you rent by the week. Cheap but clean. Kitchenette. You know."

Judith tried and failed to picture Ry in a shabby little room with a lumpy bed, a kitchenette and a TV. Was that how he'd raised Sophie, moving from one sleazy motel to another?

"He's being cooperative. Even given the history, Edgekoski didn't see him as a risk to bolt."

Alarm flared. "They don't know him."

Ry would never accept responsibility for any wrongdoing. Oh, yes, he'd be cooperative, as long as he thought he could manipulate the system into letting him off. The moment he understood that he'd lost, that he *would* be going to prison, Rylan would vanish. Defeat wouldn't be acceptable.

What Judith feared was that Rylan wouldn't be satisfied by making his getaway; he would feel victorious only if he recovered Sophie. Only if he showed Judith that he was smarter than she was. That their daughter loved him more.

Ben waited until her eyes refocused. "Maybe you don't know him anymore, either," he suggested, voice gravelly.

"I know him." She sucked in a deep breath and let it out. "I'm sorry. Here I go again. After yesterday, the last thing you want to hear is—"

"Damn it." His hand shot out to grip her wrist. "Quit apologizing. The son of a bitch stole your kid. He threatened to do it again. You hate him and you're afraid of him. Why wouldn't you be upset?"

She stared at him, surprised as much by the anger

that glittered in his narrowed dark eyes as she was by what he'd said. Was the anger on her behalf?

"You...you don't think I'm being silly?"

He muttered a profanity. "No. I don't think you're being anything but cautious." He jerked his head toward the silent house. "Where are the kids?"

"In their rooms." She made a wry face to hide the painful emotions she felt. "I chewed out Zach. Now he's sulking." Knowing she was begging, she looked up at her neighbor's strong, blunt-featured face. Surely, surely, he'd give her the honesty she sought. "He's only nine. A child. Am I asking too much of him?"

"No," Ben said harshly, "That's plenty old to help you out and to understand how serious the threat is."

Surprised again by the force of his reaction, Judith said, "*I* see Rylan as a threat. Zach sees him as his father."

Ben grunted impatiently. "Does he even remember him as a father?"

"Yes. Well, more or less. I think..." She looked down at the porch floor; it was in need of new paint. "Truthfully, he sees his father through rose-colored glasses. Ry was never all that interested in the kids or their activities. He sure wasn't out there coaching T-ball or mother-goose soccer."

Muscles bunched in Ben's jaw. His tone was odd. "Not a devoted father."

She pressed her lips together. "No."

"Why your girl? Why not his son, too?"

She knew what he was asking and explained that

Zach hadn't been at the day-care center the day Rylan had taken Sophie.

Ben listened with frowning incredulity. "You're telling me the guy couldn't wait another day so he could have his son, too?"

"I don't know! I don't know why he did it that way!" Fiercely, she held back the tears that threatened. Zach and Sophie were safe; right this minute, she knew where Rylan was. And she had an ally. Judith struggled for control. "I have coffee made. Will you have a cup? It…it doesn't matter if you track a little dirt in. The floor sweeps up easily enough. Or I can bring it out here, if you'd rather."

A silent battle seemed to take place inside him; after a moment, he bent his head in assent. "Thank you."

When Judith opened the screen door and went in, Ben followed her, so close she smelled his sweat and…maleness. It put her on edge again, and she was glad to have her back to him as she took mugs from the cupboard, got out sugar and milk.

She poured him a cup and turned to find that Ben wasn't in the kitchen at all. The low sound of his voice came from the hall. Around the corner, she saw him immediately, standing in the doorway to Zach's bedroom. Part of her wanted to sidle close enough to hear what he was saying, but she would have felt as if she were spying.

Ben nodded and quietly pulled the bedroom door closed. He turned to see her in the archway to the kitchen. Something flickered in his eyes, but his face was expressionless when he came toward her.

She didn't question him, only handed him a steaming mug. "Sugar and milk on the counter."

He accepted the mug of coffee but didn't move past her. Without inflection, he said, "Your kids need to feel comfortable with me if I'm going to be keeping an eye on them."

Hope tightened her throat. "You believe me?"

That dark brow rose again. "You mean that your husband might still come after them?"

"Yes. Even though that police detective doesn't think so?"

A muscle twitched in his cheek when he looked down at her. "You know him better. He's done it once. Yeah, I believe you."

Relief weakened her knees. How easy it would be to sag against this man, rest her forehead on his shoulder, feel his arms come around her. But she remembered...oh, all sorts of things. She recalled how much faith she'd had in the police when Sophie first disappeared. And then as the weeks went by, she'd realized that they were busy with other cases, that a noncustodial parent taking a child didn't rate a huge number of man-hours. That if she didn't keep nagging and fighting and going on TV and distributing Sophie's picture herself, she might never see her daughter again.

And she remembered how confident she'd been that her parents were wrong, that Rylan was the man for her. That he would love her forever, and be a good father, and never deliberately hurt her.

Judith made herself stand straight. No matter how desperately she wanted to lean on Ben, she couldn't.

For the sake of her children, she couldn't afford to put all her faith in Ben McKinsey. In any man. It was up to her to keep Zach and Sophie safe, to keep them with her. She would be grateful for help but not depend on it being there unfailingly.

That kind of trust had been lost with Rylan's betrayal.

"Thank you," Judith said, her gaze holding Ben's. "It...helps to know you don't think I'm crazy."

"Even if I did," he said, "it's my job to give you the benefit of the doubt."

Somehow she'd retained a sense of humor, enough to let her laugh, if wryly, at his candor. "Hasn't anyone ever told you to quit while you're ahead?"

"Quit...?" The corner of his mouth twitched. "I, uh, didn't mean to imply that I *do* think you're wacko."

Her smile quivered into life again. "Thank you. I think." Judith touched his arm but quickly drew her hand back, startled by the heat of his skin and the way the muscle under her finger tips tightened instantly. She twined her fingers together and took a deep breath. "Ben, I'm sorry I dragged you into my troubles. I rented this house partly because the agent told me you'd be my neighbor. That wasn't fair."

The crease in one cheek deepened. "You did what you had to. And once you moved to my town, it became my job to protect you and your kids."

His job. Why was that not what she wanted to hear? Did she want him to feel like the knight in shining armor, galloping to the rescue of his ladylove out of pure chivalry?

"Thank you," she said again, her voice low.

His eyes seemed to darken. "Don't worry. I won't let the bastard—" He stopped.

"It's okay." Judith tried to smile. "You can call him anything you want."

"You don't have mixed feelings?"

Was it the cop inquiring, she wondered, or the man? Either way, the answer was easy. "No," she said simply. "I asked for the divorce. That's what he's trying to pay me back for. When I married him, I was a fool."

"We're all fools at some time or other." His dark eyes were steady. "Some of us most of the time."

"Have you ever been married?" she asked on impulse.

Between one blink and the next, the momentary closeness vanished. "No." He set down the mug of coffee, untasted, on the table. "I'd better be on my way."

"Oh?" She strove to sound uncaring. "Fine. I'll walk you to the door." As if he couldn't find his own way.

He nodded and strode ahead of her. Judith didn't follow him out. He let the screen door close, then turned to face her, its mesh blurring his features.

"If it's okay with you, I promised your son that someday this week after school, I'd put him and his sister up on the horses."

Dumbfounded, she could only repeat, "On the horses?"

"I'll lead them around. Unless the boy has ridden before."

"Zach."

"What?"

"Why do you always call him 'the boy'?" Judith asked, genuinely curious.

"He reminds me of one of my brothers."

Even more astonished, she wished she could make out his expression better. "What's his name?"

"Eddie." That giveaway muscle in his cheek twitched. "Ed now."

"Are you friends?"

"Haven't seen him in years." His mouth tightened. "The horseback ride okay?"

"I...if you have time. Is it safe?"

"We'll be careful."

She gave her head a bemused shake. "Fine. You know they'll love it. Any day."

"Tomorrow?"

"You're not working?"

"I'm taking a few days of vacation."

She wanted to ask why he wasn't going on a Caribbean cruise or climbing Mount Rainier or taking a fishing trip with friends instead of hanging around home alone, but considering how grateful she was to have him near, she figured it would be as well not to sound either nosy or critical.

"Thank you," Judith repeated for about the fiftieth time.

He nodded and left. Through the screen, she watched him cut across her lawn—such as it was—and turn onto the dusty lane. His strides were long but taut, controlled, balanced. This was not a man who sauntered.

Nor a man who did anything lightly. Protecting her children was his job, as he saw it, and he'd try his damnedest to do just that.

Why had he never married? she wondered. Some woman had missed a good prospect. Maybe he didn't smile or tease, and she doubted he'd bring a woman roses or write her poetry, but she'd be willing to bet that when he promised forever, by God he'd deliver. She thought maybe Ben McKinsey could be trusted. She'd take that over flowers or poetry any day.

But he hadn't offered her anything but police protection, and that was one thing she couldn't—didn't dare—trust. Not even when a man as steady as a rock offered it.

THAT EVENING, Ben phoned his sister. He'd stayed closest to her, in part because she was the youngest and had least resented his premature elevation to parenthood. He was her big brother, and Nora had worshipped him until she turned thirteen and he refused to let her date Brad Marcovich, a sixteen-year-old stud. At sixteen, she forgave Ben. He was a cop by the time she graduated from high school, so he was able to help pay her university tuition. Nora majored in—of all damn things—horticulture and was now a landscape designer in Portland, Oregon. Eddie and John had both married and had broods of their own; Nora, like Ben, was still single.

"Ben!" she cried when she heard his voice. "Is something wrong? What's up?"

Disconcerted, he said, "Does something have to be wrong? I just, uh, wanted to say hello."

"Really."

Slouched in his well-worn recliner, he frowned. "Is that a crime?"

"You don't call very often," his sister said with a hint of tartness, "and when you do, it's usually for a reason. I just figured we'd get family stuff out of the way first."

"There's no family stuff," he said shortly.

"Oh. Well then, how are you?"

Ben grunted. "I'm okay. You?"

She'd decided to strike out on her own, Nora announced; she was confident she'd built up enough of a reputation among local gardeners and horticulturists to make a living.

"New businesses take at least a couple of years to turn a profit," Ben noted. "Can you afford that?"

"Are you offering to invest in McKinsey Landscape Design?" she teased.

"If you need help..."

"I think I can pull it off," Nora said, her voice suddenly gone soft. "But thank you."

He mumbled something, then asked abruptly, "Have you talked to Eddie recently? How is he?"

There was a moment's pause. "Funny, he asked me about you the last time he called. Maybe you're both mellowing."

"I don't need to mellow. He's the one with the problem." The oldest next to Ben, Eddie had resented his brother's authority the most. An adult now in years if not maturity, he still held a grudge.

"A little mellowing wouldn't hurt you, either, dear brother." She didn't give him time to respond. "Eddie and his wife are having problems. He told me she walked out, but you know how he exaggerates. I think they'll work things out.''

''You always were an optimist.'' A wry smile kicked up one corner of Ben's mouth. ''Everyone is always going to be okay.''

''I'm usually right.''

''Mom wasn't,'' Ben said harshly.

''No.'' The one word was as quiet as a breath released. ''Maybe if she were alive…''

''We'd be one big happy family?''

''Well…you never know.''

For once, he didn't argue. Maybe if their mother had had medical insurance and gone to the doctor regularly, her breast cancer would have been discovered in time to save her. And maybe then her grown children wouldn't have drifted apart. They might be gathering for Thanksgiving feasts and on Christmas morning to watch the next generation of McKinseys tearing open their presents.

He shook his head to dispel the storybook images. Good God, he must be getting senile to imagine such scenes with anything but horror!

''So,'' Nora asked brightly, ''what's new in your life?''

She always asked; ''nothing special'' was his invariable response. The hell of it was, ''nothing special'' was no lie. In Mad River, the greatest innovation was a novel flavor of ice cream at the café. Half to surprise Nora, he said, ''I do have some new neighbors.''

"In that rental? The one the guy turned into a marijuana farm?"

"Yep. The walls inside are pink now."

"Pink?"

He shifted in his recliner. "Well... Kind of peachy. It actually doesn't look bad."

"It's probably gorgeous," his sister said reprovingly. "What's special about these neighbors?"

Ben told her about Judith and her troubles. "The boy reminds me of Eddie. Mouthy to cover up being unhappy."

"He has reason to be."

"Looks like he has it pretty good to me."

"He's a child, not a big tough guy like you."

"He's the same age I was when Dad died." He felt like a damn fool the minute the words were out; even he recognized that he'd come to the crux of his mixed feelings toward the kid. Ever since he and the boy had had that talk out on Judith's front porch, he'd been bugged by the parallels between Zach Kane and himself as a boy.

Back then, Ben had wanted to whine and pout and throw temper tantrums, too, but he hadn't, because who else could his mother turn to? Why should he look on this boy with anything but contempt?

Ben ended the conversation with his sister abruptly, wishing he could as easily cut off the self-examination. He knew damn well that his irritation with Zach Kane had roots more tangled than mere scorn. Maybe somewhere inside he was jealous. Maybe he even wondered if he'd *had* to turn himself into a martyr.

An uncomfortable thought nudged its way onto the

tail of the last one: maybe Eddie did have reason to dislike him. After all, Ben had been self-sacrificing beyond his years. Whatever poor Eddie did must have seemed childlike in comparison. If Ben hadn't been so determined to step into his dad's shoes, to do it all, he and his brothers could have been in it together, a team.

Yeah, at first Eddie and John had been pretty young, but with time they could have helped out more, taken more responsibility, made sacrifices just as he had. But no, by then he was the dictator, so wrapped up in his own bitterness it never occurred to him to loosen the reins even a fraction of an inch, much less hand them to anyone else.

And the whole damn time he'd begrudged every minute given to his siblings.

Ben swore and rubbed a hand over his face. He thought he'd put all that behind him, his resentment and his guilt. What the hell was making him dredge it up now?

Of course, he knew damn well what it was. The trigger was a kid named Zach Kane. The boy, his cute, sad little sister and his pretty mother, whose problems had begun to absorb more of Ben's time and thoughts than he liked to admit.

Ben hadn't told his sister this part—that he had offered to spend an hour or so leading a couple of kids around on his horses. If he had, she would have laughed, and Nora had a wicked laugh.

The next afternoon, as soon as he saw Judith's van turn onto their shared lane, he headed out to the barn to brush and saddle Travis, the more patient of his two quarter horses. The van passed his place without stopping, but the kids and their mother came streaming into his barn not two minutes later. No pause for milk and cookies there.

Sophie rose on tiptoe and stuck her hand through the rails without hesitation to clumsily pat Travis's muzzle. The horse winced with each whack but endured her affection without lifting his head out of reach. Zach hung back. And their mom…

Ben swallowed. "You're not dressed for riding."

She wore a mint-green, slim-fitting dress with sleeves that just covered the cap of her shoulders and a hemline that left bare long creamy legs, shapely enough to keep a man awake nights. The shorts had been bad enough. The dress was worse. If she didn't change to jeans right now, he wouldn't sleep tonight.

Her eyes widened at his suggestion. "Me? Oh, I can't ride."

"Why not?"

"I never have."

"Everyone around here rides," Ben told her. "Go on. I can take care of the kids. You go change."

Doubtfully, she looked from him to the horse, then at her kids and back to Ben. "Are you sure?"

"Yeah." He nodded toward the barn doors. "Scat."

Judith went with a few dozen backward glances.

The minute she was out of earshot, the boy swaggered forward. "I get to go first."

Ben lifted a brow. "Yeah? Why's that?"

"I'm the oldest…" He read Ben's expression correctly. "I mean, I ought to show Sophie how to do it, don't you think? Since she's so little?"

"I think maybe we'll start with both of you." Ben

backed the gelding out of the stall. "Can you two slip through those rails?"

Now Sophie was the hesitant one, looking a little wary as she inched out into the sunlight. She'd likely just realized how enormous the horses were without a fence separating her from them.

Ben bent and cupped his hands. "Zach, put your left foot right here and I'll toss you up."

The boy obeyed, swinging his other leg over the horse's back like a pro. Once up, he gripped the saddle horn and surveyed the world from on high. "Cool," he proclaimed.

Ben squatted in front of Sophie. "Okay, I'm going to lift you up. You'll fit in the saddle right behind your brother. You wrap your arms around his waist and you'll be safe as houses."

Wide, apprehensive eyes as lucid a gray as any he'd seen fastened on Ben. "Safe as houses?" she echoed in that high, piping voice.

"Yeah." He swiveled on his heels and pointed toward his farmhouse. "See how solid it is? It never slips off its foundation. You'll be that secure up on Travis. Besides—" he lowered his voice "—I think Travis likes you."

She giggled, and he had a flash of Nora giggling just like that. He'd always been softest on her.

Like a projector bringing up the next slide, he suddenly saw another little girl, this one dark haired. Did he have a daughter somewhere with eyes that wide and vulnerable? A child lifting her arms trustingly for someone else to boost her wherever she wanted to go?

He pinched the bridge of his nose hard enough to

hurt. Hell, he knew better than to let himself think like that! Besides, if he had a daughter, she'd be a lot older than Sophie Kane. More like six—no, seven years old now.

And she wasn't his, not in any way that counted.

Sophie was a featherweight. He swung her in an easy arc and settled her into the saddle. No boa constrictor could have grabbed a snugger hold.

Her brother gagged. ''Sophie! Loosen up!''

Ben had to pry her small arms from their death grip on Zach's waist and reposition them. Travis shifted his weight just then. Her whole body quivered and her arms squeezed again.

''Easy,'' Ben soothed. ''He won't do anything but walk. The first few steps will seem bouncy, but then you'll feel the rhythm. His back is nice and wide. You won't fall off.''

''Promise?'' she whispered.

''Word of honor.''

She took a deep breath. ''Okay.''

''You doing all right?'' Ben asked the boy.

His knuckles showed white around the saddle horn, but he said scornfully, ''Of course I am! I'm not a baby like her.''

''I'm not a baby!'' Sophie cried.

''Are too!''

''Am not!''

This argument had a familiar ring to it. Ben ended it by the simple expedient of taking hold of the reins and starting Travis forward. The first rolling step brought two gasps and then silence but for the quiet thud of each hoof coming down. Ben turned his head to see two sets of saucer eyes.

As he led the quarter horse on a meandering path through the pasture, however, the kids loosened up. Zach let his body sway with the horse's rhythm and tried to look nonchalant. Sophie craned her neck to peek around each side of her brother, then twisted around to see the horse's big brown rump.

Both started when Sherlock trotted up, but when Travis did no more than stroll along, Sophie giggled. "Sherlock was lonesome."

"Yep," Ben agreed. "Horses are herd animals, you know. Pretty much like most people."

"I'm not a herd animal!" the boy protested.

"No? Before you moved here, what'd you like doing for fun? You a baseball player?"

"Yeah, and soccer. I was the striker," he boasted, then fell silent. "Well, just 'cuz they're team sports doesn't mean..."

"But we play team sports because that's what comes naturally." Ben patted Travis's neck. Despite the earlier grooming, dust rose. "A kid who'd rather stay in from recess is the oddball, right?"

"I guess," Zach agreed reluctantly.

"So you still want to argue?"

"*You* live alone."

He mostly worked alone, too. By choice. He'd always figured that after being crammed for all those years into that tiny house with three siblings, he needed solitude. He was comfortable with it.

Funny, then, that he was actually kind of enjoying

this ramble with the two kids, even the conversation. Maybe he *was* mellowing.

"When you're an adult, about the only way to have someone to live with is to get married, and that's a big step. You want to be sure you've chosen the right person. I guess I just haven't found her yet."

Sophie poked her head around her brother's side. "Mommy isn't married."

"Yeah, I know." Legs like that, and she wasn't married.

"I like horses," the little girl continued artlessly. "If you married Mommy, Zach and me could ride Travis and Sherlock lots, couldn't we?"

Ben had to laugh. At least she was straightforward. "Got it all figured out, don't you?"

Zach turned his head and burst out, "What about Dad? Have you forgotten him?"

Sophie blinked and looked confused. "No-o," she said doubtfully. "Not 'zactly. But...but I don't know where Daddy is!" Her voice rose and her face puckered.

Ben flicked a glance at the boy. "Way to go," he growled. "She's a little kid. She's just talking. Give her a break, why don't you?"

"Well, she shouldn't talk like that," Zach mumbled.

Ben dropped back to the gelding's side and laid a hand on Sophie's ankle. "Shall we go a little faster?"

Her distress vanished, replaced with delight. "You mean gallop?"

"Not quite. Just walk a little faster." He waited for the boy to respond.

Zach gave him a sulky look. "Big deal."

Ben returned to the horse's nose and urged him into a faster walk. After a while he looked back to see both kids grinning. On impulse, Ben said, "When we get back to the barn, I'll take you up with me, one at a time, and we'll canter. Would you like that?"

Yeah, they'd like that. Their mom, waiting at the water trough, wasn't so sure.

"I won't let them fall," Ben promised. Damn it, the jeans weren't an improvement. They fit her hips the way his hands would have liked to, and she'd paired them with a skinny little shirt in a shade of green close to that of her eyes. His quick survey told him that terrific as her legs were, they might take second place to a pair of high, round breasts. He shifted uncomfortably, hoping nobody noticed the way his jeans had tightened.

Behind him, Sophie said in her little-girl voice, "We'll be safe as houses."

Judith raised her eyebrows. Ben spread his hands and smiled disarmingly.

Something happened in that instant. Her smile trembled into life; her eyes softened, then shimmered as though tears had sprung into them. She looked at him as if he were the Sir Galahad she wanted to make him.

Ben felt short of air. He reached out a hand, then curled it into a fist and pulled it back to his side. "You okay?" he asked gruffly.

She gave her head a shake. "I...yes, of course. It's just..." Her eyes searched his. "You smiled. And...and Sophie trusts you."

"She can," he said quietly, then felt as if he'd been

kicked right in the gut. Who the hell was he to claim any kid could trust him, when he'd never even bothered to try to see his own?

"Yes." Judith pressed her hands to her chest. "I know." She smiled up at her children. "Who's going first?"

She believed him, just like that. Ben felt like scum. If she knew... But she didn't, and he wasn't going to tell her.

Anyway, his past didn't matter. Judith could trust him; he wouldn't let her down.

"Oldest first," Ben said, and turned to lift the little girl off the horse's back.

CHAPTER SEVEN

JUDITH HADN'T FELT SO safe—and *happy*—since she couldn't remember when. The big brown horse ambled down the lane; she relaxed in the saddle with Sophie's round warm body squeezed in front of her; behind her was Zach, his skinny arms wrapped around her waist. Judith held the reins, but Ben strolled right by the horse's head.

Tiny puffs of dust rose with each hoofbeat; the pungent scent of ponderosa pine seemed part of the warm, late-afternoon sunshine. The larch trees, which Judith had assumed were evergreen when she first came, were turning to molten gold on the hillside.

Her gaze kept lingering on Ben's straight back and broad shoulders, his short dark hair with the strands of silver, his strong brown neck, the big, competent hand that patted his horse's shoulder. *He* was a part of her contentment, more so than she was comfortable admitting. He was here, rock solid, kind—if reluctantly so—to her children, a man who kept promises.

Reminding herself that she hardly knew him failed to do a thing to filter out the rosy color through which she seemed to be seeing the world today. And what was wrong with being happy? she asked herself defiantly. Why not enjoy a few hours of peace and...okay, dreams might be too strong a word. Hope. That was it. Hope that the time might come when she wouldn't have to worry about the kids, when Sophie would no longer beg for Daddy at bedtime and Zach wouldn't look at his sister with dark angry eyes, when Judith herself could fall in love, maybe trust a man again.

There was nothing wrong with hope, was there?

"Here we are." Ben grabbed the reins down by the horse's mouth. He'd stopped the gelding not two feet from Judith's front porch. Travis shook his head, jingling the bridle and making his mane flop.

Sophie stirred in front of Judith. "Can we ride again?" she asked hopefully.

"Yeah," Ben said, "we'll do it again." He reached up for Sophie, who tumbled willingly into his arms.

"Will you have dinner with us?" Judith asked as he set her daughter down on the porch steps. "I put on a stew this morning in the Crock-Pot." When he hesitated, she coaxed, "I make wonderful sourdough biscuits."

The way to a man's heart... Judith clamped off the thought. She was *not* trying to entice him; she was merely reciprocating his kindness.

He inclined his head in assent. "Can't resist an invitation like that. My stews are usually out of a can. Biscuits, too, come to think of it."

"Real men don't cook, right?" Zach said. "Mom tries to make me learn."

"If real men enjoy eating, they cook." Ben looked steadily up at her son. "I get lazy when all the effort is just for myself. 'Don't' doesn't mean 'can't.'"

"Oh."

Even without being able to see Zach's face, Judith felt the onset of sullenness. He needed a father, she thought, someone to ally himself with. What he had was a little sister who threatened his place with his mother. And a mother who was overwhelmed by the struggle to mend a family even as she had to stand guard. Although part of her wished Ben were the fatherly kind, she was glad he didn't cater to Zach too much; all she needed was a redneck neighbor who convinced her son that men didn't cook or clean house, that women were sissies and that his mom was overprotective.

But, oh, for a man who took Zach under his wing. Her fingers tightened on the reins. If only remarrying weren't the only sure way she knew to provide him with a daddy.

As if in answer to a prayer, Ben lifted a brow at her.

"Maybe Zach would like to ride back with me, help unsaddle Travis and feed the horses. I need to shower, but he could wait for me."

"Could I?" her son breathed.

"Sure." She smiled at the police chief. "If he wouldn't be a nuisance."

Something wry in his expression told her that yes, he expected Zach would be just that, but he shook his head. "Taking care of animals is part of owning them. Time he learned that."

"We don't *have* any animals," Zach grumbled. "Mom would never let me get a dog."

"We had no yard, and you were too young to walk one alone." *And I was too afraid to let you.*

"A dog might not be a bad idea now," Ben suggested. "Good early-warning system."

"Yeah!" Zach bounced behind her, and the horse's hindquarters bunched and shifted. "Could we?"

Judith grabbed the saddle horn. "I'll think about it."

Ben hid a smile without complete success. "You can get off anytime."

"Of course," she said with dignity. "Um...how?" She couldn't fall into his arms like a five-year-old or dismount the way you were supposed to, with Zach behind her. When she glanced down, the ground seemed awfully far below. Judith swallowed and looked back at Ben.

A grin deepened the slashes in his cheeks and the lines beside his eyes. "I'll catch you," he said softly.

"I don't *need* to be caught," she lied.

"All right, help you," he amended, still with that wicked gleam in his eyes.

Where had her grim neighbor gone? Judith wondered breathlessly.

"Bring your right leg over Travis's neck," Ben suggested. "It's awkward with the saddle horn, but you can do it. Like that," he said approvingly as she took her life in her hands and followed his orders. "Now, kick free from the stirrup and let yourself slide down."

"Slide..." Judith moaned, but Ben's hands had already closed around her waist, and he lifted her and swung her away from the horse.

"There." Ben deposited her with her feet on the grass. "That wasn't so bad, was it?"

He hadn't released her. She was so close she could

see individual bristles on his chin and dark spiky lashes around his eyes. Judith moistened her dry lips. "No," she squeaked.

Still his hands lingered. His gaze had moved to her mouth. *His* was incredibly sexy, even if the smile had faded. Her knees wanted to buckle, and she didn't think it was from the riding. Her heart raced, and she felt strange, as if everything around them had become misty, indistinct.

Ben's head bent, slowly, purposefully; Judith's lips parted.

"Mommy," said a small voice, "can't you stand up?"

Sophie. Judith jerked upright. Oh, dear Lord, Zach, too! She'd almost kissed a man right in front of her children!

Ben blinked and stepped back, his hands falling away from her waist. He looked as disoriented as she felt.

Long practice at hiding the most wrenching of emotions let her say, almost evenly, "I guess my legs are a little shaky. How about yours?"

"Uh-uh! Daddy says my legs are noodles. I can pract'ly do the splits. Wanna see?"

Judith didn't dare look at Ben. "Why don't you come take a shower with me, pumpkin," she suggested. "We'll wash the horsey smell off. You can show me in the bedroom."

"Okeydokey," her small daughter said cheerily, jumping up from the porch step.

Climbing the steps, Judith wasn't so sure it *was*

Ben's touch that had made her legs wobbly. They still felt very peculiar.

Behind her, he said, "A hot bath would be an even better idea. Otherwise, you may wake up sore in the morning."

"Sore?" Despite herself, she turned.

Ben was poised with one foot in the stirrup, about to swing himself up on the horse's back.

"Yeah, sore. Human legs aren't made to be spread so wide." He cleared his throat even as she blushed fiercely. The children remained oblivious to the unspoken "except" that had leaped to both adult minds. Hastily he said, "There's, uh, a reason old cowboys walk the way they do."

Without waiting for her to respond, Ben grabbed the saddle horn and pulled himself up easily. With a minimum of awkwardness, he swung his leg forward, over the saddle horn, and settled into the saddle. Pulling on the reins, he turned Travis away. Zach was getting so confident he didn't even grab hold.

By the time Judith ran a hot bath, her thigh muscles were stiffening and she wished she did have time for a long soak. The fragrant bubbles she'd added on a whim might not be medicinal, but they made her feel feminine. Of course, Sophie had to hop in, too, dumping a few quarts of water on the bathroom floor and mat, which squished under Judith's feet when she got out.

She dried her daughter's bare, wriggly body first, then herself. Sophie went off to choose her own clothes. Judith, for unnamed, unexamined reasons, did not reach for the sweatpants or jeans she would normally have worn on an evening at home; instead, she put on snug turquoise leggings and a loosely woven white sweater with a scooped neckline.

Sophie had combined an eye-popping ensemble: bright-red gathered skirt, lace-edged pink-and-purple knit shirt and green knee socks. Tactfully not commenting on her color coordination, Judith helped her turn the shirt around so at least the tag wasn't flopping under her chin.

Then she kissed Sophie's forehead. "All right! Let's go cook."

Listening to Sophie chatter as they mixed the dough, Judith felt another swell of happiness. The five-year-old was adjusting far quicker than Judith had dreamed she would. Their new home, comfortable routines and plenty of patience seemed to be the answer. Of course there'd be setbacks—there had to be—but Sophie had come so far.

The biscuits were in the oven by the time the front door crashed open. "We're home!" Zach bellowed.

Judith went to meet them, giving her son a once-over. Hair and dirt coated the insides of his pant legs and was sprinkled over his shirt. "You have time for a quick shower, if you hurry."

"I don't need..." He looked down at himself. "It's just horsehair, Mom." Seeing her expression, he made a face. "Oh, all right."

She'd been terribly conscious the whole while of Ben waiting right behind him. With Zach racing down the hall, Judith had no choice but to meet Ben's eyes. They were dark, quiet, deep. Watchful.

His hair was still damp, and he'd obviously shaved

for a second time that day in honor of her invitation. A long-sleeved white shirt, cuffs buttoned, was tucked into clean black jeans, which she guessed were meant for dress-up. Although unsmiling, he was handsome enough to set her heart to racing.

"Hi," she said breathlessly. "Thanks for taking him."

"No problem." One side of his mouth tilted up. "He's a talker."

"Motor mouth." The almost forgotten sobriquet popped out of her subconscious. "That's what Rylan called him. When Zach was four or five, I'd swear he woke up talking and was still murmuring to himself when he fell asleep at night. He's actually been a lot quieter lately. Having Sophie back—" Judith checked herself. The five-year-old was plopping silverware on the table within hearing distance. "Well... Come on in."

She felt Ben behind her as she went to the table. With the part of her mind that functioned automatically, she saw that Sophie had placed the silverware randomly.

"Honey, we each need one fork, one spoon and one knife." She made her voice light, teasing. "I'd look kind of silly buttering my roll with a fork, wouldn't I? And Ben might have a hard time stabbing cooked carrots with a knife."

Sophie giggled. "Okay," she said obligingly, and began rearranging the silverware, singing to herself as she circled the table over and over again.

Judith folded napkins and followed her around, placing one under the fork at each place. Sophie carefully set out the plates and bowls next, then glasses for water and milk. Finally done, she gazed expectantly at Ben, who had hovered in the background.

"It looks real pretty," he said, smiling down at Judith's daughter.

In an abortive gesture in which Judith read tenderness, he lifted a hand as though to touch Sophie's coppery curls but drew it back before the little girl noticed.

"You'll be a heck of a hostess when you grow up."

Sophie's eyes opened wide. "What's a 'hosess'?"

Taking the biscuits out of the oven, Judith left Ben to offer an explanation, although she wouldn't for the world have missed a word of it.

"A lady taking care of her guests," he said gravely. "A man with guests is the host."

"Oh." She frowned. "What's a 'heck' hosess?"

"A really terrific one."

"Oh," Sophie said again. She gave a pleased nod. "Okay. That's what I'll be when I grow up."

He gazed down at her with the oddest expression, as though this child, a mere kindergartner, fascinated and charmed and repelled him all at the same time. Finally he gave his head a shake.

"You'll be more than that." His voice sounded almost hoarse. "You'll be all kinds of things. A horsewoman, maybe a teacher like your mom, a wife and mother..." He gave a grunt that might have been a laugh. "Who knows? Maybe a gardener. An ambassador."

Sophie smiled radiantly. "A princess. I wanna be a princess."

He gave another grunt. "My sister did, too. That's what she dressed up as at Halloween every year."

"*Is* she a princess?" Sophie reached trustingly for his hand.

He froze, just for a second, then his fingers flexed and closed carefully around the small hand. "No." His head was bent as he looked down at Sophie. "No, instead she makes gardens beautiful enough for any princess."

"Can I see one?"

"Well, they're not around here. But maybe someday."

Beyond them, Zach asked, "Someday what? Can I do it, too?"

Ben straightened and let go of Sophie's hand. "Yeah, someday you can mow my lawn."

Zach blew a raspberry. "You think I'm dumb or something? I know that's not what you said."

How familial this felt, Judith thought with an odd clutch of pleasure as she called, "Dinner's ready. Everybody sit down."

Sophie ushered Ben to the spot at the table facing Judith's that had been empty until now. Then she scrambled up onto her own chair.

The dinner was more formal than usual. Everybody asked for dishes to be passed, kept elbows off the table, said please and thank-you. Judith was delighted by the children's manners, particularly Sophie's. When she'd first returned, the five-year-old had acted as if she'd never sat down to a properly set dinner table or been expected to ask nicely if she wanted something. But what gave Judith a lump in her throat was the way Ben listened gravely to her children, gave quick smiles or praise and raised an eyebrow to wordlessly chide. The whole while she sensed he, too, was on his best behavior, a little uncomfortable with the niceties of spreading a napkin on his lap and asking permission to take another biscuit.

A solitary man, but he knew how to be a father.

If she hadn't promised not to ask God for anything else, Judith might have sent up a small prayerful wish right then. But she had promised, and so she didn't. She only felt the ache beneath her breastbone and wondered if fate might be this kind to her.

Ben offered to help clean the kitchen, but Judith declined. It was Zach's bedtime and later than Sophie's usual one, so Judith had the kids clear the table and go brush their teeth.

"Zach," she called after them, "help Sophie with her nightie." To Ben, she asked, "Coffee? Tea?" *Or me?* Wasn't that how the saying went?

"Sure," he drawled. "Either."

She glanced at him to be sure he hadn't somehow read her mind and taken her up on an offer she hadn't—wouldn't—make, but his expression was bland.

By the time the water boiled, the kids were ready to be tucked in. Judith excused herself and went to kiss both good-night. Her lips lingered, first on Sophie's plump cheek, then on Zach's thinner, smooth one. She switched off the lamp and paused in the crack of golden light let in by the half-opened door. "I love you," she said softly. "Both of you."

"I love you," Zach murmured, the incantation a nightly one.

"Daddy loves me, too," offered Sophie in a sleepy voice.

The stab of pain was always unexpected, as if she'd been taken by surprise. The anger was more familiar. *That bastard had better love his daughter,* she thought, *or else what was his excuse?*

"'Night," she said again, and pulled the door to the precise correct position that she and Zach had agreed on after long bargaining sessions. Not wide open, not closed. A precise four inches kept the bedroom from darkness and let him know she would hear him if he called out. Now Sophie was the one who awakened with nightmares, sometimes finishing the night in her mother's bed, but the bargain held.

Ben had poured the coffee and was stirring a teaspoon of sugar into one mug when she returned to the kitchen. He added some cream, stirred and handed it to her. His own was still black.

"Thank you," she said, surprised. "You know how I drink my coffee."

"I notice things."

"Shall we go sit out in the living room? Or on the porch? It looks like a nice evening."

"Porch."

She hesitated but left the outside lights off. Ben was the one to ease the screen door closed. When she sat on the swing, he took up his usual position against the railing. Enough light fell through the windows to allow her to make out his features.

"Is it because you're a policeman?" she asked. "That you notice things?"

"Yeah. Probably. You get in the habit. Maybe not if you were always a small-town cop, but in a city for sure. People walk down the street totally oblivious to what's around them. Not a cop. You see that alley ahead, you quietly check out who's walking behind you, you notice the license plate on a car creeping by." He shrugged. "Habit."

"Did you always want to be a cop?"

"Truth?"

She nodded.

"Nah." His mouth had a wry twist. "I wanted to be a doctor. How the hell I thought my mother would pay for all those years of school, I don't have a clue."

"What happened?" Judith asked softly.

He pushed himself to his feet and turned to gaze out at the night. His voice became curt. "Real life. It's what happens."

His answer wasn't expansive, but she didn't have the sense he was shutting her out entirely as he had the other day. So she let her curiosity have its way.

"You couldn't afford medical school?"

"Didn't even make it to college, not out of high school." The way he stood now, his face was entirely shadowed. "I grew up in Puyallup. I stayed at home until I was in my early twenties. Worked at whatever I could find. Finally went to the community college, got a degree in criminal justice."

"Why?"

He turned his back on the darkness to look at her again, his head cocked. "Why what?"

"Why criminal justice?"

Ben didn't seem to mind her nosiness. "I put a new roof on a cop's house. He liked to have a beer and tell stories. He made his job sound exciting and...oh, hell, valiant. Honorable. You don't find out that you're going to spend your life with the scum of the earth until you're already on the job."

"But you don't if you police a town like this."

"Right." This smile was genuine. "But there isn't much excitement, either."

"I suppose not." Judith wanted to know more, so much more, but she had to frame her questions to sound casual, not as if this were an inquisition.

He beat her to it. "How about you? Why a teacher?"

She found herself talking about her own childhood, about her mother, who had started as a teacher at a prep school and eventually rose to be principal, and of her father, a midlevel executive in an insurance company.

"He always made more money than Mom," Judith said, "but he never liked his job. I wanted to find something I'd love doing. Of course, I never imagined it would be teaching. I remember telling myself *I* would never be like my mother! But I did some tutoring when I was in high school, and then I got a job as a summer counselor at a day camp and..." She spread her hands and smiled. "I loved figuring out ways to convince kids that they wanted to learn whatever I was going to teach. I enjoyed their questions, their silliness, their vulnerability. So here I am."

"Here you are," he echoed, studying her.

A silence grew, not awkward but not entirely comfortable, either. She set the swing to rocking and told herself to say something. Anything. Chat. But after the spate of background information she'd offered, her vocal cords seemed to have shut down. Or maybe that wasn't it. She just couldn't think of a single thing to say.

The sound of distant crickets or frogs, or possibly just brittle autumn leaves whispering in a breeze, came from the darkness beyond the porch. She still hadn't gotten used to how dark it was here, so far from city lights. And how many more stars she could see with cold white clarity if she just stepped off the porch and tilted her head back. But tonight, the light from the kitchen falling through the windows was like a circle of firelight, making a warm, safe place against the invisible terrors of the night beyond its reach.

Somehow Ben McKinsey had become the night *and* the security of her own front porch. He made her feel safe even as he scared her a little.

He hadn't moved, just kept looking at her.

"I've been wanting to kiss you."

His voice was the darkness, deep and mysterious and frightening.

Her breath almost stopped. Wildly she wondered what she was supposed to say to that. How about a bright, interested "Oh?"

"Any chance you've been hoping I would?"

Oh, Lord. He was asking her to declare herself. *Yes, you make my knees weak.* Or *No, sorry, not interested.* If she did agree to kiss him, she would have to take equal responsibility. She couldn't pretend to herself later that she hadn't really wanted his lips on hers.

"Is it that tough a decision?" he asked roughly.

"I...no." Her heart gave a funny thump when he made a sound and started to turn away. "No, I didn't mean— It isn't that tough. I..." Her voice faded to a whisper. "Yes. Yes, I've been hoping."

Ben stopped, and she saw that his hands were knotted into fists. Slowly his fingers uncurled and he rubbed his hands on his pant legs as he turned to face her. The expression on his face made her heart give a few more thumps as it swelled and filled her chest to the point of pain.

He didn't say another word. She rose to her feet and lifted trembling hands to flatten them against his chest. He was so warm, and Judith realized she'd begun to shiver.

"Thinking about pushing me away?" he asked.

"Oh! No!" She started to snatch her hands back.

His snaked up to grip her wrists. But instead of yanking her forward, Ben carefully splayed her fingers one at a time against his chest again. "I was kidding." His voice was low, gritty. "I like the way it feels. You touching me."

"I like the feel of you, too," she admitted, so quietly he had to bend his head to hear her.

He said something else, something quick and vehement, but she couldn't make it out. She didn't even try. His ragged breath was enough to let her know what was coming, and she lifted her mouth to meet his.

She hadn't expected tentativeness, not from this

man, and she didn't get it. He kissed her with the thoroughness of a longtime lover, but he was trembling as much as she was when his tongue stroked hers and his teeth closed on her lower lip.

She must have been starved for this, because her nervousness evaporated along with her ability to think. She just felt: his body, long and hard and muscular, flattened against hers; his big hands, one wrapped in her hair, the other gripping her hip; his tongue, hot and slick and evocative. Her arms encircled him now; he was groaning, and she was making little sobbing sounds as his mouth traveled down her throat, kissing and nibbling.

Ben pushed her sweater off one shoulder, her bra strap with it. In a thick voice, he said, "This has been driving me crazy all night. You're so delicate, so pretty…"

She let out a shuddering breath that he echoed.

"I think," he said hoarsely, "that I'd better quit while I can."

"Quit?" Judith whispered, not wanting to understand.

His hands brushed the sides of her breasts, wrapped around her upper arms. More kisses softly touched her collarbone and the hollow at the base of her throat. He groaned, then kissed her mouth again, but gently this time, with finality. With aching slowness, he stepped back and let her go.

"Ben?" she asked, still not comprehending.

"Do you want me to make love to you? Right here on the porch?"

"Make love…?" Judith looked around, awareness

returning. All he'd suggested was a kiss, and she'd been all over him. She'd never been so...so mindless before! She had kids in the house right behind her. They might not even be asleep yet. And she hardly knew this man. Certainly not well enough to...to...

"No." She swallowed. "Of course not! I'm sorry, I..."

His hands shot out again and gripped her shoulders. He kissed her again, quick and hard. "What's to be sorry for? It was a hell of a kiss. Let's do it again. When your kids are out of shouting distance."

"I...yes." Did she dare? It was scary, thinking she might be swallowed by passion. She'd always been able to think logically, even in the worst days following Sophie's kidnapping.

"Good night."

He seemed reluctant to let her go, or else why did his fingers uncurl so slowly from her arms? Why did his voice sound raw?

"Thanks for dinner."

He backed up a step, then another. At the top of the stairs, he took a long look at her, then turned and left, darkness into darkness, no longer part of the cozy world bounded by the porch railing and the reaches of the kitchen light.

Judith sank onto the swing and wrapped her arms around herself. She felt suddenly very alone.

He hadn't been gone two minutes, and already she missed him. Which gave her even more to be scared about. On a soft sound of distress, she closed her eyes and hugged herself against the loneliness and the night chill.

CHAPTER EIGHT

"OKAY." HANDS CLASPED behind his back, Ben strolled between desks in Judith's classroom, a meandering route that allowed him to look closely at each fifth grader. Things had changed; instead of whispering, they were all attentive. Heads turned as he walked.

"Jimmy heard some guys were going to gang up on him after school," Ben continued. "He's thinking about taking his dad's gun and sneaking it to school in his backpack to protect himself."

The students stirred; Ben felt their interest. From her quiet post at the side of the room, Judith smiled at him, a subtle little tweak to his ego.

"Let's talk about the consequences if he carries that through. Any good things that might happen? Bad things?"

Hands shot up.

"Bryan."

"He might get caught."

"True enough. Lauren."

"He might shoot somebody." Her eyes were wide at the very thought.

"Or else somebody else might have a gun, too, and

shoot *him*," Ian added with the relish of a typical ten-year-old boy.

Ben nodded his approval. "Anything good that could happen?"

Tony, the rebel, raised his hand. "Yeah, if he showed it around, the other kids would think he was cool."

The classroom erupted in agreement and protests. Ben picked out comments that went all the way from "*I* wouldn't think he was cool" to "Yeah, everybody would be scared of him. Even that gang."

He waited until they simmered down to ask, "Do you think the gang would bother him once they heard he had a gun?"

"Nah," Tony said. "They wouldn't be that stupid."

Ben was pleased when another boy interjected, "It might make them madder, though. If he doesn't bring the gun to school every day, they'd get him some day when he didn't have it."

"Well, he could bring it every day..." Tony began.

"But what if his dad noticed it was gone? Besides, *my* mom looks in my backpack sometimes," one of the girls said. "I bet most people's moms do."

Tony opened his mouth again, then shut it. Obviously, his mother or father did indeed mount an occasional search for school notices that hadn't been handed over or carrot sticks that might be decomposing in the bottom of the backpack.

They went on to talk about the risks of carrying a gun, whom Jimmy might talk to about whether this was the best way of protecting himself and what other choices he might make. The kids were so caught up in the discussion that Judith let them go until the bell rang. Within seconds, they'd put their chairs up on their desks, grabbed packs and were jostling one another out the door.

Almost as quickly, Judith dumped a load of papers into a briefcase. With another smile at Ben, she said, "You're getting good at this."

"Thanks." He studied her. Today she wore a simple white knit shirt and a flowery gathered skirt that swirled around her legs. Her fiery hair was braided in some complicated way that lay flat against her head and looked old-fashioned to him. Fresh and young in a way that had nothing to do with actual age, she made him think of spring, not fall, despite the color of her hair. She made him imagine he could start over.

"I've got to run and get the kids," she said, interrupting his reverie.

"I'll walk you."

She made a comical face. "Walk? You ought to see me racing down the halls."

Ben didn't want her to know that he had. "You take your life into your hands out there," he said, nodding toward the tumult in the hall. "I'll protect you."

"Now, there's an offer." Her quick, teasing smile made his blood sing.

"Will you have dinner with me?" he heard himself ask.

Now, where the hell had that come from? He hadn't consciously formulated the invitation, though he supposed it had been hovering in the back of his mind.

About to head out the door, Judith stopped. When

she turned, all kinds of emotions chased across her face. After a moment, she said slowly, "I'd love to, but I can't leave Zach and Sophie. Not with a teenager."

"Maybe I can think of someone."

She worried her bottom lip. "Well, normally... But right now, if I don't really know the baby-sitter..."

Oh, hell. Maybe he hadn't planned to ask her out, but now that he had, Ben realized how badly he wanted to be alone with her.

"Yeah, okay," he said. "I don't blame you. Maybe later, after Kane's been sent away."

Judith nodded, but her expression remained anxious. "I'm sorry," she murmured, then rose on tiptoe and kissed him, just a brush on the mouth, but affecting him more than an openmouthed kiss would from most women.

"Hey, don't apologize..." Ben began, but his eyes suddenly focused beyond her and he realized the school principal had appeared in the doorway. He nodded to her. "Ms. Galindez."

Judith whipped around. "Carol!"

"Judith. Chief McKinsey." The principal's brown eyes twinkled. "Romancing my staff?"

Pink blossomed on Judith's cheeks and she said in a flurry, "It was just a thank-you. But I apologize. I didn't consider what the kids might think if they saw me—"

"I was teasing." Carol Galindez came into the room. "Nobody saw. And you weren't exactly necking, anyway."

Too bad, Ben thought.

"I couldn't help overhearing some of your conversation," Carol said. "And I have an idea. You have a minute, don't you?"

"I...I really need to collect the kids."

"I'll talk fast. My sister's bringing her family over tonight for a barbecue. Tim is in Zach's class, and Nadia is almost five—just missed the cutoff for kindergarten. With luck, they'll all hit it off and have such fun we adults won't have to listen to them whine about being bored."

"Oh, but..."

Carol strolled to the nearest bulletin board and scanned the student drawings hung on it. Over her shoulder, she said, "You could use a night to yourself. Assuming you want to turn down our revered police chief, you're welcome to come, too, but I'd be delighted to take Zach and Sophie if you want to kick up your heels a little." Her sly glance took in Ben, waiting quietly to the side.

Judith's mouth opened, then closed, then opened again in a pantomime of indecision. "Are you *sure?*"

"You bet." A woman didn't become a school administrator without knowing how to sound firm. "Why don't we go collect them right now and see what they think."

Judith turned a helpless gaze on Ben. "I guess you can't get out of that invitation now, can you?"

"Guess not," he said laconically. He winked at Carol, who laughed and went out the door. Then he took in Judith's flustered expression and frowned. "You've been pushed into this, haven't you? We don't have to do it."

"No. I want to." She didn't play coy. Her gaze was direct, her tone positive. "Really. You must have to go back to work. What time shall we make it?"

They decided on five-thirty. The Galindez barbecue presumably wouldn't last into the wee hours, even if it was Friday evening, so he figured they'd better enjoy what time they had.

Back at the station, Ben couldn't force himself to concentrate on the administrative stuff that made up too much of his job. He knew police chiefs who sat on their butts behind a desk all day, but he liked knowing what was going on out there. Since Julie Robinson had gone off on maternity leave, he'd taken extra shifts. Today wasn't one of them, but he figured having another cop on the street wouldn't hurt anything. Why not go?

He'd barely pulled out of the parking lot when his radio crackled. A break-in reported at a residence in the four-hundred block of Highland Street.

Ben grabbed his mike. "I'll take it."

The victim, a man in his twenties, met Ben at the door of the freshly painted 1930s-era bungalow. Clean-cut, the guy looked vaguely familiar. Ben searched his mental files. A checker at the supermarket? No, that didn't click. Hardware store? Nope.

"That was quick," the victim said, standing back. "Come on in."

Ben glanced around the living room. Hardwood floors, well cared for. Big-screen TV, a stack of expensive stereo equipment, two recliners and a leather couch. Two hundred or more CDs filled a wrought-iron rack on the wall above the oak stereo cabinet.

Okay, maybe the burglar hadn't taken the TV because it was too big. But why not the VCR or the tuner? Had this guy surprised him before he could make off with anything?

Taking out his notebook, Ben said, "When did you notice the house had been broken into?"

"Just now." The man held out a hand. "Josh Heyer. You're Chief McKinsey, aren't you?" Ben agreed that he was. "I just got home from work—I'm a pharmacist," Heyer continued. "Everything looked okay here." He gestured vaguely toward the audio-video equipment. "I went straight to my bedroom to change clothes. I was going to go for a run. My bedroom's...well, not a mess, but a couple of drawers and the closet doors were open, a roll of socks was on the floor.... Just little stuff. I thought maybe they were looking for money, but I don't keep any around, except for some small change."

"Jewelry?"

"Not really."

"So nothing was taken?" Ben doodled on his pad. "Just clothes."

That got his attention. *"Clothes?"*

"Yeah. Pretty weird, huh?" Heyer nodded toward the bedroom. "You can look around if you want."

"Uh...sure." Clothes?

They passed the kitchen, where a juicer, a blender and an espresso machine stood at attention on tiled countertops. The door to a den was open. There a computer shared desk space with two printers and another piece of equipment that might have been a color scanner or a small copying machine. All untouched.

Considering the era of the house, the huge bedroom could only have been achieved by knocking down a wall. A king-size bed floated in the middle of three-inch-deep cream-colored carpeting. The doors on a bank of closets were ajar; the drawers on the pale wood dresser weren't.

Ben rocked on his heels and scanned the room. Another TV, twenty-seven-inch screen. Combination CD player-clock radio beside the bed.

"Are you single?" he asked.

"For six more weeks." Heyer had stayed in the doorway, as though reluctant to enter the bedroom again. At Ben's look of inquiry, he added, "I'm engaged."

"You had any teenagers here recently? Doing yard-work, whatever?"

No teenagers. Nobody but Heyer's cleaning lady, who had worked for him for three years now.

"Can you describe the clothes that are missing?" Ben held his pen poised.

Josh Heyer could. One dress shirt, pin-striped. Half a dozen white T-shirts. And his Grateful Dead shirt.

"I've had it since I was a teenager," he said, looking really fried for the first time. "I bought it when I went to see them play down in Oregon. Eugene. I don't suppose you went?"

Ben shook his head.

"Damn it, I liked that shirt! The rest of the stuff I can replace, but not that. The Dead T-shirts in catalogs now are so commercial looking. They're just not the same."

He described it in minute detail, down to the rip

near the hem, apparently sacred because he'd torn the shirt that same day in Eugene.

Ben didn't have any trouble figuring out how the intruder had entered the house. The screen had been removed from the kitchen window, which was wide open. Some branches had been broken off the rhododendron below the window, and footprints were visible in the flower bed but weren't clear enough to tell Ben much.

Heyer walked Ben to the front door, where he assured the pharmacist that they'd do everything they could, although he didn't hold out much hope. "Did you monogram your dress shirt?"

Heyer shook his head.

"Laundry marks?"

"I don't think so."

"Then there's probably no way to prove it's yours even if we spot someone walking around town in it. Same goes for the T-shirts. Still, I'd like to know why someone would break into a house just to steal clothes. And why just shirts? Once he was here, why not pants or socks? Why not a CD player or a VCR? At least those he could sell."

"*You'd* like to know? What about me?" Heyer grimaced. "It's damned kinky. And...oh, hell, I guess it makes me feel insecure. You know? I mean, I'll be more careful to lock windows, but still...."

Ben understood; the reaction was typical. Although this had hardly been a devastating break-in, the idea of someone poking through your drawers and trying on your clothes might hit you harder emotionally than the more impersonal burglary of a TV or stereo equipment. They shook hands, and Ben repeated his assurances.

By this time, it was after four. The radio was quiet, and Ben headed back to the station to write a report. By the time he'd finished, he had all at the station shaking their heads over the bizarre break-in.

Once he was home, Ben showered and changed with lightning speed. He hadn't been on a date in a while. A year, maybe? He wondered if it had occurred to Judith that, in a town this small, by tomorrow morning everyone would have heard that she'd had dinner with the police chief.

When he drove to her house she was ready. She wore a simple little dress the color of mint juleps, and all those auburn curls were gathered on top of her head in a snug knot, leaving her slender neck bare. He was glad she didn't wear much jewelry; he liked seeing her creamy skin unornamented. Hell, he'd like to see her in nothing *but* creamy skin and fiery curls.

On the drive back to town, Judith asked about his day, and he told her a thief was walking around town in someone else's Grateful Dead T-shirt.

"Damnedest thing," he said. "Why go to all that trouble for eight shirts, six of them plain white T-shirts?"

Tension crept into her voice. "What size were they?"

He shot her a glance. "You're thinking about your ex? Why the hell would he arrive in town desperately in need of eight shirts?"

"I can't imagine," she admitted. "Still..."

"Size fourteen neck. Small guy. Sleeves were only a thirty-two length."

"Oh." Her relief was obvious. "Ry wears a much larger size than that. It was a silly thought anyway. No, it's a silly crime! Do you think you'll ever find out why those shirts were stolen?"

"Probably not. There are a few cases I've spent years wondering about. This'll probably be one of 'em."

They speculated about the thief's motive. Perhaps he was in love with the victim or wanted to impersonate him. But why just shirts?

"Maybe the pharmacist's covering up a crime he committed himself," Judith suggested, eyes sparkling. "Let's see. He murdered someone and got blood all over his shirt. The dress shirt, that is, with one of the T-shirts beneath it. But it would sound funny if he reported only two shirts missing, so he threw in the others to be more convincing."

"He wouldn't need to report the shirts missing in the first place," Ben said. Though if the pharmacist's fiancée turned up missing, he thought wryly, he'd keep this bizarre episode—and Judith's farfetched explanation for it—in mind.

After some discussion they decided on a new restaurant in town, one that Ben privately figured wouldn't make it. This was cattle country, and folks liked a big slab of steak when they went out to dinner, cholesterol or no. This new place, called The French Invention, was just a little too fancy for the locals. The idea of having their chicken or steak wrapped inside a skinny pancake hadn't gone over so far. Ben happened to like crepes, and he wasn't surprised that Judith did, too.

Terra-cotta tile floors, wallpaper with tiny sprigs of lavender and white antique tables and chairs gave the place a feminine ambience that made Ben feel large and clumsy, but the hostess seated them at a booth in the nook formed by a bay window, where there was plenty of leg room. Only two other tables were occupied, neither of them close by; the room was romantically dark, with short fat candles flickering on the tables. Their light gave Judith a golden cast, as if she had stepped from a Renaissance painting.

Not a man given to compliments, he cleared his throat. "You're beautiful."

Her smile was soft and pleased. "Thank you. You should have seen me at eight years old, skinny and covered with freckles. Thank God, they seem to have faded away." She hesitated, then amended, "Mostly."

Was it his imagination, or had her cheeks pinkened? That made him wonder where she might have freckles, and the speculation had him shifting in his seat.

Fortunately, he was distracted by the necessity of ordering. He asked for the burgundy beef crepe, and Judith chose one with Swiss cheese and chicken and broccoli.

The waitress melted into the darkness.

"This is nice, Ben." Judith gestured gracefully with her small hand. "I haven't been out to dinner without at least Zach in…oh, ages. I've been too busy being Mommy."

"You have good kids."

"And you're wonderful with them. Why haven't you had your own?"

He usually found a way to avoid answering that one directly. But this time...oh, hell, he didn't know where this thing with her was going, but he knew that he, too, wanted to be honest.

Honest enough that she'd see right away that he wasn't stepdaddy material. Any more than he'd been daddy material, he thought grimly.

"For one thing, I've never married," he said. *Yeah,* his inner self mocked, *but if you were any kind of decent man, you would have.* He ignored that voice. "I have two younger brothers and a sister. After my father died, when I was Zach's age, I had to help raise all of them. My mother worked two jobs to support us. I did most everything else. By the time Nora, the youngest, made it safely to eighteen, I figured I'd done my part." He shrugged. "I've never wanted to do it all over again."

"I can see why you'd feel that way," Judith said with a solemn nod. "But, you know, it's not the same when the children are your own. It's..." Her brow crinkled as she sought the right word. "It's so *primal*—almost scary—how protective you feel. You know from that first moment that you'd do anything for this baby. Even die." She heard her own intensity and gave her head a shake. "I'm getting carried away, aren't I?"

Would she love a man as wholeheartedly? He steered away from the dangerous thought.

"Not everyone reacts to becoming a parent the same way," he remarked. "In my job, I see some parents who don't give a good goddamn. I don't want to become a father and find out I resent the obligations."

"But..." She stopped and with a visible effort made her face and tone expressionless. "No. I guess you're right."

"I may yet change my mind." The words came out unbidden, and he had no time to yank them back. He despised himself immediately; damn it, he was lying to her, giving her hope that he might be a man she could have a future with, when he wasn't.

Whoa! He didn't have a reason in the world to think she might want a future with him. This was a first date, for God's sake! Maybe he'd lied, maybe not; all he'd really done was soften his earlier statement. And a man never knew, did he? Famous last words were called that for a reason.

Lie or not, it worked. A smile reappeared on her lips and she said, "You'd be a great father."

Somewhere out there was a kid who'd dispute that. Judith Kane would despise him if she knew about that child.

There wasn't a damn reason she should ever find out.

"I can be pretty brusque with them."

"I thought so the first time I met you." Her wide, candid eyes searched his. "But you're so good with Sophie and Zach now that you know them. And I have to tell you, Tony Fiorentino has a bad case of hero worship for you."

"What?" Ben was genuinely startled. Trouble-in-the-making Tony?

"Mmm." He noticed the faintest hint of dimples when she smiled. He'd never noticed them before. "He's decided he wants to be a cop."

"So he can carry a gun," Ben said dryly.

"That could have something to do with it," Judith admitted. "But he also thinks it's so cool that people have to call you 'Chief.' And that even though you probably arrest *dozens* of people every day, you still come and talk to our class. He likes to imitate the way he's sure you throw a crook up against the wall. If he had a pair of handcuffs, he figures he could have them on a suspect in ten seconds flat."

"Good God," Ben muttered.

"Yes, I know, but it wouldn't hurt if you encouraged him. His dad is in the penitentiary in Walla Walla for armed robbery. His mother came home to live near her parents, who apparently make a habit of telling Tony he's just like his father. He's going to be a good-for-nothing, too, if he goes on the way he is, according to Grandma." Judith looked seriously steamed. "I heard the woman right out in the hall in front of my classroom!"

He imagined the scene. "Did you give her hell?"

"Darn right I did!" She made a face. "Of course, it didn't do any good at all. That poor boy. He's really sweet, you know." Her eyes beseeched him. "He just doesn't have a good role model."

Her words sank in. "Exactly what do you have in mind?"

"Well, if you could just take an interest in him."

Now she was treading delicately, apparently reading his stupefaction right.

"Maybe he could ride along with you in your police car someday. If I had him do a report about it..."

"Should I let him handcuff someone, too?"

"I was thinking more when you were off duty."

He could just picture the kid grabbing the radio, sticking his fingers through the grille, wanting to know if there were any bloodstains on the seat. He'd be a pain in the butt.

Reluctantly, Ben remembered thinking it would be a good idea to get to know kids like Tony, ones who seemed headed for trouble. He doubted he could have any lasting influence, but maybe if he got to know the boy well enough, he'd come to Ben before he did anything really stupid. Anyway, Tony would be sure to lose interest once he realized how dull Ben's job was. How rarely he handcuffed anyone, never mind slammed somebody up against a wall.

"Maybe," Ben said grudgingly.

"Oh, good." Judith smiled. "And here's dinner."

Over crepes they discussed life in general: baseball—neither cared about it; movies—most cop ones drove him crazy, while she admitted to liking them; and even Christmas—she went whole-hog, he ignored the entire season.

"But you have family!" Judith said, aghast. "Don't they invite you to join them?"

"Yeah." He sipped wine, partly to hide his discomfiture. The past few years, he'd known that if he went to the family get-together, Eddie wouldn't. It was more important that Eddie's kids know their relatives than Ben celebrate a holiday he didn't give a damn about with family who resented him. "Sometimes I go, sometimes not."

"But to spend the holidays alone when you have a choice..." She stopped, obviously astonished at the idea.

"I'm a loner."

"Oh."

She seemed to consider his words. He waited for her to decide optimistically that all he needed was a family of his own to cure him. To his surprise—and disappointment?—she only nodded and applied herself to her meal. She'd written him off, Ben speculated.

"Your kids want to ride again tomorrow, before the weather turns cold?"

Now what was he doing? he wondered. Talk about sending mixed messages! The honorable part of him was pushing her away, while the selfish part was afraid she'd agree that he was a lost cause.

She studied him with a perplexity he fully understood. After a long moment, she said, "Well, I suppose. If you mean it..."

"Sure." Incredibly, he did mean it.

Ben took a big gulp of red wine. If he didn't shut up, he'd find himself volunteering to take in foster kids or become a Big Brother. Something about this woman across the table from him had triggered an alarming shift in viewpoints that he'd thought were set in stone. Could you have a midlife crisis in your thirties? Ben wondered.

Over coffee, he asked Judith if she missed Boston. Mad River had been culture shock for him, and he'd grown up in a smallish town.

"You know," she said thoughtfully, "I really don't. Except for my parents. And even Rylan's, although that relationship is awkward. But the city itself...well, Boston is beautiful, and historic, and...*alive.* But I like the quiet here, and the lack of traffic, and I *hated* always hunting for parking places. Besides, I'm not that big on night life." She sipped her coffee, her expression far away. "The schools had problems we don't have here. More opportunities, too—better special services, for example—but classes were bigger, and even the elementary schools had more smoking and drug use and vandalism and kids who were really snotty to adults." Her eyes focused on him. "No. I'm actually a little surprised to discover that I like it here. What about you? Any second thoughts?"

"Aw, sometimes I miss having more challenges on the job. But I don't miss dealing with the pathetic excuses for humanity that we spent half our time arresting over and over, wasting time in court only to see them walk off or get probation." He shook his head. "No regrets."

"I don't suppose you liked the crowds."

Maybe that's what he'd hated about Seattle. All those people. But actually, he wasn't that antisocial; he got along fine with most of the folks he dealt with here on this side of the mountains.

"I like having the horses right here, not boarded an hour away from where I live." He took a last swallow of coffee and nodded at her cup. "More?"

"Oh, I don't think so. I should get the kids soon in case they're miserable."

"Shall we go pick them up now?" Ben signaled for the bill.

"But…why don't you just take me home? I can run back into town to get them."

"Why should you have to?"

What he really wanted to do was take her home and carry her up the stairs to his bedroom—or down the hall to hers—and hunt for the freckles that *weren't* on her nose. But he knew damn well she wouldn't go for a visit to either bedroom, not yet. And it would be just plain stupid for her to have to set out all over again in her own car. Besides, he'd only pace until he saw her returning headlights.

They argued about it for a minute, but he was adamant and she gave in at last.

He knew where Carol Galindez lived with her husband, who owned the town's one furniture store. The house was a nice place, cedar and glass, built into a rocky hillside among the larch and pine, with a drive way that wound up to it. By Mad River standards, Carol and Paul had money.

Cars lined the asphalt drive. Ben eased his pickup to a stop where he wouldn't be blocked in and cut the engine. Judith didn't hop out immediately. He rolled down the window. Muffled voices and laughter came from around the house, where the deck overlooked the valley. On this side, only a porch light and golden squares from a couple of smaller windows pierced the dusk, which was deeper here under the trees.

He turned to Judith and laid his arm across the back of her seat. "You would have enjoyed Carol's barbecue."

"She's nice. But I had fun with you."

"You're easy to talk to."

"So are you," she murmured.

His voice roughened as he touched her chin, tilted it up. "You're easy to kiss, too."

"Kissing you is…a little scary."

She said it so softly he hardly heard her. But her words stopped him dead. "Scary?"

"The way I feel. The way you make me feel."

She was admitting vulnerability. To him. His heart cramped. "Yeah," he admitted gruffly. "Maybe *easy* wasn't the right word." Maybe *earthshaking* was closer to the mark.

"I like it anyway," she said, even more quietly. "You kissing me."

Ben closed his eyes for an instant as powerful emotions buffeted him. When he could speak, he growled, "I like kissing you, too."

He made out her smile, the sweetest damn thing he'd ever seen, as she touched his cheek with her fingertips. Ben tunneled his fingers through her hair and took her mouth with a kind of ferocity that disguised what lay beneath it.

Kissing her didn't scare him. It terrified him. Because he'd just discovered that he wasn't suffering from a midlife crisis. He was falling in love.

CHAPTER NINE

JUDITH CLICKED OFF the lamp that stood on the bookcase separating the two beds in Zach's room. "Okay,
it's late. I'm glad you guys had fun at Mrs. Galindez's.
Now sleep."

"Mommy," Sophie said drowsily, "I don't remember how come Daddy is gone."

Judith stood rigid for a moment, her hand inches
from the lamp switch. "What made you wonder, punkin?"

"Nadia was talking about her daddy. I told her my
daddy is gonna come for me. That's what he said,
anyhow. But he's been gone forever. Do you think
he'll come?"

Sophie had cried for her father at first, and sometimes she still asked for him, but she'd never talked
about what had happened when she was taken from
him. Judith didn't know how much the five-year-old
understood or should be made to understand.

She sat down on the edge of her daughter's mat-
tress, conscious of Zach, quiet and listening, only a
few feet away in his bed.

"Do you wish your dad would come for you?" she
asked, striving for a tone of sympathy and warmth,
hiding her own hurt.

Sophie tugged her thumb from her mouth. "Yeah," she murmured, even closer to sleep. "I guess."

"I'd miss you." Judith bent over to kiss her daughter's silky head.

"Can't Daddy live here, too?" asked the small voice.

"No, your daddy and I aren't married anymore. And I sure like having you with me." She almost lied and said, "Zach does, too," but what if he declared loudly that he didn't?

Sophie popped her thumb back in her mouth and sucked furiously for a moment. Then, around it, she said, "I don't think I want to go away."

"Good." Eyes stinging, Judith kissed her again. "'Night, sweetheart."

She rose and went to Zach's bed. She could just make him out, lying on his back, staring up at the ceiling, his sheet folded neatly over his covers. He could be messy and uncaring about many things, but his bed had to be just so for him to climb into it, and the door precisely ajar. Judith had long recognized his need to control important parts of his environment. The sight of him in bed, so still, as if he were afraid of movement, always made her sad.

"Good night," she whispered, bending over him.

"Mom?"

His voice was so quiet she doubted Sophie could hear him. "Yeah?" She sat beside him on the bed, close enough to allow her to smooth a hand through his hair.

"Dad's like the bad guys on TV, isn't he?"

She was torn, as she'd been a thousand times before.

Rylan had done the cruelest thing possible to her, short of killing one of the children. Yet she could never let herself forget that he was their father—their blood, their genes, an important presence in their early years. How could they grow up with healthy self-esteem if they'd been taught to hate a part of themselves?

She glanced toward Sophie. Her thumb had slipped from her mouth and she made a small grunt and burrowed beneath her covers.

Judith looked back at Zach. "No. Your dad's not a bad man," she said quietly, rumpling his hair again. "I loved him once, you know. He…was funny, and very handsome, and he could charm your socks off. People always like your dad when they meet him. Things went wrong between us, but it wasn't all his fault." Her fingers momentarily went still. "I don't understand how he could do such a terrible thing to us, taking Sophie the way he did. He's so angry it's as if he's gone a little crazy. He scares me now. But that doesn't mean he's a bad man, only that he's done bad things."

Zach lay silent, staring up at the dark ceiling. "Oh," he said finally, offhandedly. "I just wondered."

"When you're older, if you choose, you can get to know him again."

"Like he wants to know me."

"You were his favorite." Ironically, that was true. And it made Rylan's decision to leave with only Sophie all the more puzzling.

Zach made a jerky movement with his shoulders. "Yeah. Sure."

He sounded as if he didn't care. But he must. No child could be indifferent to a parent's rejection.

"Maybe," Judith said tentatively, "he didn't take you because he knew how hard it would be for you. Sophie was little. She'd have missed me, but she could get used to changes. You were seven. To get you to cooperate, he'd have had to tell you that I was dead." She pressed her lips together. "That...would have hurt. Maybe..."

"Right, Mom." His tone was scathing. "I don't need bedtime stories anymore."

"I wouldn't lie to you."

Zach turned his face away.

Judith tried again. "I'm only trying to make sense of things your dad did that I don't understand, either. I know he loved you. He didn't leave you because he didn't want you."

The nine-year-old didn't say anything.

Judith bent over and kissed his cheek. "You're all that saved me. I couldn't have stood it if you'd gone, too."

With startling speed, Zach rolled over and hugged her, his arms squeezing her rib cage so tightly it hurt.

"I love you, I love you, I love you," she murmured against the top of his head.

"I love you, too," he whispered, and let go of her just as suddenly, lying back against his pillow.

She hesitated a moment, but when Zach said nothing else, she rose to her feet. He immediately straightened and smoothed his covers anew before folding his arms on top of them.

Judith slipped out of the room, positioned the door and through the opening said softly, "Good night."

"'Night, Mom."

His voice drifted from the dark bedroom. Was he still upset? She couldn't tell.

Troubled, she made her way through the house, checking window latches and turning out lights. Why had she never realized before just how hurt Zach had been that Rylan hadn't wanted him? How could she comfort him when the only blessing she'd had was that Zach was still with her?

She hadn't seen Rylan in almost two and a half years, but she found fresh reason every day to hate him with a passion that frightened her.

Judith got ready for bed, then went back into the hall. At the children's bedroom, she whispered, "Zach?"

No answer.

She clicked off the hall light and went to bed, though she lay awake for another hour or more, worrying about her son, what Rylan's plans were and why she felt so much for Ben, who had made it all too clear he had no intention of being a father to anyone's children, including hers.

THE NEXT COUPLE OF weeks Ben was always around: taking Sophie and Zach riding, letting Zach help re-roof her garden shed, showing up with a pizza or sitting on her porch evenings. He was the perfect family man. After a while Judith convinced herself that Ben had been telling her how he *used* to feel about having children, before he met her. All he'd been doing, she decided, was explaining why he didn't yet have kids of his own. Otherwise he wouldn't be courting her children as patiently as he was courting her.

And he *was* patient. Judith and he never had a chance to be alone, except for stolen moments on her porch after she'd tucked the kids into bed. Those moments were sweet and intoxicating. Any sourness she'd felt toward men was washed away by Ben's kisses.

Having him around so much eased her worries about Rylan, too. Being alone, having no one to rely on, had heightened her fears. Now she wasn't alone; Ben was here.

She was cleaning out the flower bed along the front of the house with Sophie's help one Saturday. The previous weekend, when he'd roofed her shed, Ben had taken a long disapproving look at the lawn mower that came with the house. Today he was changing its oil and sharpening the blades and replacing the spark plug and probably half a dozen other things. Zach, of course, had eagerly asked if he could help. As usual, Ben gave one of his easy nods.

"Time you learned these things."

Now Zach was crouched beside Ben, who sat on his haunches with his back to her. The lawn mower lay on its side in the driveway. The whine of metal on metal suggested they were doing the blade sharpening right now. All Judith could see was Ben's broad back in a gray T-shirt, the muscles bunching in his upper arms as he honed the edges of the blades. Sweat darkened a patch on his back and under his arms, even though the air had an autumn nip to it.

Every so often, he'd let Zach take a turn. Zach was like a lion cub being initiated into hunting, its mock leaps and growls a perfect imitation of its mother's. From an occasional grunt to the safety glasses and the way he squatted over the mower, Zach was copying the big man beside him. Just as he would a father, if he had one. A real father.

In the act of gathering up a heap of withered leaves from the lilac bush, Judith stopped, watching them. The sight of Ben tutoring her son was all it took to bring a quick stab of happiness so sharp it hurt.

All of a sudden, her love for her son was all mixed up with what she felt for Ben McKinsey.

I love him. It came to her with the abruptness of a winter storm, and Judith wasn't sure the realization was any more welcome.

Well, why not? she asked herself. Was there a reason in the world she shouldn't fall in love? Some law that said she shouldn't be happy? And Ben showed every sign of returning her feelings, or else why was he here? Why was he bothering with her son?

But she sensed the danger in letting herself believe it would be that easy. How could she be sure Ben would be any different from Rylan? He *had* said he didn't want children.... *But look at him. He knows how to be a father. He's good at it. He's ready.*

She hoped. She prayed.

"Mommy," Sophie said, "the phone's ringing."

Judith blinked and turned her head. Sure enough, a muffled ring came from inside the house. Judith hurried up the porch steps, Sophie tagging along.

"Can I get a boxed juice?" she asked.

"Sure." Judith picked up the receiver. "Hello?"

"Hi, Judith? This is Susan Robb. We met at my sister Carol's the other night. I'm Nadia and Tim's mother."

"Oh, yes," Judith said warmly, remembering the dark-haired woman with merry brown eyes. "Tim's been including Zach in basketball games at recess since then. That's so nice of him."

"He likes Zach. In fact," Susan said with a rush, "that's why I'm calling. Carol explained your situation—I hope you don't mind. And...well, I wondered if your kids could come and sleep over tonight. Nadia and Tim are both excited about the idea. I'd take good care of them. And I figured you could use a break."

"Oh, but that's asking so much of you...."

"My kids have friends sleep over all the time. I order a pizza, rent some videos, maybe a Nintendo game for the boys, and they're all out of my hair for the evening. Nadia has a brand-new board game she's dying to share."

"You're sure?" She said that dismayingly often these days, Judith thought wryly. She seemed to have a bottomless need for reassurance.

"Are you kidding? I can beg if you want."

Judith had to chuckle. "That isn't necessary, I assure you. Let me ask them." She covered the phone. "Honey, do you remember Nadia, the girl at Mrs. Galindez's house? Her mom wants to know if you'd like to spend the night at her house."

Sophie's face lit up. "Can I?" Then the brightness dimmed and she edged closer to her mother. "Will Zach be there, too?"

"Yes, Tim invited him. Shall we go ask him?"

Her daughter nodded.

They went out on the porch. "Zach," Judith called, "Tim and Nadia want you and Sophie to spend the night. Would you like to go?"

"Cool!" he said, swiveling on his heels.

But it wasn't her son Judith was looking at. Ben straightened and turned at the same moment, a wrench dangling from one hand. The jeans and T-shirt clung to his big, lean body. Grease smeared his hands and one cheek; he wiped the sweat from beneath his eyes with his forearm. The whole time, his gaze didn't leave Judith. She remembered that night when he'd asked how she would feel about a kiss: the quiet, the darkness, the waiting reflected in his eyes. The same expression was there now, and her stomach somersaulted.

Judith heard her son—she even understood him—but still she looked only at Ben. "I...I'll tell Tim's mom," she said.

Ben was still waiting, but she didn't know the answer to his question. Was she ready? With her eyes, she begged him for time, for understanding, for more patience. *Maybe,* she said silently, and he gave a brief nod, as if she'd spoken out loud.

She was able then to tear herself away, to go back to the telephone lying on the kitchen counter. As if glued to her mother, Sophie went, too.

Judith brushed Sophie's hair back from her forehead before she picked up the receiver and said, "Yes. An emphatic yes."

"Oh, good. The troops will be happy. If I run over to get them, can they be ready in an hour?"

An hour. So soon. Her stomach took another tumble.

"I could drive them...."

"But then we'd just have to go back out to choose videos, so we may as well do it in one go. If we exchange directions, maybe you can pick them up tomorrow and we can have coffee and tell each other gory stories about the trials and tribulations of rearing children."

"Sounds like fun," Judith agreed, smiling. Susan's good humor was infectious. "Do you have a pencil?"

Judith gave directions, then wrote Susan's down. After hanging up the phone, Judith said, "Well, punkin, you need to get packed. What do you want to take with you?"

She went out on the porch and called Zach in to clean up and pack, too. Ben said something to him but stayed hunkered over the lawn mower. Judith left him to it and went to supervise Sophie's packing.

"Of course you can take your blanket!" she said. "I'll bet Nadia has one, too."

"What if I don't want to stay?" Sophie asked, clutching the blankie, her eyes newly fearful.

"Then you can phone me. In fact, I'll call and wish *you* good-night and sweet dreams. How would that be?"

Sophie nodded.

"You'll have a good time." Judith hugged her. "I'll bet you won't even miss me."

"She's a baby," Zach said from the other side of

the room, where he was stuffing clothes into a duffel bag. "*I* won't be homesick."

"It wasn't so long ago that I had to rescue you from a friend's house in the middle of the night," Judith reminded him.

"That was years ago!"

"Sophie is *years* younger than you." She smiled down at her daughter. "Just because he talks big doesn't mean he'd mind if you go wish him goodnight, too."

Zach didn't say anything. Sophie smiled.

It seemed like only minutes before a car horn honked out front. Bag bumping on his back, Zach skidded down the hall and raced outside, screen door banging behind him. Sophie and Judith went out at a more civilized pace. By the time they reached the foot of the porch steps, Tim had already slung Zach's bag in the rear of the station wagon and the two boys were hopping in. Nadia came shyly to meet Sophie, who hung back.

In the act of wheeling the lawn mower into the shed, Ben stopped to exchange greetings with Susan. After a polite exchange, he disappeared into the small outbuilding.

"You've got our police chief working for you?" Susan asked, the hint of a smile dimpling her cheeks. "Good going."

"Strictly volunteer." Judith lifted her hands to proclaim her innocence. "He's bored without enough challenges on the job. He had to take us on to add some excitement to his life."

"Well, if he needed to raise his blood pressure, winterizing the lawn mower is the way to do it," Susan agreed cheerfully. "My husband always swears and throws a few tools when he does ours." She smiled at the girls, still eyeing each other from their mothers' sides. "You guys ready to pick out a movie?"

Sophie nodded.

Nadia said, "Do you like *Homeward Bound?* I think it's really funny."

Sophie nodded again but still clung to Judith's leg. Was she going to chicken out? Judith was ashamed to realize that she almost hoped Sophie did. That would postpone the decision she needed to make about Ben.

But Sophie gave a last squeeze to Judith's thigh and ran to the car. Nadia took her hand and the two girls climbed into the front seat. Judith watched as Susan buckled them in side by side.

"Have fun, guys!" she called as the station wagon pulled away. All four kids turned to wave.

Feeling absurdly bereft, Judith stood watching until they turned onto the main road and vanished. It was so quiet without them. So peaceful, she admitted guiltily.

She sensed more than heard Ben come up behind her. His voice was husky.

"We're alone."

"Yes." She drew in a deep breath and turned. Meeting his dark eyes, she saw what she'd expected: the banked desire. But his face gave away more: his vulnerability, the tension he tried to hide. "So," she said, "care to entertain a lonely lady this evening?"

"Yeah." His mouth curved into a smile that sent her heart into a tailspin. "I care."

"Good," she whispered.

Ben lifted his hands but stopped short of touching her. "I'm filthy. I don't want to get grease all over you."

"Shall I make us dinner? Or do you want to do the town?" she asked, the lightness in her tone disguising *her* nervousness. Dinner wasn't the kind of entertainment he had in mind.

"You'd probably like to go out, wouldn't you?"

The coward in her would. The mother wanted to stay home. The woman in love wanted the same.

"No," she admitted. "I'd rather have dinner here."

His brown eyes caressed her. "We haven't had much chance to be alone."

"No." Which was exactly why she was so nervous. In one way, she knew him well. But she knew him best as a neighbor and father figure for her kids, not as the man who kissed her as if she were his salvation.

"I'll go home and shower. What time do you want me?"

Anytime leaped to mind. *Now.* Judith swallowed. "Whenever you want to come back."

There was that word again. *Want.*

Ben read her mind. "Soon," he said roughly. "As quick as I can clean up." He backed away, one step, two. His eyes never left hers. When his feet hit the gravel lane, he stopped, took one last long, hungry look at her, then finally turned away. Ground-eating strides carried him toward his house.

Judith pressed her hands to her chest. Oh, he was beautiful! She'd never been a woman given to admiring the finer points of well-built men in jeans, but since meeting Ben, she hadn't been able to help herself. He moved with such effortless grace, muscles synchronized like finely tuned machinery. His biceps and thighs didn't bulge like a weight lifter's; instead he was long and lean. Even his rear end was taut. She imagined those muscles tensing as he lifted himself over her...

Judith's face heated and she wheeled around, making herself take the time to put away her rake and shovel before dashing—well, okay, stumbling—up the porch steps and into the house. For Pete's sake, if she didn't corral her thoughts, next thing she'd be staring at the part of his anatomy that *did* bulge and imagining herself easing down the zipper and...

Judith mumbled a word she wouldn't have said around the kids. Maybe being without them wasn't healthy. She never had thoughts like this! For all that she'd rebelled as a teenager, she'd been raised to be prim and proper, a girl from a good Bostonian family. Not a prude, but not a wanton, either.

Judith had to roll her eyes over that one. Honestly. A normal desire for sex with the man you'd already admitted you loved didn't mean you belonged on a street corner in hot pants. And maybe she and Ben wouldn't make love, anyway. She could say no. Ask him to wait.

But she knew she wouldn't, and that was why her hands were still shaking when she started dinner half an hour later. The shower hadn't relaxed her; the makeup hadn't given her confidence.

Footsteps on the front porch announced Ben's arrival even before he knocked. Heart pounding, Judith

went to let him in. He wore his good black jeans and
a white shirt again, cuffs buttoned. He'd shaved, she
noticed. A tiny fleck of dried blood marred the smooth
line of his jaw. Maybe his hands had been shaking,
too.

She backed away. "Come on in. I was just putting
dinner together." She was all too aware that her retreat
into the kitchen resembled a fugitive fleeing the law
more than a hostess gracefully welcoming a guest.

She'd been busy layering ingredients from half a
dozen bowls and pans and jars on the counter into a
casserole dish. "This is one of my favorites," she said
brightly. "Except for the chopping, it's no work at all.
It's called Chicken—"

"I'm not that hungry," Ben said.

Oh, Lord. She swallowed, unable to turn and face
him. "I can…I can put it in the refrigerator for a
while. Until you are."

"Why don't you do that," he agreed, his voice a
rumble.

Feeling panicky, Judith slapped the last layers heed-
lessly together. She'd expected to have time to work
up her nerve, to get in the mood, to have second and
third thoughts, if necessary.

Why so scared? she scolded herself. If she didn't
want to make love with him, all she had to do was
say so. She was acting like a timid virgin, not a divorced mother of two. She'd done it before. She would
insist Ben use a condom, so there wouldn't be any
consequences if…well, if she realized she'd made a
mistake. Or if he realized the same.

She looked down at the casserole and saw that it was ready to go in the oven.

"There!" How perky she sounded. Maybe she should have her own cooking show on TV: "How to Put Together the Perfect Dinner for the Postcoital Meal." Desperately, she said aloud, "It's all set. Just let me cover it with tin foil and pop it in the fridge. Would you like a glass of wine?"

He raised a dark eyebrow. "If you would."

She hesitated, then shook her head. She wouldn't let herself be that big a coward. If she was going to do something this reckless, she would be sober, in her right mind. "Um...shall we go sit down?"

Ben's mouth twitched. "Sure."

When they reached the living room, he took her hand and led her to the couch. As she sank down next to him, his arm came around her. For a moment she sat stiffly, but his warmth seeped through the thin fabric of her shirt and leggings, melting her resistance no matter how hard she tried to hold on to it. When his fingers began kneading her upper arm, she relaxed against his side and with a sigh laid her head on his shoulder.

"That's better," he said, his mouth against her hair. "Scared?"

"Petrified," Judith admitted.

"Of me? Or you?"

"Both. Everything. I'm afraid of making a fool of myself." She nibbled on her lower lip, glad she didn't have to look him in the eye when she made her confession. "I'm really not very experienced, you know."

His chuckle vibrated in his chest. "You've got two kids. How long were you married?"

"Eight years." She hesitated, then confessed in a rush, "Rylan was the only man I ever...you know. I was a virgin...well, not when we got married, but when we fell in love."

Ben tilted her chin up so she had to look at him. "Sex is pretty basic. Far as I know, I don't do it any differently from any other man."

"But...but it must be different."

A muscle in one cheek twitched. "Is that necessarily a bad thing?"

Startled, she examined the thought. "No. No, I guess not. I mean, Rylan did sour me on romance. So I suppose..."

Ben made a rough sound and captured her mouth with his. The kiss was hard and sure and more intoxicating than any glass of wine could have been. Her hands flattened on the muscled wall of his chest; his found her breasts, cupped them and massaged gently. He made a muffled sound, and she whimpered.

All that agonizing, and it was so easy. She no longer thought, only felt. Heat, thick and slow moving, flowed through her veins, starting in her belly and her chest, traveling out to her fingertips and her toes. His mouth did glorious things to her as it moved from her lips to her earlobe, down her throat to the hollow at its base, over the sensitized skin on her chest, until he ran up against the limits of her shirt. Judith lifted her arms willingly when he peeled it off. She stared down in fascination as his big brown hands wrapped around her breasts again, contrasting with the cream of her skin and the shimmery white satin of her bra.

"Lovely," he said, his voice hoarse.

With a sigh, she arched her back so he could unfasten her bra. When he had done so, he dropped to his knees in front of her to nuzzle her breasts, kiss them, tease them, suckle them. She curled her fingers in his thick dark hair and let out tiny gasps as he tugged awake unfamiliar sensations.

Rylan had thought her breasts too small; his caresses there had been perfunctory. But she seemed to be giving Ben as much pleasure as he gave her.

When he lifted his head to look at her, his eyes were hot and intense. Gaze never shifting, he unbuttoned first his cuffs, then the front of his shirt. Dark hair curled on the flat, muscular planes of his chest. Of their own volition, her hands reached out to him. The hair was silky, the nubs of his nipples as hard as her own. His heartbeat drummed under her palm, not steady at all, but frantic. She bent forward and kissed his neck, where his pulse beat. The skin was salty, feverishly warm. She moved lower, over the strong, jutting collarbone. When she closed her eyes and rubbed her cheek over his chest hair, Ben groaned and tangled his hands in her curls, lifting her face to meet his for a hungry kiss.

Her head was swimming by the time it ended. His fingers caught in her waistband and stilled.

"Your bedroom?" he asked thickly.

She tried to think. The children weren't home. It didn't matter.

He made the decision for her, rising to his feet in

one smooth motion that took her with him. Judith squealed and wrapped her legs around his waist.

Ben made a ragged sound and shifted his grip on her bottom, lowering her until she was wrapped around the hard ridge beneath the zipper of his jeans. Her shaky exhalation was close to a sob. Oh, he felt so good! She wanted…she wanted…

He muttered an obscenity. "I could take you right now, right here."

"Yes."

Whatever else he said, she didn't hear. He strode down the hall and shouldered open her bedroom door. Three more steps and his legs bumped the bed. He began kissing her again, openmouthed, bold, tongue sliding over hers. He lowered her onto the coverlet, peeled off her leggings and panties, then yanked down his own pants without taking his mouth from hers. Judith arched her hips in a need so primeval it shocked her in the distant part of her brain that was still dimly conscious.

He laughed and touched her there, his hand so big, so *knowing*—another difference. He'd made her as bold as he was—she even reached up and stroked him, felt him quiver.

She opened her body to him and he entered her slowly, shaking with the strain of holding back. And then, suddenly, she felt how deep he was, buried in the center of her. She loved the way he filled her, and the way her body wrapped around him, squeezing him.

"No," she whispered when he started to withdraw. She clutched at his upper arms, sweat slick and knotted with hard muscles.

"I can't come back if you won't let me go."

She wanted him back, so she loosened her legs and arms and felt his agonizingly slow retreat, shivered with the power of his surging return. He did it over and over, giving her a pleasure so overwhelming she could only ride it helplessly, knowing that this time *was* different, and she was fiercely glad.

And finally it was too much. The pleasure coursed through her blood. She called Ben's name once, twice, again. He was thrusting hard and fast, growling her name in her ear, groaning, trembling, finally collapsing on top of her.

Judith smiled and kissed his damp skin. She could have laughed out loud with pure joy. If only she'd known making love could be like this!

And then a fugitive thought edged its way into her consciousness, a wisp of alarm. Had he used a condom? She couldn't remember.

For all her usual caution, she'd been as foolish as a teenage girl. What if he'd just made her pregnant?

The alarm evaporated. Delight almost as potent as her climax rippled in her belly and between her legs. He would be a magnificent father. She'd never even considered having more than two children, but with Ben... Judith smiled again, closed her eyes and rubbed her cheek against the smooth, cooling skin on his shoulder.

She wanted to have a baby. With Ben.

CHAPTER TEN

BEN SLIPPED OUT OF bed the next morning and left Judith sleeping, even though he really wanted to kiss her awake and slip his fingers between her legs and then wrap those legs around his waist as he eased into her. The sleepiness in her eyes would become a different kind of dreaminess. He'd like to see her face when she cried his name again. It made him feel ten feet tall. It made him feel like a good man.

Which was one thing he wasn't.

As he pulled on his pants, the questions rose unbidden. Did he intend to marry this woman? Raise her children as his own? And if not, what in hell was he doing in her bed?

He wouldn't steal out of the house; that would be too low, even for him. How would she feel when she woke up and found him gone? He knew the answer: used.

He could lie, leave a note saying he'd been called into work. But he'd have to face her sooner or later.

Not that she'd ask his intentions, but the question would be there in their minds. It wouldn't have to be spoken aloud.

And he didn't know the answer.

Ben took a last lingering look at her face, relaxed

in sleep. Her rosy cheeks and the pout of her lips almost drew him back to kiss her. In the morning light, he discovered new delights. Her closed eyelids were the creamy white of alabaster; her auburn lashes weren't straight and spiky like his, but actually curled naturally. That glorious coppery hair was everywhere, tangling over her pillow and cascading over her cheek and throat. Ben's hand rose to brush it away from her face, but he stopped. No. He'd wake her, and he needed some time to think.

He'd watched Judith cook enough to know where she kept most everything in the kitchen. He started with coffee. Just instant, but he needed the rich aroma and the acrid taste to get him going.

It was only seven-thirty in the morning. She might sleep for a couple more hours. Trying not to bang pans, he scrambled himself some eggs and buttered two slices of toast. While he ate at her kitchen table, morning sunlight pouring over him, Ben asked himself some hard questions without coming to any conclusions.

He liked Sophie and Zach; he even enjoyed the time he spent with them. Zach reminded him of Eddie, always wanting to help, wanting to know why, wanting to be a man even though he was a little boy. A kid himself, Ben had pushed Eddie away, hadn't taken the time with him that he should have. Sometimes, when Judith's son was dogging his footsteps, he'd turn his head and see Eddie there instead of Zach, hear his little brother's voice.

Ben wasn't sure whether the time he spent with the kid was for the boy's sake or his own. Did he think he could atone for past mistakes, win some kind of cosmic forgiveness? He gave a grunt of disgust and pushed his empty plate away.

"Hi," a voice said shyly from behind him.

He swung around, scraping the chair legs on the vinyl floor. Judith stood barefoot in the doorway, eyes still drowsy, wearing a prim cotton nightgown that was therefore all the more provocative. Just the sight of her made him hard. Ben cleared his throat. "Good morning."

No questions yet, just the shyness, as if she didn't know what to expect from him this morning. Maybe she understood him better than he realized, Ben thought on a wave of self-revulsion.

"That nightgown is made to be ripped off," he said roughly.

Her cheeks pinkened. "It's...it's not very sexy. Just warm."

He stood and went to her. There was plenty he should have said, starting with, *Last night was the best thing that ever happened to me. I love you* would be good, too. The first was true—he knew it was. But what about the second part? *I love you.* He thought he did. But was that love enough to encompass her children, too, and all the obligations they brought with them? He just didn't know.

So he didn't say a word. Instead, he kissed her.

Of course they ended up making love again, a slow, leisurely journey of pleasure and tenderness that frightened him some because it made him even more certain of his feelings for her. *I love you.* Every time the words rose in his throat, every time his lips started to shape them, he recalled his helpless rage at being stuck with responsibilities he didn't want. He made himself remember his resentment at the endless demands. Sleepless nights when one of the little ones was sick; the cooking, the cleaning, the hurrying home after school instead of playing football; the lessons in tying shoes, the homework, the whining. He couldn't let himself be seduced into forgetting. He couldn't let himself be trapped again. He'd done the unforgivable to avoid it.

Judith didn't seem to expect the words, for which he was grateful. Come to think of it, she didn't say *I love you,* either. He wondered if she did. Wasn't it a given, when she'd never had sex with any man besides her husband until now?

Maybe, he thought with a sinking feeling, she'd just decided her life needed a little excitement, and he was handy.

Or else she was trying to tie him to her so he'd stay close and defend her children from that scum Rylan Kane.

No. Ben rejected the second notion. That was too calculating for her.

They talked—just murmured words about this and that. He gave her a back rub, and she reciprocated. They made love again. He remembered she hadn't had breakfast and insisted on getting up to grill a couple of cheese sandwiches and make a salad. Then they took a shower together, which led to some more shenanigans. Personally, he could have gone on that way for the rest of the day and all night, too, but Judith insisted on calling to see how her kids were doing, and Sophie decided she was ready to come home.

To avoid questions, Ben didn't go with Judith. Instead, he tucked his shirt into his jeans, put on socks and boots, remembered his watch where he'd set it on her nightstand and kissed her goodbye.

She stood on tiptoe to reciprocate.

"I'll see you," he said gruffly.

He thought her smile was just a little uncertain, though her tone was light. "Can't seem to get away from us, can you?"

He could give her this much, at least. "I don't want to," Ben declared, kissed her again, quick and hard, and walked away.

He had just reached his own porch steps when she passed him in that cherry red van. He lifted a hand. She waved back. For the first time, it occurred to Ben that what they'd done together in bed hadn't changed anything. He couldn't be sleeping over there or kissing her in front of the kids. He was still just a neighbor. Last night might as well not have happened.

Except now that he'd had her, the wanting would be edgier, more urgent. It was just sex, Ben tried to tell himself. He'd had it before; he'd have it again. For God's sake, he wasn't being kept out of heaven if she wouldn't have him again!

But he couldn't fool himself with feigned indifference, because next thing he knew, he was trying to figure some way to get those kids out of the house again. He didn't know Carol Galindez or her sister well enough to beg them to extend further invitations, so he tried to remember who had kids more or less the same age as Judith's. Damn it, all his friends seemed to have older or younger ones or none at all.

Of course, he kept an eye out his kitchen window for the van's return. An hour went by, and he started to worry. She'd probably stayed to chat, Ben figured; two women, that's what happened. Another hour passed. He remembered she'd been low on milk. So, okay, a stop at the grocery store made sense. Two hours and fifteen minutes. Two and a half hours. He started to pace.

He had picked up the phone to call in and have the officers on duty keep an eye out for her, when the red van turned in and went on by his place without slowing. Ben looked at the clock. Almost three hours. Where in hell had she been? Why hadn't she told him she intended to dawdle all over town?

He went to his living-room window and pulled aside the lace curtains—they'd been on the windows when he moved in, and he never had liked them, he realized irritably. From here he could see Judith unloading children and then bags of groceries. Which still didn't explain three hours.

Among those rights he didn't have was the right to demand an explanation. He could go offer to help with the groceries, but he wasn't sure he was up to pretending in front of the kids that nothing had changed. Tomorrow, maybe, but not today.

He'd go for a ride, he decided. Ben changed shirts and went out and threw a saddle on Sherlock. Travis nipped his arm, just to show that he was put out at being left behind. Sherlock pranced a little as if to brag. Ben wondered if he married Judith, whether she'd enjoy leisurely trail rides or whether her interest in the horses went no further than keeping her kids happy.

Just across the highway, a well-worn track wound up the canyon, twice fording a small stream, near bone-dry at this time of year. Ben rode it often. The elevation didn't rise much, so snow didn't close the trail for more than a few months during the worst of the winter. Come spring and early summer, it ended up at a real pretty waterfall. He'd take Judith and her kids there once winter had replenished the streams.

His saddle creaked under him; Sherlock grunted when he had to scramble up a bank or jump a fallen log. They opened into a lope a few times but mostly jogged or walked. The air smelled like autumn: the musty scent of fallen leaves, the dryness, maybe a foretaste of winter storms. Bare branches silhouetted against the blue sky, which darkened as the afternoon wore on.

The ride cleared his mind but didn't resolve any of the issues churning in it. With no oncoming traffic, Ben sent the palomino clattering across the road. As soon as Judith's house came in sight, he checked for her van. Still there.

Irked at himself, Ben stripped the tack off Sherlock, rubbed down the gelding's golden coat and fed both the horses.

Once in the house, he did what he knew he had to. He got out his address book, flipped through the pages to the M's, picked up the phone and dialed Eddie's number.

His brother answered. "Yeah?"

Ben hunched his shoulders. He should have planned out what to say. "This is Ben."

Eddie didn't say anything. But he didn't hang up, either.

Ben grabbed for the first subject that came to mind. "I hear you and Anne are having problems."

"Called to set me straight?" Eddie asked, tone belligerent.

Ben rubbed the back of his neck. "No. My record in that department isn't too great." He hesitated. "I'm sorry."

"Sorry for what?" his brother asked, voice uncompromising.

For everything. "About you and Anne. Did she take the kids?"

"Yeah." Heavy breathing. Then, abruptly, Eddie said, "But we've been talking. I think she's coming back this week."

"Do you enjoy being a father?" The question was asked on pure impulse. He probably sounded like an idiot, but he really did want to know. Eddie had been seven when their dad died, so he probably had nothing but vague memories of him. The only other father he'd known was Ben, who'd let him down big-time. If he could overcome that and still like raising children of his own, anything was possible.

"Why are you asking?" Suspicion crackled like static.

If that didn't sound like the Eddie Ben knew and loved.

Ben massaged the back of his neck again. "I've been doing some thinking. Mostly about my mistakes.'' He let some irony sound in his voice. ''Not surprising my thoughts turned to you.''

After another pause, his brother gave a grunt that might have been laughter. ''You're right about that.''

''So? You going to answer my question?''

''Yeah,'' Eddie said. ''The kids are the greatest. When I get home from work, they come running to meet me, and I feel like a king. They can be noisy— obnoxious sometimes—but I can't imagine being without them.'' He grunted again. ''Check that. I know what it's like being without them. I call every night, but it's not the same.''

Eddie, the Father of the Year. Ben closed his eyes and squeezed the bridge of his nose.

''I haven't seen them since they were babies. How old are they now?''

''Sheila is seven. Smart as a whip. Just tested into the school's gifted program. Jay's five. Started kindergarten this September. He already knows his letters and his numbers. Smart kid, too.''

''I'm not surprised,'' Ben heard himself say. ''You were a good student. I always told you that you could do anything in the world. If you'd wanted to be a lawyer, you could have done it.''

''Well, probably a good thing I didn't. Who'd have paid for my tuition?''

''We'd have figured out a way.''

''No one figured out a way for you to go on to school.''

''I've done okay,'' Ben said. ''I like my job.''

''You never complained,'' Eddie said unexpectedly. ''I used to wish you would.''

"Why?"

"If you'd just once bitched, I could have listened, at least. I could have said, 'Well, why don't you let me help out?'"

It had only taken Ben twenty years to figure out that Eddie probably would have liked to shoulder part of the burden of keeping their family going. The fact that he hadn't been allowed to probably explained much of his resentment.

"Well, I wish I'd let you," Ben admitted. "I turned myself into a goddamned martyr. Got so I hated all of you, and Mom, and especially Dad...."

"You were a kid. Mom asked too much."

"Did she have a choice?"

"Yeah, she had a choice." His brother sounded angry. "Her trouble was, she had too much pride to accept charity. Wouldn't even take food stamps. Remember? She used to drum into us that you had to make your own way. Well, if she'd lowered her pride a little, you wouldn't have had to be a man when you were nine years old. You were the smartest one of us. You should have gone to college."

For the first time Ben could remember, Eddie had silenced him. He'd never thought of his mother's pride at getting by without welfare as selfish, but maybe her children would have been better off if she'd humbled herself some.

Or maybe not. What twisted in Ben's gut now was the fact that, even with all the bitterness between them, his brother was still willing to excuse him.

Ben opened his mouth to say again, "I did okay,"

but just in time he realized that Eddie would see it as a refusal to be honest. To share. To ask for help.

Yeah, he *had* done okay. Eventually. But at first, he'd believed his life had been ruined by having to raise two younger brothers and a sister.

So instead Ben asked Eddie if he remembered Pete Black, Ben's best friend in high school.

"Sure," Eddie said, sounding puzzled.

"He got a scholarship to Willamette University. The middle of the night after he left, I got out of bed and jogged a mile into the middle of the woods between us and Dellwing's dairy farm, and I screamed and cried and beat my hands against a tree trunk until they were bloody."

"And then you came home and pretended you didn't give a damn."

Ben grimaced. "That was *my* pride."

His brother growled an obscenity. "You know what? I turned sixteen that summer. What was John— thirteen, fourteen? Even Nora was almost a teenager. We'd have done okay. You weren't indispensable."

"Nobody told me that," Ben said simply, realizing how foolish that sounded but also how true it was. It had been beaten into him that he was needed, that he could keep the family together, that his mother couldn't do it alone. So he'd done what he had to, wearing blinders to prevent being tempted from the path of righteousness. He'd just plodded on like an old horse in harness, waiting for somebody to pull on the reins.

Ben guessed it was too late to get mad at his mother, but thinking back, he couldn't imagine why she hadn't said, "Go! You've been great with your brothers and sister, but they'll be okay now without you. Eddie can do what you've been doing. You apply to Willamette, too."

Maybe she'd been wearing blinders, as well, plodding along in her own rut. Maybe she'd hardly realized that her children were growing up. Or that her oldest was a kid, too.

Definitely too late for anger, Ben thought. She'd done her best. It was time he quit being mad.

"You shouldn't have needed to be told," Eddie grumbled. "I figured you were so used to playing God you didn't want to give it up."

"I'd have given my right arm to leave home."

Another long silence. "I wish you'd said something."

"I can't change what I did."

"Okay." Eddie's voice held a challenge. "You haven't said why you called."

Ben's mouth had been running away with him lately. Now was no exception. "I thought I'd have the family Christmas this year. I wanted to ask you first."

Silence sizzled like oil in a hot pan. Or maybe it was only in Ben's imagination, because his brother sounded downright amiable when he replied, "All right. It's your turn."

That easy.

Well, maybe not easy; the conversation hadn't been a comfortable one for Ben. And if he'd thrown this Christmas thing out first, Eddie would probably have told him where to go. The holidays hadn't been the point anyway; the conversation had been.

"Good," Ben said. "I'll ask the others, then. I hope you'll let me know when you work things out with Anne. I'd like to see your kids at Christmas."

"One way or another, they'll be with me," Eddie promised. He hesitated, adding awkwardly, "I'm glad you called."

"Yeah. I'm glad I did, too."

That was it. Something he'd put off for too long was done. One weight lifted from his shoulders, mostly thanks to Eddie's generosity. He'd been a good kid, as well as a smart one. Too bad Ben hadn't let himself appreciate his little brother then, when it would have done both of them a lot of good.

"RAT A-TAT CAT!" Judith announced triumphantly.

Zach groaned. "I get one more card."

"Me, too," Sophie chimed in.

"Yes, you do." Judith waited while they each drew again; Zach kept the new card and discarded an old one. Sophie's draw was a nine, illustrated with a sneering rat. She wrinkled her nose and put it down on the pile.

They all turned over their cards at the same time. Judith had won, although not by much.

"Let's play again," Zach pleaded.

"I've already won two out of three."

"Let's go for four out of seven," he suggested guilelessly.

Judith was in such a good mood she agreed. Watching him laboriously shuffle the deck of cards, she said on impulse, "I've been thinking. Remember how we talked about maybe getting a dog?"

His head shot up. "Can we?"

Sophie's eyes shone. "Can we get a puppy?"

"Probably not a puppy." She smiled at them. "There are always so many grown-up dogs that need homes—I'd rather take one of them. Puppies are cute, but they have to be house-trained and they chew stuff up and they whine at night and…" *They don't bark at intruders. Or bite them.* But she couldn't say that, not when it was their father she hoped the dog would attack.

"How come you know so much when you've never had a dog?" Zach asked.

"I checked out a book from the library," Judith admitted. "I read all about owning a dog and training it and what to feed it and all that."

"Oh." He fastened a hopeful look on her. "Can we go pick one out right now?"

"The shelter is closed on Sunday and Monday. Tomorrow after school, we'll go to the store and buy food and bowls and a leash, then Tuesday we'll choose a dog."

"Hey, cool." He launched himself across the coffee table, tumbling her back on the couch. "Thanks, Mom!"

Sophie piled on. "Thank you, Mommy! Thank you!"

Judith tickled them both. They ended up in a wrestling match that she lost, only partly on purpose.

"I give up!" she cried breathlessly.

Sophie bounced on her stomach. Zach gave one last tickle to the bottom of her bare foot. Then they helped their defeated mother up. The cards were scattered over the table and floor.

"Can we still play Rat-a-tat-cat?" Zach asked.

"Oh, let's go make dinner," Judith said. "I'm starved."

"We ate lots at Nadia's house," Sophie told her. "Nadia's mom made pancakes. Piles and piles and piles of 'em."

"Good for you." She didn't tell them she'd skipped breakfast and eaten only a scanty lunch, because they'd have wanted to know why.

Sooner or later, they'd catch on that something was happening between their mom and Ben, but Judith would just as soon go for the later. Or maybe never, if...well, if the whole thing fizzled out.

She opened the refrigerator door and scanned the contents without really seeing them. Instead she was remembering the way Ben looked at her as they made love: his face taut, eyes dark and glittering. Such hunger, but tenderness, too. And, oh, the pleasure, not just because the sex was so good. She had loved the feeling of contentment that came from holding him and being held by him, the joy she felt in knowing he wanted her.

Fizzle? How could feelings so incredible die?

"Mommy? Can we have pancakes again?"

Judith blinked and looked down at her daughter, who was peeking into the fridge, too.

"Again?"

"I like pancakes."

"I don't like 'em *that* much," Zach said. "I want lasagna."

"It's too late for lasagna. Let's see." She made herself concentrate for a moment. "How about...omelettes? We have cheese and ham and broccoli."

Her kids considered that for a moment. "Okay," Sophie said agreeably, and Zach shrugged his consent.

"They won't take long. You guys go wash up."

She set the carton of eggs on the counter and got out a bowl and the beater. But the moment Zach and Sophie left the kitchen, Judith looked out her window at Ben's house. His kitchen window showed light, too. Just knowing he was there, so close, made her heart squeeze. She had to shut her eyes.

She loved him. Forever and ever.

It wasn't *her* emotions that she feared. It was his. She could have sworn she saw love in his eyes, felt it in his touch, even heard it in the way he groaned her name. But he hadn't said a word about how he felt. No *I love you*. No *I can't live without you*. Not even *When can we be alone together again?* What was it he had said? "I'll see you"? Did that sound like a man in love?

Maybe he really didn't want to be a parent to Zach and Sophie. Maybe he was just attracted to her, and she'd made herself available, so he'd taken her up on it. *Want to entertain a lonely lady?* she'd asked him. How blatant could she have gotten?

Judith let out a soft sigh. *Don't jump to conclusions,* she told herself. *You always knew he wasn't a man given to poetry and bouquets of roses.*

At this point in her musings, the phone rang. Ben, she thought immediately. She picked up the receiver.

"Hello?"

Silence, then a slight rasping sound—an indrawn breath?

The hair on the back of Judith's neck prickled. "Hello?" she repeated. "Who is this?"

A soft click was the only answer. She slowly hung up, too.

Just a wrong number, Judith told herself. Nothing to feel uneasy about. Why would Rylan call? He had no reason.

The telephone rang again. Judith stared at it, her heartbeat accelerating. She picked it up as if it might bite. "Hello?"

"Hi."

At the sound of Ben's voice, reassuringly calm, Judith's anxiety vanished, and she felt silly to have reacted so strongly. "Hi," she said. "Did you try to call a minute ago?"

"No." His tone sharpened. "Why?"

"Oh...a wrong number, I guess." She shrugged, even though he couldn't see her. "It's just that I'd no sooner hung up than the phone rang again."

He accepted her explanation and they talked for a few minutes as she cooked. The conversation felt stilted, though. She wished he were here, instead, so she could see his face. She suggested he come for dinner the next night; he had a meeting.

"City council. We've had some vandalism of city property."

"They're not mad because you didn't prevent it, are they?"

"Nothing like that. I recommended a chain-link

fence and some barbed wire around the equipment yard, and tonight they're going to discuss paying for it.''

"Speaking of preventative measures, I've decided to take your advice," Judith told him. "We're going to get a dog. Zach's thrilled.''

"Good. I know some breeders if you want a pure-bred.''

"I thought we'd just go look at the shelter. A mutt makes just as good a pet, doesn't it?''

"As long as you don't bring home something twelve inches high and yappy. Do you want me to come with you?''

Judith thought about it. She'd rather not get too dependent on him. And although she wanted a guard dog, she was hoping for an animal that would be a pet, too. A dog she and the kids would fall in love with. She was pretty sure Ben would scoff at such an emotional consideration.

"No," she decided. "We'll be fine.''

"Okay. Listen, I'll talk to you later.''

"Right.'' She bit her lip. "Goodbye.''

"Yeah.'' She felt his hesitation, ached for him to say, "I miss you.'' But finally, almost brusquely, he added, "Bye,'' and hung up.

Judith stuck out her tongue at the telephone.

CHAPTER ELEVEN

JUDITH LINED UP the camouflage fabric and fed it under the needle of her sewing machine. Halloween was only a week away. They had found the perfect pink-spangled princess costume for Sophie at the town's one department store, thank goodness, but Zach insisted on being a dinosaur à la *Jurassic Park.* The coarse material—gray, green and brown—had struck Judith as most realistic. Now all she had to do was figure out how to give him stegosaurus plates that would stand upright.

She'd cut out the fabric before dinner, then set up the machine on the table as soon as the kids had cleared the dishes. Pinned pieces were laid in a logical order, waiting to be sewn together. The kids were off playing in the bedroom.

When the phone rang, she called, "Can one of you get that?"

"Yeah!" Zach yelled back.

She heard the thunder of feet, the crash of her bedroom door bouncing open, then the ring was cut off. Instead of him bellowing, "It's for you, Mom!" she heard only the murmur of his voice.

Her attention was snagged back to the sewing machine when the thread snapped. "Damn," she muttered, lifting her foot from the presser bar and reaching for the scissors.

She rethreaded the machine and finished the seam, then set aside the left leg of the costume. Who was Zach talking to? Even if one of his new friends had called, nine-year-old boys weren't given to chatting. What was up?

Her heels clicked on the wood floor; she arrived in her bedroom doorway just in time to hear Zach say, with some urgency, "I gotta go." Sprawled stomach-down on her bed, he spotted her and added hastily, "Okay," and hung up.

"Who was that?" she asked.

"Who?" Oddly, he looked flustered. "Oh. Um. It was just Tim."

"Big secrets?" she asked.

He sat up sharply, his expression accusing. "You were listening, weren't you?"

"No," she said, astonished. "Of course not."

"Then why'd you ask about secrets?" Zach demanded.

Her interest piqued, she sat down on the bed beside him. "Because you and Tim don't usually talk very long. You're action kids."

Apparently appeased, he relaxed. "Oh. Well, Tim just had stuff he wanted to tell me. We're making plans. For things we're going to do next time I spend the night at his house."

"That's fine," Judith said mildly. "I didn't mean to sound like I was conducting an inquisition."

He shrugged without looking at her.

Something was wrong, she thought. He could be a brat, but he was usually open about it.

The tinny sound of Sophie's tape player came from the kids' bedroom. The music from Disney's *Aladdin*. Sophie was currently enamored of it.

Looking down at Zach's bent head, Judith said tentatively, "There's something I've been wanting to talk to you about. Maybe this is a good time."

Although they weren't touching, she felt him stiffen. "Yeah?"

"About your father. It's important that you let me know if he ever tries to contact you. Especially if you see him, but even if he just calls and says he wants to talk."

Zach flung his head up. "You think that was him, don't you?" he cried, jerking away when she held her hand out. "I suppose you think I'm lying about it being Tim!"

"I didn't say that—"

"But you think it! I can tell." He leaped from the bed, quivering with outrage. "Why won't you just believe me?"

She stayed sitting in the hope of provoking him less. "I never said you were lying. The phone ringing just reminded me that I'd been wanting to talk to you about your father. That's all."

"*Now* you say that's all!" He sneered as if he were fifteen instead of nine going on ten. "Anyway, would it be so bad if I talked to my own father? Like that would hurt anything."

"It could. He's not in jail, you know." She pressed her lips together. "I'm afraid he'll try again—"

"You're always saying Dad wouldn't want me, right? It's precious Sophie he's after. So why are you worried he'd call me? Why don't you talk to *her?*"

She'd never realized he hurt so much. Or could hurt *her* so much. "I've never said that he'd only want Sophie," she explained quietly. "He's just as likely to come after you. I..." Judith had trouble finishing. "I don't want to lose you. Like I did her."

He stared at her, eyes wide and filled with an emotion she couldn't decipher. For an instant, she thought she'd gotten through, that he would fling himself at her for a hug, say he was sorry. But instead, in a hate-filled voice, he said, "Well, it was Tim. Not Dad. *I wish.*" And he left the room so precipitately she guessed he had begun to cry.

Judith sat on the edge of the bed, paralyzed. She was losing her son as surely as if Rylan had taken him. Losing him to resentment, because she was trying so hard to protect him.

No! She wouldn't let herself think that. He'd just reached a difficult age. She had sounded as if she were questioning his truthfulness. Well, all right, she *was* questioning his truthfulness. Of course he'd taken offense! He wasn't such a little kid anymore. He'd been wanting more privacy lately, was less chatty about what went on at school each day. That was normal at his age.

In the past, parents of her students had told her the same thing. All of a sudden, their son didn't come home chattering about his teacher and what they'd done in class and what Chad or Joey or Kyle had said. When asked how his day had been, their son would grunt, "Fine," and head for his room. They didn't know what to make of it. Now Judith understood their bewilderment and hurt feelings.

Zach was going through the same thing, she told herself. Maybe it was a little harder for him, and for her, because of the situation with Rylan. It didn't help that Zach had had to go from being an only child to sharing his mother with a little sister, too.

She was worrying too much, Judith decided. She'd better go check on his whereabouts, make sure he hadn't stomped off down the lane in a fit of temper, knowing that running away would upset her even more. Especially with it getting dark outside. But if he was around, she'd let the incident go. Work on his costume, have him come try it on as soon as she had enough sewn together. He might have an idea for the plates that would run down his back. By bedtime, this quarrel would be forgotten. Tomorrow they'd go pick out a dog, which would keep Zach busy for the foreseeable future. Everything would be fine.

With a sigh, she rose to her feet. Why couldn't life be simpler?

IN HIS OFFICE, the ratty blinds pulled down and his door firmly shut, Ben stared at the phone number he'd scrawled on a message pad.

Calling wouldn't achieve a damn thing. Kelly would not be delighted to hear from him, and Lord knows he had nothing to say to her. All he had were a few questions, and he wasn't altogether sure he wanted to be burdened with the answers.

What if he knew he had a daughter, blond and blue-eyed like her mother? Or dark like him? He'd start seeing her in every child's face, start wondering if she'd inherited his family's musical ability, which had skipped him for some reason, or his mother's and sister's love of flowers.

Worse yet, what if the child had the same tangled feelings Zach Kane had about his father? Then Ben would have to face up to his responsibilities, and wasn't that exactly what he had refused to do seven years ago when Kelly told him she was pregnant?

So why was he so damnably tempted to call?

He gave a gruff laugh. *Tempted* wasn't exactly the right word; *tormented* came closer. Sometimes, for months on end, he had almost buried his guilt and the simple curiosity that walked with it. But all it took was a glimpse of a pretty blonde who reminded him for a fleeting instant of Kelly, or maybe a child's wide-eyed stare in a grocery checkout line, and then he'd wonder. Had the birth gone all right? Was the kid healthy? Pretty? Homely? Smart? Did he—or she—have a temper like Nora's when she was little? Was the child loved?

He'd heard from a former neighbor that Kelly had gotten married. Pretty damn quick, too. Ben didn't know the guy, but Kelly had drummed him up from somewhere when she'd decided she needed a husband and a father for the baby Ben refused to acknowledge.

Actually, that wasn't quite true. He'd never denied his part. He'd been present and enthusiastic during some wild nights of sex. Maybe the pregnancy even had been an accident, as Kelly claimed, although he doubted it.

But she didn't want what he was willing to offer: money. She'd wanted him to be her dream husband and a father to her child. Ben had told himself that the decision to have a baby was hers; in offering to pay child support, he'd done all that he was obligated to do.

Goddamn it, he didn't want to be a father! And Kelly had damn well known that.

But somewhere out there a kid was growing up knowing that her own father hadn't wanted her. That sense of guilt had started small, just a drop now and then, easily ignored, but the drops were acid that corroded and weakened and ate their way through his defenses and justifications.

He hadn't taken a hard look at how full of holes they'd become until Judith and her children moved in next door. Now...

"Oh, hell," Ben muttered, and squeezed the bridge of his nose. Face it. He was the wrong man for Judith. He was a son of a bitch who wasn't good enough to be a father to his own kid, let alone someone else's.

When that even bigger SOB Rylan Kane was safely behind bars, Ben should gracefully let Judith go. Let her find a decent man. Wallow in his guilt without mucking up her life.

He crumpled the paper with the phone number in his fist and shoved his chair back. A DARE class was waiting; the fifth graders needed his moral guidance to grow into good citizens. Today, the irony was almost more than he could stomach.

In his present mood, he just thanked God the class wasn't Judith's.

BEN LEANED his forearms against the top rail of the stall and watched Travis lipping up hay from the full rack. To each side of Ben was a kid. Glancing at them, he saw that both were mimicking his posture, right down to the foot resting on the bottom rail.

It gave him the strangest feeling, seeing that. Sophie looked especially funny in this manly position dressed in her pink corduroy overalls and sparkling purple canvas shoes. How could he help feeling touched? What was that saying—something about imitation being the sincerest form of flattery?

Ben abruptly shoved himself away from the stall partition. God almighty, he didn't deserve their adoration.

The quick movement was enough to make the Kanes' new dog flinch. Some kind of collie and lab mix, the damn mutt was scared of his own shadow. Hell, he'd run with his tail between his legs if someone broke into the house in the middle of the night!

The kids both looked startled, too, but followed when he stalked out of the barn.

The boy clicked his tongue. "Come on, Hercules."

Out of the corner of his eye, Ben saw that the dog scooted along with them, his chin bumping Zach's heels. Hercules!

"Time to go home," Ben said curtly.

"You'll walk us, right?"

Sophie's trusting gaze was enough to drive the stake straight into his heart. How easily he'd been able to forget, to whitewash himself!

"Yeah." He started across the yard. The kids fell into step, the dog glued to Zach. After a moment, Sophie's small hand wormed into Ben's clasp. As always, he stiffened for an instant, but how could he reject her advances. After all she'd gone through?

Zach began talking about something or other to do with his friend Tim and heroics Hercules was going to perform. Ben tuned him out.

A week ago he'd loathed himself. He'd actually picked up the phone to call Kelly, before chickening out. But, hey, given a day or two, he'd had no trouble burying his guilt again and sliding back into his daily routines—which had mysteriously come to include Judith's children.

And Judith herself. Telling himself that she needed him right now, he could easily excuse the fact that he was probably leading her to believe marital bliss was in their near future.

The truth was, he was letting pure selfishness rule him. He wanted Judith, whether he was good for her or not.

She came right out on the porch to meet them, probably alerted by Zach's continuing chatter. The mutt instantly abandoned the kid for his goddess. When she bent to pet him, Hercules rolled over, dribbling pee. Ben made a sound of disgust.

Judith gave him a reproving look and murmured reassurances to the dog. But when she straightened, she'd apparently forgiven him. "Stay for dinner?"

How did a woman look so beautiful in plain chinos and a turtleneck? Her turtleneck was a warm brown that showed off the fire in her hair, which tumbled over her shoulders. That small dimple quivered at the edge of her mouth, as tantalizing as a lacy bra.

Noble as always, Ben surrendered without so much as a battle. "You sure you have enough?" he asked. "You don't have to always be feeding me."

"I like to feed you." Her smile deepened. "But we've got to hustle tonight. You're sure we won't get any trick-or-treaters here?"

"Positive."

"Go wash up," she told the kids.

When they raced inside, Hercules damn near knocked them over to make sure he got in the door, too. The dog had a self-esteem problem. Low self-confidence, Ben reflected, did not make for a powerful protector.

Judith lowered her voice. "Have you ever had any cases of candy being tampered with around here?"

"Worst thing about Halloween is cleaning up the eggs come morning. If you're nervous, though, the hospital x-rays the candy free." He kissed her, just because she was close enough. The sweetness of her lips always drowned out his conscience.

"Are you going to come with us?" Judith whispered.

He nuzzled her neck. "Can't. I have to get back to work. We do get a rash of calls about teenagers out kicking up a rumpus."

He'd always detested Halloween. Well, not always; as a kid, he'd had as much fun as everyone else. He and John and Eddie and Nora had had to come up with their own costumes, but they hadn't minded. An old white sheet had made Ben into a hell of a spooky ghost one year. They'd taken turns being hobos and hippies and clowns, whatever they could put together themselves. The annual gorging after Halloween was especially memorable since both shortness of money and their mother's convictions meant they hardly ever had candy in the house.

Of course, in time he'd wanted to drive around with his friends instead of walking his little sister from house to house, waiting with the parents out on the sidewalk. He did remember one fight with Eddie, who had wanted to go with his friends and refused to take Nora and John. Ben smiled wryly. He'd have to remind Eddie of that one.

But as a cop, Ben had come to think of Halloween as trouble with a capital T. What in hell possessed someone to put cocaine in a chocolate bar, he'd never know. But it happened. Not here in Mad River, although urban sickness tended to migrate here eventually. So far the problems were old-fashioned ones: teenagers throwing eggs, scaring little kids and vandalizing the high school. His nightmare was a kid in a dark costume getting hit by a car. Everyone on the force would be out tonight, slowing down speeders and patrolling the neighborhoods where most of the trick-or-treating took place.

Over dinner Zach talked nonstop, excitement fizzing inside him. He was like a can of soda someone had shaken up, Ben thought. God help the fool who opened it.

Sophie didn't know whether to be excited or a little scared. Apparently she'd never been trick-or-treating. Her brother launched into a story about a house back in their old neighborhood where the lady had dressed up as a witch to hand out candy. Weird music could be heard half a block away.

"But I didn't let it scare me," the boy boasted. "I just walked right up to the porch. I reached for the doorbell and—guess what?" His voice lowered and he leaned forward. "Out of the darkness came..."

Eyes saucer wide, Sophie breathed, "What? What came out of the darkness?"

"A bony hand!" he shouted, groping for her, his fingers writhing.

She squealed and shrank back in her chair. "Mommy, I don't want to tick-or-teat! I don't wanna!"

Judith opened her mouth.

Zach didn't even notice. He said cheerfully, "It's okay, Soph. The thing is, it was just a plastic hand. And that lady gave out practically whole *scoops* of candy. Most people are really stingy and give only one candy bar, or else they act like they're so generous when they give you two of these eensy teensy ones. She was cool." He stopped in remembered admiration.

"Oh," said Sophie.

"So you wanna go trick-or-treating, right, Soph?"

"Right," she decided.

"Well then." Judith looked around the table. "Let's get this show on the road!"

She hadn't let the kids put on their costumes before dinner, in case they spilled something on them. Ben hung around long enough to admire the princess and the stegosaurus, then headed for work while they loaded into their van for a night of trick-or-treating.

As Halloweens went, this one was a breeze. No hit-

and-runs, no poison or razor blades in candy, not even any broken windows. There were just the usual egg yolks and slimy whites dripping from car windshields and mailboxes, a few front yards strewn with toilet paper and—his personal favorite—the bejesus scared out of that busybody Ruby Santoya.

Quivering with fury, she'd snapped, "I almost had a heart attack! There I was, standing in the kitchen washing up the dishes, when this...this skeleton rises up out of my lawn! There was just enough light from the back porch for me to see it—shining white. *Oh!*" The last was an exclamation of rage. "Steven went right out there to check, and of course it was one of those silly plastic ones you can buy as a joke from mail order catalogs, but it was rigged with strings going over the branches of the apple tree so they could make it move."

He suppressed a grin. "Which means they had to be sitting right under your kitchen window to pull the strings." And to hear her scream.

"They laughed!" she declared in outrage. "What a...a *mean* trick!"

The perps were long gone, of course. Ben figured this was a payback for one of a couple dozen phone calls Ruby had made to 911 reporting various misdeeds on the part of local teenagers. Ben thought the prank was actually funny, though he didn't say so.

It must have been midnight by the time he turned down his dirt road. The squad car bounced into a rut and he swore. He should have had the lane graded this fall. Monday morning, Ben told himself.

He slowed as he reached his house, but damned if

there weren't still lights on at Judith's. He kept right on going, rolling to a quiet stop in front.

Maybe Halloween made her nervous and she'd left a light on for security when she went to bed. But no, the kitchen was lit, too.

By this time he knew where every squeak on her porch steps was. Adrenaline pumping, he made his way carefully up them, his hand on the butt of his revolver. She was probably staying up to watch a late movie—tomorrow was Saturday. But the logical explanation didn't wash. She never stayed up late. She liked to get up when the kids did, even on the weekend. Right now, worrying about her ex the way she was, he couldn't imagine she would burn the midnight oil.

Instead of knocking, he eased over to the kitchen window and craned his neck. The dinner dishes had been cleaned up, but there was no sign of Judith.

Maybe one of the kids was sick. Probably throwing up after too much candy, Ben thought reminiscently. Judith would be holding Zach's head and bathing his sweaty forehead with damp washcloths.

He stepped back from the window and bumped the porch swing. The chains groaned as it swung away from him. From inside the house, barking erupted.

So Hercules was good for something after all.

Ben figured he might as well knock. He wasn't sneaking up on anyone, that was for sure.

Judith came to the door immediately. "Hi," she said shyly. Hercules the heroic stopped barking, peeked around her, then flopped to the floor.

She obviously wasn't upset about anything. Ben's

heartbeat might have settled back down if the sight of her in those snug jeans and turtleneck hadn't given him a new burst of adrenaline.

"You shouldn't open the door without knowing who's here. What if I'd been your ex?"

She smiled. "I could have taken great pleasure in telling him what a bastard he is."

"The kids…"

"Aren't home."

"Ah." With a surge of intense satisfaction, Ben stepped across the threshold. "So the blazing lights were like a flare?"

She blushed. "More of a welcome."

"I like feeling welcome." Deliberately, he shut the door and turned the lock. "Where are Zach and Sophie?"

"We trick-or-treated with their friends Nadia and Tim. Their mom suggested another sleepover. She followed me back here and they packed with lightning speed."

"How did Sophie make out tonight?"

"She had a lovely time. She couldn't believe all those people were just giving her candy."

"Yeah." A reluctant grin twitched his mouth. "I remember feeling pretty stunned, too. Our mother wasn't much for candy, and there I was with this huge grocery sack full, all mine."

"So you ate until you got sick."

"Right." He shot her another grin. "Brave woman to have a sleepover."

"Four kids with tummy aches instead of two."

Humor fled and he took that last step. "God, I need

you.'' Without giving her time to respond, he snatched her into his arms and captured her mouth with his.

She responded so naturally, body yielding, lips parting, that fierce pleasure filled him. The other night had been as good for her as it had for him; she'd summoned him tonight, waited up, melted into his arms. She must love him.

A part of him pulled back in alarm—what did love have to do with this?—but it failed to rein in his primal need to possess her, to claim her as his. She was his woman, and by God, he had to have her. Now.

He swept her into his arms and carried her down the hall, just as he had that first time. Blood was roaring in his ears, deafening him to anything but his need.

He tumbled her onto her bed, stripping her of clothes even as his mouth explored every inch of flesh he bared. She was gasping, clutching at him, murmuring his name. *My woman,* Ben thought with primitive masculine triumph, as though he were a caveman who'd snatched her from a rival tribe.

His own clothes disappeared with clumsy haste. Her arms were waiting to receive him when he came down on top of her, found the entrance to heaven and entered.

He'd never lost control like this, plundered instead of coaxed. But no woman had ever shaken him the way she did.

She convulsed around him, ripples of pleasure so intense he could only plunge once, twice, three times more before shuddering and calling out, ''Judith!'' in a voice so raw it couldn't possibly be his.

In the still eye of the storm, he lay on top of her

for long minutes, even though he knew his weight must be crushing her. At last he rolled to one side, taking her with him. Judith murmured something indistinct and nuzzled his neck.

The words "I love you" crowded his throat. He swallowed heavily and managed not to say them. Not yet. Not until...

Until what? Until he'd decided to become a family man?

A chill crawled up his spine. He stared blindly over Judith's head, still buried under his chin. God almighty. He hadn't used a condom.

He had one in his back pocket; he always did these days, just in case. But he'd been so damned horny he'd turned off his brain.

What if she was pregnant?

His eyes stayed open, but he no longer saw Judith's bedroom. In living color, Ben relived the scene when Kelly had told him she was pregnant.

She'd picked him up at work, insisting they go somewhere new, not to the sandwich shop around the corner where half the clientele were cops. She'd been subdued once they were seated in the small café.

Finally he had to know. "What's up?"

"I..." Her cornflower-blue eyes shimmered with tears. "I know what you've always said, but I hope you didn't really mean it. It's not as if I meant this to happen...."

He felt sick. "What to happen?"

Tears formed glittering diamonds on her lower lashes. She'd never been more beautiful. "I'm pregnant."

Her words ricocheted like a stray bullet. "Pregnant," he repeated without understanding.

"It was an accident!" Kelly cried. "You have to believe me! I know how you feel. But—"

"Pregnant."

"Yes! Is that so terrible?"

"Goddamn it, yes!" he roared, blundering up from his seat. A glass fell over, scattering ice cubes and sloshing cold water over the white tablecloth.

Her face was just as pale. "I love you," she whispered.

Ben had walked out.

Later, of course, they had talked. She insisted that it was an accident, but he remembered the packet of pills he'd seen recently in her bathroom drawer. It was the kind where you popped one out each day. Ben had noticed that it hadn't been touched and he'd wondered why. Vague disquiet hardened into angry suspicion. He'd made it clear he didn't want children. Ever. She'd pretended to understand, claimed she could live with that. Now, conveniently, she was pregnant and wanted him to marry her and settle down to cozy domesticity.

He declined with an offer of child support.

Her shock had metamorphosed into anger, maybe even hatred. It glittered in her eyes when she spit, "You don't want to be a father? Fine! You're not one. But I won't take your money. And changing your mind down the road isn't an option." Her voice was hard. "This baby will never be yours."

Kelly walked out. Ben had never heard from her again.

The movie played out, but no credits ran. What if Kelly *had* gotten pregnant by accident? Ben had wanted to believe it was deliberate, that she was trying to trap him. Maybe he'd wanted to believe it so bad he hadn't given her a chance.

She could be coy. She played little mind games. But she was basically honest. She probably figured that, like plenty of other men who weren't ready to have a family, he'd love his son or daughter once the baby was born.

She hadn't understood that his reasons were different from other men's, that he meant what he said.

And selfish bastard that he was, Ben hadn't thought about the kid at all. So what if Kelly had lied and schemed? It wasn't the baby's fault. A decent man would have seen that. He'd played the tune; he should have paid the piper.

Judith stirred in his arms. He ran a hand over the silken waves of copper that flowed over her shoulder and across his chest, mingling with the dark hairs that grew there. God, what if six weeks from now she told him she was pregnant?

Judith's sleepy, contented little wriggles abruptly ceased. He felt her stillness and lifted his head. She tilted hers back on his arm and gazed at him with fathomless gray-green eyes.

"We didn't use a condom tonight, did we?"

We. Both of them taking responsibility, not just him.

"No. I didn't."

"Oh." Her expression became thoughtful, and she nibbled on her lower lip. He doubted she realized how provocative that simple action was, small white teeth denting her lip, already swollen from his kisses. "You know," she said, "the first time we made love, I didn't see you put a condom on."

"You thought I didn't use one?"

Judith gave a small nod. "The thing is..." She hesitated, then finished in a rush, "I was glad. I'd like to have your baby."

The rush of intense pleasure that knifed through him shocked him as much as her words. It also scared the hell out of him.

Maybe that was his excuse. He shot up to a sitting position. "You know I don't want children."

The color leached out of her face.

"I didn't believe you." Judith sat up and reached for the sheet, tugging it up to cover her breasts. He'd made her feel naked.

He wasn't proud. "Why not?" he asked tightly. "How much clearer can I be?"

Spots of hot color appeared on her cheeks. In contrast, her voice was an icy shard. "You could stop spending half your time with my children. You could refrain from holding Sophie's hand or teaching Zach how to grow up and be just like you. You could convince them *not* to love you! That's how you can be clearer."

He'd done all those things. He knew he had. He'd wanted them to love him, just as he wanted her to. It didn't make any sense. He knew it didn't. Why did he want what he *didn't* want?

Ben shook his head, like a cornered bull, and stumbled to his feet. "I told you," he repeated, stubborn insistence overruling logic. "I didn't want you disappointed. Why the hell do women never listen? Why do they always think they can remake a man?''

Judith rose to her knees, clutching the sheet to her breasts with white-knuckled fists. ''What do you mean, women *never* listen? Am I just one of many?'' Temper sparked in her eyes. ''Do we all misunderstand you?''

It took him thirty seconds to find his goddamn pants. Like his underwear, they were inside out. He had to stand there buck naked, turning them right side out, while the woman he loved stared at him with eyes that burned with newfound hate.

She was just like Kelly, he told himself. She'd thought she could turn him into whatever she wanted him to be. Soften him up a little bit and he'd become Father of the Year.

''Do you all misunderstand me?'' he snarled. ''No. Just two of you.''

She actually flinched. If he hadn't been so full of rage and self-contempt and fear, he couldn't have finished saying what he had to.

But if he didn't drive her away, he was going to do what he'd sworn not to, and then he was going to let her and the kids down, just as he'd let down his brothers and sister.

''Yeah,'' he said cruelly, voice raw with self-disgust. ''Somewhere out there I already have a kid. But, damn it, I told Kelly not to get pregnant! I didn't want a kid, so she's not mine in any way that counts.''

Judith stared at him for the longest moment. His soul shriveled. Then she inched backward on the bed, as though his presence might contaminate her.

"Leave," she said clearly. "Please…" She clapped her hand over her mouth and her words came out muffled. "Please go now."

She leaped to her feet and ran from the room. The bathroom door slammed. The lock clicked.

Anguish ripped through Ben. He sank to his knees beside her bed, his mouth open in a silent howl.

CHAPTER TWELVE

JUDITH THOUGHT SHE might die. Back against the door, she slid to the bathroom floor, gripping the sheet as if it were her shroud. She had hurt worse only once in her life, when she knew she might never see her daughter again.

One of the worst parts of that day had been the knowledge that Rylan had done it to make her suffer. The realization that he could be that cruel.

She would have sworn Ben was everything Rylan wasn't. In her dreams, she'd endowed him with strength, unflinching integrity, kindness, compassion. She had believed with all her being that he would never hurt her or her children deliberately.

Tonight, he'd done just that. The idea of having a baby with her was apparently so horrifying he'd lashed out as viciously as Rylan at his worst. Was it so terrible that she'd let him see how she felt? Why had he found himself compelled to disillusion her so brutally?

And, dear Lord, why then? What a moment to tell her his darkest secret! Or maybe he'd created it out of whole cloth, she didn't know. Either way, the story made him a contemptible creature, a monster on a par with her ex-husband.

She was a fool to have let herself fall in love again.

With burning eyes, Judith stared at the bathroom cabinet without seeing it. She must have the world's worst taste in men. Was she one of those women who walked through life with a sign around their necks saying Kick Me?

What should she do? Where should she go? She had run away from Rylan, and she wanted even more desperately to run away from Ben, never to see him again.

"I hate you," she whispered, and buried her face in her arms when she felt the tears start. "I hate you." She would not scream it, however much she ached to; she wouldn't give him the satisfaction of knowing how badly he'd hurt her.

Judith cried for a long time, wrenching sobs that left her drained but not numb. She wished for numbness, but no matter how she tried to empty her mind, the tearing pain remained. Her legs began to cramp from the position, but she didn't move.

She dragged herself up and went to the sink, where she turned on the cold water. For a long time she stared down at the water splashing into the sink, unable to remember why it ran. At last she lifted her head and stared into the mirror.

The puffy, splotched face that stared back at her was unrecognizable. It couldn't be her. But whoever it was, she needed to blow her nose. Judith closed her eyes and took slow, deep breaths through her mouth.

As though she were a small child who had to figure out how to do the simplest thing, she took a tissue and blew her nose, splashed cold water on her face and then dried it. She even brushed her hair, with slow, mechanical motions.

What she saw in the mirror now was scarcely an improvement, but she didn't care. It didn't matter what she looked like. Zach and Sophie wouldn't see her. Thank God they weren't home.

Judith made herself think.

She and the children couldn't leave Mad River. She had to work, and she'd been lucky enough to get a job with such short notice in the fall. What were the chances of finding one mid-term?

Besides, she couldn't let Carol Galindez down. The principal had hired her, helped protect Zach and Sophie, become a friend.

But she couldn't live here. She'd find a rental in town. Yes, Judith thought, pouncing on the idea. Tomorrow. There'd been other places available. If they moved, she would scarcely have to see Ben.

Judith had no idea how much time had passed. Surely, surely, he would be gone. But still she opened the bathroom door cautiously, listening for any small sounds. Lying in the hall right outside the door, Hercules lifted his head. The tip of the dog's tail waved and his brown eyes were soft and sympathetic.

"Is he gone?" Judith whispered.

The dog rose to his feet.

"He is, isn't he?"

Hercules wagged his tail.

Even so, Judith crept down the hall, the sheet clutched around her, part of it trailing like the train on a wedding dress.

She would not think about wedding dresses. Ever.

The house was still and silent. She didn't want to

go back into her bedroom, but she couldn't wander around naked all night.

In the doorway she had to stop for a moment, frozen by the sight of tumbled sheets and strewn clothing and the scent of sex. Memories clawed at her. The way he'd torn her clothes off and fumbled with his own, the look in his eyes, the exquisite sensation of him filling her... And, oh, God, the pitiless tone of his voice when he said, "You know I don't want children."

Clapping her hands to her ears, Judith cried out in anguish. She would never understand him. Never trust herself to love a man again.

Judith scuttled into the bedroom and snatched a pair of panties and a nightgown from her drawer, fleeing then as if these walls harbored demons. She took a shower, scrubbing herself until the water grew cold. Armored by the flannel gown, she made the familiar rounds of the house, turning off lights and making sure windows were locked. The back door was just as she'd left it. She approached the front door reluctantly.

The knob didn't turn.

It was locked. He had locked it on his way out. Not the dead bolt—he couldn't—but the button on the knob. He had made sure that she wouldn't be left vulnerable. What did that mean?

She crept into the children's room, choosing Sophie's bed. The scent of bubble bath pervaded the sheets. Closing her eyes, burrowing her cheek into the pillow, Judith imagined that she held her daughter in her arms, soft, squirming, sweet scented. Miracles happened. She had Sophie back. She had survived one of the most terrible things that could happen to a parent. She would survive this.

If only she understood why he had done this to her.

HE GAVE IT his damnedest, but Ben couldn't quite convince himself that he'd done the right thing. His motive for telling Judith the ugly truth hadn't been to save her from himself. He'd done it out of panic. The fates closing in.

He muttered a profanity and bolted out of bed. The clock told him it was 4:00 a.m. The cold wood floor chilled the soles of his feet. Naked but for shorts, he didn't reach for jeans or a sweatshirt, even though he shivered. He deserved any discomfort he could serve up.

God. He remembered the moment when he'd felt the intense, purely masculine satisfaction at planting his seed in a woman's womb. Not *any* woman—his. She'd actually made him want children.

It wasn't anything she'd said that had scared the hell out of him. No, he'd done that all by himself.

He wanted her. He wanted to father her children. He wanted to *be* a father to Zach and Sophie.

There was nothing in the world he wanted less than to be a father.

Ben swore again and flattened his palms on the bedroom windowpane, resting his forehead against its smooth chill. Judith's rental house was a darker bulk against the night sky. He would never be welcome there again.

A harsh sound escaped his throat. He was the biggest fool in Mad River, and that was saying a lot. A good woman loved him, he loved her, he was even getting kind of attached to her kids—and he'd gone out of his way to make sure she discovered what a bastard he really was.

A man who deserted a woman pregnant with his child.

He could explain... *You mean excuse,* he mocked himself harshly. *Justify.* And what was his excuse? He was tired of bandaging skinned knees and turning on night-lights. He'd been there, done that, didn't want to do it again.

Fine excuse.

Eventually Ben went back to bed. He even slept, if the nightmarish images could count as dreams rather than memories and fears. The hatred staring out of Kelly's blue eyes suddenly switched to Judith's gray-green ones. A child taking his hand was first Sophie, then Eddie, then nobody he knew. And that small boy with the dark eyes—was that him an aeon ago?

Come morning, he fed the horses, ate a bowl of cereal, then sat around feeling hung over, waiting for a decent hour to make a phone call. One he should have made a long time ago.

When he finally dialed the number for directory assistance, it occurred to Ben that he must have written down that same number a dozen times over the years. Whatever scrap of paper he wrote it on always ended up in the wastebasket.

This time he dialed it.

The third ring was cut off. "Hello?" said a childish voice.

A noose closed around Ben's throat. He couldn't

breathe, couldn't swallow. The hand that held the phone receiver shook. He could not do this.

"Hello?" Now the child sounded uncertain. "Is somebody there?"

Ben hung up. Air rasped into his throat. He was goddamn crazy to think he could make any difference after all these years. Kelly would slam the phone down. He deserved to be haunted by unanswered questions. A man who sold his soul didn't go to hell; he spent an eternity in perdition.

Outside, a dog barked. Ben swung around. Unwillingly, he went to the kitchen window. The damn windows in this house were starting to feel like the bars of a prison cell. He could look longingly out, but never leave. He'd closed the cell door himself.

That pathetic excuse for a dog Judith had chosen was running in frenetic circles on her front lawn, barking the whole while. Wrapped in a white robe, Judith stood at the head of the porch, watching the dog. She held something, a cup of coffee, maybe. After a moment she leaned her head against the post, as if holding it up were too much effort.

Ben turned around, went straight back to the telephone and picked up the receiver. He didn't have to look at the number to dial it.

This time a woman answered. "Hello?" she said crisply, a hint of suspicion coloring the single word.

"Kelly." He squeezed the bridge of his nose. "This is Ben McKinsey."

He heard her shocked intake of breath, then silence. But she hadn't hung up.

"I'd like to talk to you."

"We have nothing to say."

"Maybe you don't, but I do."

"Oh?" she said sarcastically. "Do you have demands now? Or...let me think. You've had another child who needs a bone marrow transplant, so you're scraping the bottom of the barrel in search of a donor. Or maybe you just want me to absolve you, sprinkle your head with holy water."

He'd take number three. *Give me forgiveness.*

"I just...wondered...about her. Or him."

"What did you wonder?" There was no sympathy in her voice.

Exasperation swept him over the edge. "Goddamn, which is it? A boy or a girl?"

"Why do you want to know?" she asked uncompromisingly.

Why? He hardly knew himself. So his kid had a chance to deal with the son of a bitch who walked out on his mom? To make amends?

"I should have stood by you," he said.

"Yeah? Well, you didn't. It was too long ago, Ben. My daughter has a father." The finality in her voice warned him even before he heard the click as she hung up. She'd meant what she said all those years ago. The child would never be his.

But she'd told him something, at least. He had a daughter.

Ben knew he had to see her.

TOO BAD SHE COULDN'T use a glue gun to keep her smile in place, Judith thought grimly. She stood at the back of the classroom, doing her best to look attentive and pleasant as Police Chief Ben McKinsey talked about alcohol and drugs with her students.

Last week she'd felt an inner glow when he was in her classroom. She'd tried not to think about making love with him; it wouldn't do to have one of her students catch her blushing. She'd occupied herself by observing how far he'd come as a teacher and mentor for the kids. His body language was easy now, his dark stare compelling, his rare smile reward enough to have the children's hands waving eagerly when he asked a question or wanted a volunteer. He knew how to pace the flow of information, when to switch to role playing or ask them to come up with ideas. The other fifth-grade teachers had commented on how good he was. Previous years, they said, the kids were often bored and had less chance for input.

"Less chance to show off," Judith had said, laughing, and they agreed.

"But it's good for their self-esteem to have that chance," Linda Mayfield remarked, "and isn't that part of the purpose of the program?"

Today, all Judith wanted was for Chief McKinsey to get out of her classroom. It was bad enough that she had to pass his house twice a day, hear his car, know how close he was. She didn't understand why she'd put off looking for a rental in town. Maybe she feared the effect another move would have on the children, though it couldn't be anything but beneficial for Zach, she thought wryly.

How had her reliable, kindhearted, talkative son turned into a sullen, angry child? He'd been worse this week, defiant, mean to his sister, sulky. She knew why, of course; the reason stood at the front of her classroom. Zach had idolized Ben; no matter how often she explained that Ben's absence had nothing to do with him, it left Zach feeling rejected again.

She sensed Ben's gaze on her, knew the expression she would see if she let herself look at him. His mouth would be wry, his eyes troubled, his brow furrowed. A muscle in his cheek would jerk when their eyes met. She would swear he was silently asking her a question. Asking her *for* something.

Understanding? A chance to explain?

No! *How much clearer can I be?* he had asked. She was a fool to imagine he hadn't already said everything he wanted to say.

Don't think about him, she told herself. He was looking away now, sparring with Tony. The discussion was about what to do if you'd always wanted to belong to a popular group of kids and they finally asked you to a party, with the kicker that you had to bring a bottle of booze.

Judith returned to her brooding. Here she'd thought Sophie to be the problem child! Instead, it was worries about Zach that kept her awake nights. He hadn't been the same since the move. On one level, she blamed Ben. Hadn't he realized what he was doing, encouraging Zach to emulate him? But Zach's problems weren't all because of Ben. Her fight with Zach over the phone call the previous week had been the catalyst. Since then he had been…secretive. It was hard to relate that word to her son, but she couldn't deny that he seemed to be hiding something. Twice more she'd heard him talking on the phone, and both times he'd claimed the callers had the wrong number.

She wanted to believe he was telling the truth. But at least three times that week she'd answered the ringing phone, only to hear a click the moment she said hello. Five wrong numbers in a week?

Dread filled her. Was it Rylan calling?

No. Please let there be another explanation, she prayed. Maybe somebody at school was bullying Zach and he didn't want to tell her. But Judith had spoken with his teacher and she didn't know of anything like that. He was doing fine with his schoolwork and making friends, Becky Allen had assured her.

Apparently, Judith thought, his anger was all saved for her.

Maybe she *had* favored Sophie, the way he'd accused her. Probably it was true. Sophie was vulnerable. She had lost her father and was living with a family she barely remembered. The nightmares, the tears, the silence—all had demanded that Judith give her that extra time and attention. Having her daughter back with her gave special meaning to everything she did with Sophie. Somehow that must have made Zach feel she didn't want him as much as she did his little sister.

What could she do to show him how much she loved him? Was it too late?

"Ms. Kane?" Ben's deep voice cut through her troubling thoughts.

She snapped back to the present, no pasted smile on her face this time.

"Yes, Chief McKinsey?"

"They're all yours."

Twenty-six ten-year-olds stared at her. She could see the wheels turning. Why was Mrs. Kane acting so weird?

"Fine," she said with cool efficiency. "We'll see you next week, Chief McKinsey. Class, start cleaning up your desks."

Ben didn't leave. Instead he followed Tony, who went to the coat closet to retrieve his pack. Out of the corner of her eye, Judith saw Ben lay a hand on the boy's shoulder and bend his head to talk quietly to him.

What was he saying? Tony grinned and obviously agreed to something; Ben clapped him on the back, then with a furrow between his brows, he looked straight at Judith. A tight nod, and he was gone at last.

The bell rang and her students started streaming out. Judith waged a brief battle with herself and lost. She had a right to be curious, didn't she?

"Tony," she called. "Can you come here for a sec?"

He came, his brown cowlick as unruly as ever, his thin face wary.

"I really like the way you participate in the DARE program," she said, then smiled. "Now, if you'd just put as much enthusiasm into your spelling homework."

He screwed up his mouth, as though he'd bitten into raw onion. "Who cares about spelling?"

They'd had this discussion before. Rather than recap the many benefits of learning to fluently read, speak and write English, she settled for a simple "I do."

"You have to," he said impudently. "You're the teacher."

Judith laughed and rolled her eyes. "Get going or you'll miss your bus."

He slung his backpack over one shoulder. "See ya, Teach."

Judith let him get almost to the classroom door. "Tony?"

He turned his head.

"What did Chief McKinsey want?"

It was like turning on a light switch. Tony's brown eyes shone and his voice held wonder. "He said you told him that I'm gonna be a cop when I grow up, and he asked if I wanted a ride in his car. Like I'd say no!" He marveled at the very idea. "If I bring a note from Mom tomorrow, he's gonna drive me home."

"Lucky him," she teased.

"It's so cool!" Tony gave her a shy, almost sweet smile, devoid of his usual sarcasm. "Thanks, Mrs. Kane."

She smiled back. "You're welcome."

She needed to collect the kids, but once Tony was gone, she sat behind her desk, frowning at the empty doorway. What was Ben up to? If he so detested kids, why encourage first Zach and now Tony? A week ago, she'd have thought he was trying to please her. Obviously that wasn't the case.

And yet she'd have sworn he had made a point of talking to Tony where she was sure to see.

She gave her head a shake and reached for her purse. He was a hopelessly complex man, but she wouldn't be the one to untangle his motives. After all, she was fatally burdened with children.

He was a jerk, she told herself; she'd had a lucky escape.

Somehow, Judith didn't believe a word.

BEN STEPPED OUT OF the squad car and circled around to the passenger side. He'd pulled up to the curb right in front of the main entrance to Lincoln Elementary. His timing was flawless; the doors all popped open at once, as if a bomb had exploded inside, and the teeming masses spilled out.

Adopting a relaxed pose, Ben leaned against the car, arms crossed, and waited.

Maybe the kid's mother wouldn't have given her permission. With her husband in prison, she probably was no fan of cops. Ben wondered if Tony had told her what he wanted to be when he grew up.

Along with smiles and greetings from passing parents, he got plenty of stares from the shorter set. A few of them lingered.

"Hey, Mr. Policeman," a young boy was finally bold enough to ask, "are you going to arrest someone?"

Just then, Ben spotted Tony sauntering toward him. "Nope," Ben said. "Just giving a friend a ride home."

Tony struggled not to look too pleased. "Hi," he said.

"Tony." Ben nodded solemnly. "Got the note?"

The boy handed it over. By this time, twenty or thirty students had gathered to watch.

"Dear Chief McKinsey," it began in a round, child-ish script. "Tony says you want him to ride with you. That's okay with me. Just so he's not in trouble and that's why you want him." Signed, "Shelly Fioren-tino."

"Looks good," Ben said, and held open the pas-senger door. "Shall we go?"

The crowd murmured as Tony, head held high, climbed in and Ben slammed the door. He tipped his hat at them and went around to his side. In the car, Tony sat with his back straight, hands on his legs, as if he were afraid to move. He was taking in every-thing, though, his gaze darting over the array of knobs and buttons.

Ben noticed belatedly that the boy was dressed a little better today than usual. Those were his best jeans, Ben guessed, less baggy than current style called for, and he actually wore a button-down shirt instead of an oversize T-shirt. A warm feeling envel-oped Ben.

Annoyed with himself, he turned the key in the ig-nition. What kind of sap was he turning into, touched because a kid had made an effort to look decent for the occasion? Good God, his mother had probably made him!

"Seat belt?" Ben said.

"Oh, yeah." Tony scrambled to put it on.

Ben checked his mirrors and they pulled away from the curb. "Where to?" he asked.

"What?" The boy blushed. "Oh. You mean, where do I live. Um, over the other side of the highway. You know where those stockyards are? Past that."

Ben knew the area well. Thirty-year-old single-wide mobile homes sagged on cement-block foundations, the acre parcels they occupied defined by rusty, barbed-wire fences. Junk cars clustered around the houses like nursing babies. Any horses in the rocky pastures tended to be skinny, rib cages and backbones showing. Eighty percent of the domestic disturbance calls received by his department came from that small section of town farthest from the river.

The trip wouldn't take five minutes. Looking at the kid's big eyes, Ben gave an internal sigh. "You want to go straight home or ride along with me for a while?"

"Can I?" Tony breathed.

"Wouldn't have asked if I didn't mean it."

"Yeah! I mean, sure." His eyes widened. "Do you think you'll chase somebody?"

Ben glanced at him. "Well...you never know." Hell, if he saw someone going two miles over the speed limit, he'd pull 'em over, just to make the boy happy.

In no time at all, Tony warmed up enough to start asking questions. Ben showed him how the radio worked with the frequency selectors and the emergency channel and the microphones.

"How do you make the lights go on?" Tony's stubby fingers reverently caressed buttons without actually pushing any. "And the siren?"

Ben showed him how they worked, along with the radar unit and the CB radio. Tony happily rattled the cage and was disappointed to find out that a stain on the back seat wasn't blood.

"Let's just hunker down," Ben said, "and see if we can't catch a speeder."

He had a few favorite spots where success was damn near guaranteed. One was right behind some concrete bulwarks where the highway came into town. They'd no sooner aimed the radar than a red Mustang with a dent in the fender shot by going fifty-five in a thirty-five-mile-per-hour zone.

Ben pulled right out. "You turn on the lights," he said.

Tony was aglow. "Can we sound the siren, too?"

They'd probably scare the hell out of the driver, but what the heck. "Why not."

The car pulled over right away, much to Tony's disappointment. He'd apparently hoped for a high-speed chase. He was even more disappointed when Ben made him stay in the car. The pimply-faced driver, maybe twenty years old, sank into a funk when he saw what the ticket cost.

In contrast, Tony begged, "Can we do it again? That was cool!"

Despite his better judgment, Ben kept the boy with him for about an hour. He marvelled that he'd ever thought Zach Kane was a talker. Zach was a downright peaceful companion compared with Tony. Ben's ears were ringing and his throat was hoarse from answering questions by the time he parked the squad car in front of the rusting single-wide Tony said was his grandma's place.

Tony was still going at it. "Cops have to be really brave, right? So you can beat up bad guys and kick in doors and whip your gun out...." He gave a longing look at Ben's.

Ben turned off the engine and faced the boy. "Yeah, sometimes you have to be brave, but the most important thing a cop does is notice every little thing." His voice was dead serious. "For example, your mother is waiting right inside the door, I bet. I saw her take a peek out the window and then shy back. Now, if I were here to issue a warrant and I thought she might have a gun, that would be good to know. I can tell you what make and color the two cars we passed on your road were. I saw the mailbox that had been bashed in, and the greenhouse on your neighbor's place that looks too expensive to go with the house. I won't forget your grandma's taste in curtain fabric. That's what I mean by noticing."

He was a little surprised that Tony didn't seem disappointed that a cop's most important skill was observation, not martial arts. He only nodded, his brow puckering. "Does it take practice?"

"Yeah. You can start anytime."

"I will then," the boy said eagerly. He hesitated. "I guess I've got to go now."

Ben walked him to the door and said hello to Tony's mother, who looked about twenty-two, although she had to be older. She wore frayed jeans and a men's flannel shirt that hung on her skinny frame. Smoke curled from the cigarette in her hand.

But he was surprised again when she thanked him graciously and, after sending Tony inside, admitted that the boy's father was in prison and that she was happy to have her son dreaming about being a cop and not a felon.

"Tony's a nice boy," Ben said, realizing it was no lie. "He'll do fine. Uh, when's his father's release date?"

"Not for a couple of years." Desperation flitted over her face. "It's hard making it without him. I just lost my job. I was working at Dick's Burgers, but they're shutting down now, you know. They always do for the winter, but with that new burger place out on the highway, they're giving up. I don't know what I'll find next. We're lucky to be able to live with my parents."

He could tell she didn't feel lucky.

"You know how to work a cash register?" he asked.

Her head bobbed. "With my eyes closed."

"Seems to me I noticed a sign in the window saying that Food Mart on Tenth needs a checker. I know the manager. I'll put in a word for you."

"Would you?"

No one should have to look so incredulous at such a small favor, Ben thought with a twist of pity. But as he drove away, her renewed thanks chasing him like tumbleweed, he half regretted his promise. Hell, he didn't know if she was a good worker or a slacker!

Yeah, but maybe all she needed was a chance, his Good Samaritan side argued.

He swore out loud. He was starting to sound like a social worker, not a cop. And he knew who he could blame for the idiocy. Judith Kane. She just had a way of nudging him into...what?

Ben had to pull to the side of the road as the answer hit him harder than the windshield in a head-on collision.

She had a way of nudging him into caring, he thought with sudden comprehension. First for her. Then her kids. Then for his own brothers and sister. Now for Tony and his mother. Who knew where it would end?

Not to worry, he told himself bleakly. Without Judith around, he'd find her influence fading.

He'd better start getting used to it.

THE TELEPHONE HAD a way of bringing bad news. Ben sat in his office, receiver to his ear. "Rylan Kane has disappeared," he repeated, a cold knot in his belly. "You're sure?"

"No, I'm not sure," Detective Edgekoski said. "Maybe he rented a new room and just didn't bother to tell us. He isn't due in court until next week. All I'm saying is, I stopped by to check on him and he's gone."

"Car?"

"For sale at a used-car lot. He'd taken cash for it. Didn't buy a replacement."

Ben swore.

"If he flew out of here, it wasn't under his own name. I don't know what else to tell you right now."

"The bastard is on his way here."

"We can't say that for certain." Edgekoski sounded as if he were convincing himself. "Will you warn Ms. Kane, or should I?"

Ben snatched at the excuse. "I will."

His impulse was to surge to his feet and find the kids. Stand guard. But they ought to be safe enough at school for the day. He would be more usefully employed looking for Kane.

Ben left a message at the school office for Judith to call him about Rylan as soon as possible. He figured that would get her. As soon as he talked to her, he'd make the rounds of motels and bed-and-breakfasts to learn what he could about any lone male customers— and to ask the proprietors to let him know if anyone meeting Kane's description showed up.

His line rang. He picked it up. "McKinsey."

"It's Judith. Do you have news?" *You'd better*, her tone suggested.

"Yes." He kept his tone businesslike, although his gut churned. "Edgekoski just called. They've misplaced your ex-husband."

There was a pause. "Misplaced?" she echoed in disbelief.

"In other words, no confirmation that he's bolted, but he left his last place of residence without informing them, and he sold his car."

"Oh, God."

"We'd better assume he's on his way out here, if not already in town. We'll watch for him, but you need to be extra careful."

"Yes." She sounded dazed. "Yes, I will."

"Would the kids go with him willingly?"

"I...I have no idea." Judith let out a long, despairing sigh. "I hope not. I've talked to them about it, but he is their father. I just don't know."

"Okay. I'll come over this evening—"

"Please don't," she interrupted.

Hell. "About the other night..."

Her breath hitched. "Don't do that, either."

"That?"

"Don't say you're sorry or tell me we can talk about it or explain again that you warned me. Yes, you did. You were right. I didn't really listen." She noticed that her voice was rising and took a moment to collect herself. "Enough said. But I don't want you here, Ben. If we need the police, I'd prefer you send another officer."

Feeling as if a thousand-foot drop yawned beneath him and his fingers were slipping from the only possible handhold, he said stubbornly, "I'm the law in this town."

"You have an eight-member police force. I asked. Ben, I don't want to see you." Judith took a shaky breath, but her voice remained tremulous. "Please give me that much."

There had to be something he could say. He could only think of one possibility. "I'm going to try to see my daughter...become part of her life."

"I hope you do. That won't change the fact that we want different things out of life. Thank you for the warning, Ben. Now please stay away." A resounding *click* sounded in his ear.

Ben swore viciously. He was an even bigger bastard than he'd given himself credit for: he had made damn sure she couldn't trust him now that she really needed him.

CHAPTER THIRTEEN

CORDLESS PHONE TO her ear, Judith peered around her to be sure the kids were out of earshot. She hadn't hidden the fact that she was calling Grandma and Grandpa; she just didn't want them hearing the question she had to ask.

"Have you heard from Rylan lately?" She tried to phrase it casually. Why upset his parents unless something happened?

Something. The unthinkable. The unnameable.

She must not entirely have succeeded. Her mother-in-law's anxiety was audible.

"No, not for a week. I've been afraid—" She broke off, then added in a strained voice, "He loves the children so."

Was what he'd done to them "love"? Not in Judith's book. But Mary Kane had to excuse him. How else could she live with what her own son had become?

"Does he?" Judith strove for a noncommittal response. "Well, I doubt there's anything to worry about. I just like to know where he is."

"He complained about the room he was renting," her mother-in-law said. "He was paying an awful lot for it, and half the time there wasn't any hot water, and the tenant upstairs was terribly noisy, and the bed wasn't very comfortable...." Her voice held less and less conviction, but, like Judith, she tried to sound as if she were convinced by what she was saying. "I'm sure he just found a better place and hasn't let us know yet."

"Oh, I imagine you're right," Judith agreed. They chatted briefly, but a minute after hanging up the phone, she couldn't have told anyone what either of them had spoken about. She was back to asking the same unproductive questions that had been hounding her for the past twenty-four hours.

Should she tell the children or not? She didn't want them living in fear—or looking for their father. Should she ask Carol Galindez for a couple of weeks off? The district could hire a substitute, and she and the children could flee again. Just temporarily. If Rylan didn't show up for court, there would be a warrant out for his arrest, and they'd get him sooner or later.

It was the possibility of "later" that frightened her.

It took them two years last time, an inner voice argued. *You'll lose your job. You have to keep it, unless you want to keep running.*

"No," she said softly, restoring the phone to its cradle. Rylan had done his best to ruin their lives. She wouldn't let him succeed.

She would go on doing just what she had been doing, only more obsessively: never let her kids out of her sight, except at bedtime and during school. Her glance strayed to Hercules, whose tail started to thump on the floor the moment he noticed her attention. He was definitely not an attack dog, but he did bark when he heard strange noises. He wouldn't let a man break into their house in the middle of the night unnoticed.

If only she could turn to Ben...

Judith opened the dishwasher with unnecessary force. She wouldn't let herself think that way. She was doing fine on her own. Just fine.

Later, she moved the dog's bed to the hall between the kids' bedroom and hers. When Zach asked why, Judith bent over to smooth Hercules's silken yellow ears between her fingers.

"He sleeps here anyway. Haven't you noticed? The wood floor must be awfully hard." It was true, but she couldn't swear that he stayed in the hall all night. Yesterday she'd gotten up from the couch and discovered she had dog hair all over her backside. Maybe that was where he spent the night. He did like his bed, though, so she hoped if it was near them, he'd use it. She wanted him as close as possible while she slept.

If Ben had been with them that day at the animal shelter, he would have wanted them to adopt the big German shepherd with a deep-throated woof that had scared Sophie, or maybe even the Doberman mix. But Judith didn't regret their choice. Hercules had crowded to the front of the cage, huge brown eyes beseeching, his whole bottom wagging along with his tail, and her heart had melted. When they opened the cage door, he'd erupted out and slobbered kisses on both kids' faces, squirming in pleasure at their tentative pats. He needed *them,* and he was a big dog. Big enough to be some protection.

Now Zach said, "Oh. Sure. *I* wouldn't want to sleep on the floor, either." He lay down experimentally on the rectangular dog cushion, which was stuffed with cedar. Making a face, he observed, "It's kinda lumpy."

Delighted at having someone down at his level, Hercules licked him. The pink, wet tongue worked Zach over from his neck to his ear. Zach laughed, the first time Judith had heard him do so in too long.

"He loves you."

He buried his face in the dog's ruff. "He loves you better."

"Oh, I don't know," she said lightly. "He's just smart enough to recognize the hand that wields the can opener."

"I feed him sometimes."

"But not as often."

He hugged Hercules with a fierceness he didn't seem to realize, still not looking at her. "Would he be just my dog if I was the only one who fed him?"

Judith's heart stilled. She crouched so that she could stroke first Hercules's head, then Zach's. "Why does he have to be just yours? Why not ours?"

"'Cuz then *she* gets him." He rolled violently away from the dog and jumped to his feet. "I can't even have my own bedroom!"

"I didn't know you wanted..." Judith began helplessly, but he had gone into his room—his *shared* room—and slammed the door. Apparently even his sister's company was better than hers.

What would he do, she wondered with dread, if his father asked him to go away with him, promising a special father-son bond that Zach seemed to need? He was only nine—impulsive, angry about the changes in his life, resentful of Sophie and the loss of part of his mother's attention. Rylan could be so charming, so...compelling.

She closed her eyes to shut out the chasm of fear that had opened before her. Zach wouldn't do that to her.

But children never thought about what they did to their parents; that was the nature of childhood. Zach was too young for empathy. He was so utterly wrapped up in his own problems right now he would be ripe for an approach from Ry.

Maternal fury rescued her from the feeling of hopelessness that threatened to overwhelm her.

Rylan wouldn't have that chance. He wouldn't get near either of their children, Judith vowed. She would die rather than let him take one of them again.

THE ONE PLACE SHE HAD always felt they were safe was at school. In her heightened state of fear, Judith no longer was so certain.

Her students hunched over a spelling test. She watched them write, waiting until enough faces looked up to move on to the next word.

"Messages," she said, speaking slowly and emphatically. Foreheads puckered and her students scribbled.

For the hundredth time today, her eyes strayed to the clock on the classroom wall. She knew to the minute when kindergarten and fourth-grade lunches and recesses were. Two grades went out at a time: eight classes in all. Close to two hundred kids. The aides couldn't possibly watch any one child all the time.

There were squabbles on the tetherball court to claim their attention, skinned knees, lost jewelry, swearing and insults. The handful of aides were fully occupied. Judith had seen parents strolling across the playground on their way to the office or a classroom. Nobody paid them any attention.

Zach and Sophie were most vulnerable then, among the crowds of other kids. And she couldn't do anything about it. If only the windows in her classroom looked out on the playground, she could at least reassure herself sometimes. But instead they looked out at the street.

Every day, she tensed when their recesses ended, waiting for a call from the office or a knock on the classroom door. "Zach didn't come in from recess," the secretary would say. "He's probably in the bathroom, but we thought you should know."

Judith shuddered, earning some curious stares. She shook off her dread. "Ready?" she asked.

"Wait!" cried several voices.

The minute hand on the clock clicked forward one notch. "Immerse," she said, strolling between desks.

Was Rylan really here in Mad River? Maybe watching their house with binoculars from the wooded hillside? Or even, this minute, sitting in a car across the street from the school, noting when bells rang, waiting for the moment when Zach or Sophie strayed close to an opening in the chain-link fence.... Ice seemed to fill her veins.

Her students were waiting. She had to pretend. "Imagine," she said, enunciating each syllable.

Tony waved his hand. "I gotta go to the bathroom."

"You can't wait?" she asked in exasperation.

"My stomach doesn't feel so good." He clutched it in graphic illustration.

"Do you need to go to the nurse?"

"Nah." He grinned cheekily at his friends. "I just gotta go. When you gotta go, you gotta—"

"Yes, yes," she said, interrupting both him and the general laughter. "Take a pass. Try to hurry."

They resumed the spelling test; she watched the clock. Zach's class was out right now. A quarter after two o'clock came. Tony strolled back in the door and went right to his desk. Another minute passed. Two minutes. The tension ebbed from her shoulder muscles. Afternoon recess was over. They'd be safe until tomorrow.

At the end of the day, she was collecting Zach and Sophie from their classrooms when she saw Ben down the hall. He was coming out of one of the other fifth-grade classrooms. When he turned in her direction, her breath stopped. Judith backed into the girls' bathroom, murmuring apologies as she bumped a girl on her way out.

Just as Ben went by in the hall, someone pushed open the door. Judith caught one good glimpse of his face. He looked weary, preoccupied, the lines carved from nose to mouth deeper than usual. A frown had settled as if it meant to stay between his dark brows. The harsh expression fit the man she had first met, not the one she'd come to know.

Which was he? she wondered on a wave of intense depression. Could his smiles, his kisses have been mirages?

He was gone by the time she stepped out in the hall again. Zach just shrugged when Judith asked how his day had gone; even Sophie was quieter than usual. It was similar to the day that thunderstorm struck, Judith thought; tension hung in the air like the electricity that presaged lightning.

On the drive home, her eyes strayed frequently to the rearview mirror, looking for a car that stayed behind her too long, but she didn't spot one. Rylan probably already knew where they lived.

Hercules was thrilled they were home. Zach ran around the yard with him, seeming his normal self. The boy chased the dog, then the dog the boy. Watching them, Judith was able momentarily to dismiss her secret fear that he would choose his father over her. Zach would be acting differently, wouldn't he, if he had already talked to his dad and planned to leave forever?

Their bedtime ritual seemed more precious than ever. Her lips lingered on Sophie's cheek, then Zach's. "I love you," she whispered, and he answered, "I love you, too," like always.

When she woke up in the morning, Zach was gone.

INSOMNIA HAD RULED the first hours of the night. Not until 3:00 a.m. did Judith fall into a heavy sleep. The shrill of the alarm clock at seven was not welcome. She groaned and turned it off, then stumbled into the bathroom. She showered every morning before waking the kids. Her preparations for the day always took longer than theirs, and this way, she got a head start.

Usually a hot shower swept away the cobwebs of sleep, but not this morning. She felt dull when she went into the kids' bedroom, a towel still wrapped around her head.

Zach's bed was empty and...well, not made, but neat. He was such a quiet sleeper. He must have gotten up while she was in the shower. Sophie slept soundly, her lips pursed and her knees drawn up to her tummy, so she formed a small round lump under the covers.

Judith started toward Sophie's bed to wake her, when a sense of disquiet penetrated her tiredness. The house was awfully silent, she realized uneasily. Zach usually came into the bathroom as soon as he got up. Where could he be?

And then something she should have noticed right away struck her. Hercules had not greeted her at her bedroom door. He lived for her to get up! Where was he? Her heart stumbled over a beat and she rushed out of the bedroom.

"Zach?" she called. "Hercules?"

Silence. The kitchen was dim and quiet; the living room the same. Back to the bedrooms. Her breath came in panicky gasps now. He wasn't in her room. The bathroom was just as she'd left it, the damp bath mat still on the floor. Sophie's Barbie dolls sprawled across the floor of the spare bedroom, most half-dressed, arms and legs poking up, naked torsos twisted. As always, Zach's toys were tidily ordered on shelves.

Mindless with fear now, Judith returned to the children's bedroom and peered under beds and in the closet. On her knees beside Zach's bed, she lifted his pillow with a shaking hand. His pajamas were neatly folded there. The same pajamas he'd worn last night.

Then he had gone deliberately.

She clapped a hand to her mouth to quell the rising nausea. No! She wouldn't believe that! He was outside; he had to be. He'd done something without thinking, like the time Sophie had wandered over to Ben's barn without telling anyone.

She found the front door unlocked. She knew she'd checked it before bedtime. So Zach had gone out. Please God, just to play or walk the dog.

But he was nowhere. She called and called without hearing an answering voice or bark. How could the dog have vanished, too? And so silently?

Think! she ordered herself. *What should I do?*

Judith ran back into the house and grabbed the phone. Her hands trembled so that she had to try twice before she succeeded in dialing Ben's number.

He answered on the first ring. "McKinsey."

"Ben." Her voice was high, shaky. "This is Judith. Is Zach there?"

"Not that I know of." He didn't hesitate a second. "I'll search the barn. Shouldn't he still be in bed?"

"Yes, but he's gone. His pajamas are folded under his pillow."

"The dog didn't bark?"

"He's…he's gone, too."

"I'll look here and be right over."

She could do nothing but stand beside the phone, quaking all over. *No. It couldn't be happening again. Not this. She couldn't endure it.*

Not more than two minutes passed before she heard footsteps bound up the porch steps. She met Ben at the door, hope and terror warring within her.

He shook his head. "I've reported him missing. We'll start hunting immediately. You have no idea when he went?"

Her teeth began to chatter. "Oh, God—oh, God..."

Ben grabbed her upper arms and gave her a shake. "Help me here, Judith. Don't fall apart."

She nodded, gritting her teeth to stop the chattering.

"When?" he repeated insistently.

"I don't know." She closed her eyes. "He went to bed at nine o'clock. No! Wait! I couldn't sleep. I was awake till three so he couldn't have crept out before then or I would have heard him."

"We'll find him."

Without warning, his arms closed around her, and for a few seconds, she let herself lean against his big, solid body, drawing strength. She straightened and he set her aside at the same moment.

"I'll make some more calls," he said.

Judith hurried back to check on Sophie, but her daughter still slept. For a moment she sat on Zach's bed, smoothing her hand over his pillow, touching the flannel of his pajamas. "Please come home," she whispered, and went back to the kitchen.

The day was as terrible as that other one she remembered too well. She had to call her in-laws first; they hadn't heard from Rylan and were clearly shattered by the news. Her parents were equally shocked and ready to rush to Mad River. Judith put them off for the moment. She didn't have the energy to reassure anyone else.

Uniformed police were everywhere; eventually search-and-rescue volunteers joined them. After studying the pictures of her son that she took from an album, they fanned out from her house in well-spaced lines, searching the dry hillside and pasture, crossing the highway to the hiking trail on the other side.

When they started out, Judith protested. "Rylan must have him! They won't be out in the woods! Can't you put up roadblocks or something?"

"The state patrol is watching for him," Ben said heavily, "but we can't do much when we don't know what kind of vehicle they're in. And we have to hunt here...just in case."

In case what? But Judith didn't want to think about the possibilities.

Sophie cried when she found out her brother was gone. Judith called Carol Galindez to tell her why she wouldn't be in; in an impossibly short time later, Susan showed up with Nadia.

After a quick hug, Susan said, "I'm home with Nadia anyway. I'll keep both the girls with me today—and tonight, if Zach hasn't been found. You need to concentrate."

Part of Judith wanted to cling to her remaining child. Another part knew how emotionally fragile she was. She'd only frighten Sophie. Besides, there had to be something she could do, some way of helping to find Zach.

So she nodded, hugged her daughter so hard that Sophie squeaked a protest, and watched with hot tears in her eyes as the station wagon drove away.

She turned to find Ben behind her. She felt him take in her distress with one glance. His own face showed a strain that echoed hers. "We'll find him. That bastard isn't going to get away with—'' He bit off the end of his sentence.

On a trembling breath, Judith nodded. "Thank you for coming. Considering…''

He swore. "I'd be here no matter what. My God, Judith, you must know how I feel about you.'' A spasm worked down his jaw muscles. "All of you.''

"You didn't want them.'' The words spilled out without volition, stark pain in her voice. Unreasonably, she felt the two things were connected: Ben had walked out because he didn't want children, and now she had lost her son. If Ben had been here…

Ben swallowed hard. "Did he miss me?''

She hurt too much to acknowledge that he hurt as well. "Do you care?'' she asked bitterly.

His eyes darkened. "I care.''

"Yes!'' Judith cried. "Yes, he missed you! He didn't understand.'' Tears burned her eyes again and she turned away, hunching her shoulders. "He's been so mad at me. But he trusted you!''

Ben's fingers bit into her upper arms. She felt the steel, heard the raw agony in his voice. "I will find him if it's the last thing I ever do.''

He disappeared again for a while. She made coffee for the searchers and numbly answered the questions they asked. Eventually Ben returned and had her go through Zach's drawers and closet to see what might be missing. She had to hunt through the dirty laundry, too, before she was certain: he wore a pair of jeans and a red-and-blue-striped T-shirt.

"And his basketball shoes.'' On her knees in front of his closet, she looked up at Ben, waiting in the doorway of the bedroom. "But he didn't take anything else. He loves his Boston Bruins jersey. He'd never leave that. He can't have packed anything!"

"Maybe he didn't intend to go far or be gone long," Ben said.

She felt stirrings of hope again. "Then where is he?"

"And where the hell is the dog?"

Her fingers twined together. "You don't think… Rylan would have…"

Ben spared her from putting the horror into words. "Killed the dog? Not if he wanted Zach to go willingly."

"That's true." More cause for hope.

Rylan had hated anything with hair. No pets, he'd insisted from the beginning. She hadn't argued; that was before she began to resent the fact that he always had to have his way. Rylan wouldn't like Hercules. He might hide his feelings for a few days, but eventually he would want things his way, and that wouldn't include the dog. Unlike Sophie, Zach was old enough to sneak away from his father when he got the chance. Judith had made sure he'd memorized their new phone number the first week.

Depression descended again like a thick fog, all the grayer because she'd momentarily glimpsed a light through the clouds. Even if Zach changed his mind, he might be afraid to call, convinced she'd be mad. Besides, he'd always been stubborn. He wouldn't want to admit he was wrong.

Earlier, Ben had asked Judith if she had a photograph of Rylan. She'd kept some for the kids' sake, so they could see their faces in his as they grew up. She handed him the best one. She overheard him talking with one of his officers about faxing it to the state patrol. After making a phone call in the late afternoon, he left again, Rylan's photograph in his hand. She watched him go without curiosity, so encapsulated in sorrow and fear that the activities around her seemed meaningless.

He came back swearing. At the sight of the anger tightening his face, Judith rose slowly to her feet, fright clutching at her. He had news. Oh, God, he had news. She pressed her hands to her chest, trying to hold back the sickness and the terror rising within her.

His eyes met hers and he came straight to her. "No, no, Judith." He drew her roughly into his arms. "We haven't found Zach. I did get confirmation that Kane was here in town, though."

She drew back and echoed numbly, "He was here."

"For the past four days. I checked all the motels, but I didn't go far enough. He rented a room for the week. The landlady IDed him from the photo." Ben swore viciously. "If I'd just checked the rooms for rent, too..."

"You didn't really believe he was coming, did you?"

He jerked his head to one side, as though his neck hurt. "Yeah," he said roughly. "I believed it. I was just so goddamned arrogant I told myself the son of a bitch couldn't snatch any kid out from under *my* nose."

A tiny arrow of understanding and compassion penetrated her grief. She reached a hand out to him. "Ben..."

"I screwed up big-time, didn't I?"

"No. It's not your fault." Angry as she had been at him, she had to make him see the truth. "Rylan's the bad guy, no one else."

His eyes showed his disbelief. "The worst thing is, the landlady never saw his car. He said he'd gotten off the Greyhound bus. In case that's true, we're checking used-car lots and ads from last week's paper, but we haven't come up with anything yet. So we're no further ahead than we were. And it's my goddamn fault."

Before she could protest again, he swung away to answer a question from one of the other police officers. She didn't know what she could have said, anyway.

Would it have made any difference if he had been around? Would Zach still have wanted his father? Judith had no way of knowing.

By nightfall, the search-and-rescue team had given up. Without any reason to believe Zach had set out on foot, they wouldn't expand their search radius.

Susan called, offering to keep Sophie. Judith agreed. She was exhausted, her strength sapped by the emotional roller coaster she'd been riding on all day. She couldn't be a parent to Sophie, not yet. It was an effort to hold the telephone, to get up to go to the bathroom, to thank the men and women who'd spent their day searching for her son. One by one, they touched her hand or paused in front of her to say a few kind words on their way out.

Eventually only Ben was left. "Are you hungry?" he asked.

"Hungry?" She had to force her sluggish thoughts to focus on the question. "No. No, I'm not hungry."

"Have you had anything to eat today?"

"Eat?" she repeated dully.

"I didn't think so." He left her sitting in the living room, her knees drawn up to her chest, her arms circling her legs. The closer she hunched within herself, the less she had to be aware of what happened around her. It was possible to float in limbo if only the world didn't keep intruding. Annoyingly determined not to let her withdraw, Ben returned with a mug full of a steaming liquid.

He set it on the coffee table in front of her. Soup. Noodles floated in the broth.

"I told you I wasn't—"

"You've got to eat. Just sip it."

Ben sat next to her, his large body curiously comforting. Too weary to argue, she followed the urgings of his strong hands and put her feet back on the floor and wrapped her fingers around the handle of the mug.

"Okay, now take a sip," he said gruffly.

Liquid heat flowed down her throat, bringing life with it. But life hurt terribly, and she whimpered a protest, trying to set down the mug of soup.

"No," he said in that tender, gravelly voice. "Come on, another sip. You've got to stay strong."

Why? she wanted to ask him. She couldn't do anything. Rylan had gotten to Zach despite her vows to protect her children. She was a failure as a mother;

otherwise this wouldn't be happening again. She wasn't strong—she couldn't be.

But she sipped because somehow the mug was at her lips, tilting toward her, and the soup was spilling into her mouth. Ben insisted she drink the entire cup, making a sound of satisfaction once she'd finished. Before she could curl again into her fetal position, he leaned back against the couch and drew her into an embrace so all-encompassing she felt as if she were part of him, his heat and strength enveloping her.

It was nothing like the times they'd made love, she knew; his gentle touch held no passion. With a sigh she rested her head on his chest. Her eyes closed, and she focused on the beat of his heart, steady and strong. The rhythm was something to cling to in the midst of her turmoil; every time disturbing, terrifying thoughts crept into her mind, she tugged herself back by listening to the beat of Ben's heart.

He kissed the top of her head and murmured something against her hair; she didn't even try to make it out. She must have slept, because she opened her eyes suddenly and was disoriented. Where was she?

She must have whimpered, struggled, because a voice the texture of velvet whispered, "Sh, sh," and a hand massaged her back, soothing her like a frightened animal that could only be calmed by a familiar kindly touch.

And the heartbeat was still steady beneath her ear, the vibration rocking the very wall of his chest. Ben.

Oh, God. *Zach*. The horror overwhelmed her. She cried out, "Zach, please be all right, please come home, oh, God, please," and the tender voice murmured comfort. Ben held her through racking sobs, then blew her nose, wiped her cheeks, kissed her wet eyes.

The night passed that way, although she was unconscious of time. She slept, woke, remembered, imagined the worst—*Rylan wasn't monster enough to kill his own son to pay her back, was he?*—cried hot tears and slept again. At one point Ben turned off all the lights, and terror rose in Judith's throat.

She struggled upright. "Zach likes some light! Please! If he comes back, the house can't be dark. Please," she begged.

Immediately Ben switched on a table lamp. Golden light spilled from it, and she sagged from the release of tension. "He likes his door open four inches," she explained, sensing she was being irrational but not caring. "That's enough to make him feel safe."

The knowledge that he hadn't been safe, that she hadn't kept him safe, was enough to bring tears again. Ben's shirt was damp from the last bout, but the weave of the cloth and every wrinkle were familiar now, her own security blanket.

Eventually she awoke to gray dawn coming through the windows. This time Judith knew where she was, and why. Ben's arms were heavy around her. His deep, slow breathing told her he slept. She drew back. His face was slack, his lashes thick and dark against his cheeks. His mouth softened in repose; the rigidity left those broad shoulders. She touched his hair, bemused by the sprinkles of gray. Were there more?

When Judith slipped away, Ben's arms fell to his sides, and though he shifted on the couch, he didn't

awaken. The kitchen clock said it was seven-thirty,
later than she'd thought. She went quietly to the front
door, unlocked it and stepped out on the front porch.
From a seat on the top step, she gazed toward the road,
where Zach must have stolen in the early morning.

*Yesterday. Only yesterday morning. It seemed like
forever since she had discovered him missing. Could
it really be so recently?*

Had Rylan somehow signaled Zach that he was
waiting? Or had they made an assignation? Surely,
surely, Rylan wouldn't have asked a nine-year-old to
walk alone in the darkness all the way to the main
road! Emptiness yawned inside Judith. *Had her son
wanted to go that much?*

The air held a bite and she wondered when the first
real snowfall would come. The one dusting of white
they'd had didn't count. Only days before, she and the
kids had anticipated snowball fights and sledding, but
now Judith couldn't bear the idea of snow blanketing
the landscape. Not with Zach out there. If Rylan hadn't
kidnapped him, if he'd…

She physically jerked from the picture that formed
in her mind. No! Not that! That wasn't what she
meant. She'd meant if they'd fled on foot. Yes, that
was it. If they were trying to get away on foot and by
hitchhiking, she dreaded the weather turning cold.
Zach hadn't even taken a jacket.

Why hadn't he? Did he think his mother wouldn't
want him to take his things? It made no sense that he
hadn't packed even the duffel bag he'd taken to Tim's
when he spent the night. Could Rylan have dragged
him away?

But then she remembered the pajamas. No. He'd gone by choice. Still...

Had Rylan actually been in the house? Maybe looked down at Sophie and decided she'd be too much trouble this time?

Judith wrapped her arms around herself to stop the shaking. With a violence she hadn't known she harbored, she wanted to kill Rylan Kane. She should be shocked at herself, but she wasn't. He deserved it!

Still she sat there, unable to achieve yesterday's numbness, shivering because she *wanted* to suffer. How could she go about day-to-day life, eat breakfast, sip a cozy cup of tea, shower and dry her hair, when inside she was hollow, hurting, as if her heart were ulcerating?

A footstep sounded behind her, and the screen door opened. "'Morning."

At least he hadn't said *good* morning. She hunched her shoulders and didn't respond.

"What are you doing out here?"

She turned slowly to face Ben and saw the shock on his face before he succeeded in hiding it. She must look dreadful. She didn't care.

He spoke gently. "I'll make us something to eat—" The ring of the telephone interrupted him, and tension sharpened the lines of his face.

The sound quivered through her body like live wire. Was there news? Could they—*oh, God, please*—could they have found him? But how, when they didn't know where to look?

"I'll get it," Ben said, and vanished inside.

She froze, paralyzed by the need to follow him and her fear of hearing the worst.

The conversation was short. He reappeared, an odd expression on his face. "That was Carol Galindez. I guess Tim told the other kids about Zach disappearing, and Tony came to the office and said he might know something."

CHAPTER FOURTEEN

BEN INSISTED THAT Judith shower, although she didn't want to waste precious minutes, but a glance in the mirror told her he was right; she couldn't appear at school like this. She didn't take the time for makeup or to dry her hair, just ran a comb through the wet strands and bundled them into a scrunchie.

Neither spoke on the drive to town, which was made in record time. Ben swerved to a stop at the red-painted curb right in front of the main entrance.

Carol waited in the doorway to the administrative offices, her brown eyes warm with compassion. Taking Judith's hands, she said, "I'm so sorry. You know we'll do anything, anything at all."

Thank God she hadn't asked how Judith was. The answer must be written on her face.

Judith nodded, the sting of tears in her eyes.

Seeing them, Carol said swiftly, "Come on in. Tony's waiting."

At the sight of them, he jumped up from the cushiony visitor's chair beside the principal's desk. When his gaze reached Judith, his eyes widened with the same shock she had seen in Ben's. So it hadn't been only tangled hair and puffy eyelids that had taken him aback. The horror inside her must show on the outside.

Carol stopped just inside the door, letting Ben take control. He wasted no time on niceties. "What do you know, Tony?"

"I...the other day when I went to the bathroom..." Tony faltered, his gaze sliding away from Judith. "See, the boys' bathroom is right by the doors going outside to the playground, you know. And I, well, I just kinda looked out."

Ben raised an eyebrow in disbelief. "All you did was look out."

"Well...maybe I went outside, just for a minute, see. We were having a spelling test, and I hurried...." Nobody said a word. He sounded desperate. "It really was just a minute. I swear!"

Judith wanted to scream, *I don't care what you did! What did you see?* Ben shot her a glance.

"Tony," he said, "we appreciate you coming to us like this. You won't be in trouble, no matter how long you were outside. I promise, no punishment."

"Oh." The boy stole a look at her. His Adam's apple bobbed. "Anyway, it was fourth-grade recess. And I noticed Mrs. Kane's son over by the fence, talking to a man outside. Zach had his back to the fence, and the guy was out on the sidewalk just kind of leaning against the building. Like he was waiting for something. You know? But I could see that even though they were pretending not to have anything to do with each other, really they were talking. And...and Chief McKinsey said I should notice things." Shyly, he added, "If I want to be a cop like him."

Ben gave an approving nod. "Sounds like you're already pretty observant."

Tony's cheeks flushed with pleasure.

Ben laid the photograph of Rylan down on the principal's desk. "Was this the man?"

"Yeah!" Excitement shot through his voice. "Yeah, that's him! Who is he?"

"Zach's father."

"Oh." Bewilderment clouded his face. "Then why were they pretending they didn't know each other like that?"

Judith heard herself say calmly, "Because he's not allowed to see Zach or Sophie. He...is not a good parent."

"Oh," the boy said again. He was thoughtful a moment. "Then why did Zach...?"

"He hasn't made up his mind how he feels about his father. I guess when it's your own dad, deciding not to love him anymore is hard."

Clearly, Tony understood that one. "Uh, I'm sorry, Mrs. Kane."

Tears in her eyes again. Through them, she said, "Thank you, Tony. And...and thank you for coming to us."

"I don't know if it helps," he said uncertainly, looking at Ben.

The police chief leaned against the desk. "The thing that would help most, Tony," he said almost casually, his intensity banked, "is if you saw the man leave. Maybe get in a car."

"Yeah. Sure I did." Tony looked from one to the other of them, as though he felt the instant electricity.

"I mean, they were acting weird, you know. I went outside because I saw them. The guy left after just a minute. That part was weird, too. I mean, there were lots of places he could have parked along the street right there, but he crossed and went, like, halfway down that other street...."

"You mean the cross street? Gilman?"

"Yeah, that one. And then he looked around real careful, like he wanted to make sure no one saw him, before he got in this car. It was blue and real shiny, like maybe he'd rented it. My grandma had to rent one once, and hers was the same car, except red. A Chevy Caprice. I remember it, because it was cooler than her real car—the one that was broken down when she had to rent," he explained.

Hope, real hope, swelled in Judith, glorious and intoxicating. They could find him now, couldn't they?

Ben gripped his shoulders and looked straight into his eyes. "A blue Chevrolet Caprice. You're absolutely sure?"

Tony nodded. "I even saw the license plate, 'cuz then he drove by." A frown crinkled his earnest expression. "I don't remember all of it, but the first two letters were UG. Like ugh, you know?"

"UG." Ben's teeth showed in a predatory smile. "Good boy. Now we'll get him."

"I did help?" Tony watched in bewilderment as the police chief strode out.

"Yes." Judith's smile trembled on her lips. "Bless you, Tony. You'll make a very fine police officer."

MORE WAITING, Judith realized. By the time Carol sent Tony back to class with a quiet word in his ear, Ben had already commandeered the office telephone to put out an all-points bulletin on a blue Chevy Caprice, license plate UG—the rest unknown.

After her first euphoria, Judith's optimism began to wane. Zach had disappeared more than twenty-four hours ago. If the car was a rental, Rylan could have turned it in and gotten a different one, or—if they no longer had Hercules—they could have taken a bus or train or even a plane. In that length of time, they could be two states away or more.

Once the essential calls were made, Ben suggested they get home, just in case Zach phoned. Judith went straight to the kitchen. No red light blinked on the answering machine. When the phone did ring, it was for Ben, just as all the calls that came in throughout the morning were.

Judith had to do something. Anything. She began cleaning windows, rubbing in furious circles as though every smear she obliterated was Rylan, or her fear, or every mistake she'd ever made.

At eleven, Judith heard a car door slam. She glanced in the kitchen, but Ben was on the phone again, a map spread out on the table. He seemed not to have heard the car out front.

Hesitantly she opened the door. Susan had parked her station wagon right in front of the steps. Sophie hopped out, Nadia right behind her.

Judith rushed out onto the porch. "Sophie?"

"Mommy!" Face alight with joy, Sophie dashed up the steps and flung herself into Judith's arms. "I mithed you," the five-year-old whispered from her mother's fierce embrace. "And Zachawy, too."

"Zacha..." Crouching to be at her daughter's level, Judith drew back, swiping at her tears. "You lost a tooth. No, two teeth!"

"Yeth." Sophie grinned proudly. "Nadia bumped me, and they both fell out!"

Susan smiled ruefully over Sophie's head. "The tooth fairy visited. How could she resist? I bet she doesn't get two in one trip very often."

Judith felt a surge of unreasonable jealousy. She'd missed so much because of Rylan. Now this, too!

She summoned up a big smile. "You look just like our Halloween jack-o'-lantern. If only you'd lost those teeth sooner, we wouldn't have had to dress you up to go trick-or-treating!"

"Mommy!" her daughter reproved.

The front door stood open as Judith had left it. Now Ben came out, letting the screen snap shut behind him.

Sophie went right to him. "Thee," she commanded, baring her teeth.

He cocked a dark eyebrow. "Thee?"

"Thee!" she repeated more emphatically, pointing at her mouth.

He crouched in front of her and inspected the evidence. "Where in tarnation did your teeth go?" He pretended to scowl. "Okay, who punched you?"

"Nobody!" Sophie trilled with laughter. "Nadia. But she didn't mean to." She smiled happily. "The tooth fairy came and brought me two whole dollars!"

"Thank you," Judith murmured to Susan. "You've been wonderful."

"Any news?"

"We...we know it was my ex-husband, and what car he was driving. Ben is hopeful now."

Susan gave her a quick hug that said more than words.

Judith looked back at Ben in time to see Sophie wrap her arms around his neck and kiss his cheek. What had he said? She was more startled yet when he kissed her small daughter back on her round, soft cheek.

Satisfied, Sophie promptly whirled away. "Let's go get some Barbies, like we said."

Smiling shyly at the adults, Nadia followed her inside.

Ben swiveled to watch the girls go, his expression peculiar. The screen door banged and their chattering voices became more distant. He gave his head a shake, then rubbed his fingers under his eyes. When he turned to face Judith, his eyes were red. Tiredness, Judith couldn't help wondering, or an emotional reaction to Sophie's unbidden gesture of affection?

"More news," he said quietly, those dark eyes steady on Judith's face. "The Seattle PD tracked down the seller of the Chevy Caprice. Private owner, had an ad in the *Seattle Times*. Now we have the full license-plate number. And since the car's not a rental, the likelihood is good that Kane is still driving it."

"But he could have gotten so far already. He could be in California or Arizona or Montana." Judith hesitated, then put into words one of her worst fears. "What if he took Zach into Canada or Mexico? Will I ever get him back?"

The desolation in her voice brought him across the

porch to grip her hands. Out of the corner of her eye, she saw Susan go quietly into the house.

"Chances are they're still in the U.S. Canadian and Mexican customs are supposed to check ID. If a child is with only one parent, they require a letter from the other parent giving permission for the child to leave the country. I know it's not foolproof," he admitted, forestalling her. "The letter can be forged, but your ex-husband wouldn't have any ID for Zach at all."

"That's true," she said hopefully.

"Besides—" Ben's jaw had a grim set "—we have to ask ourselves what Zach is doing and thinking right now. Is he a willing passenger? If not, his father won't dare approach a border crossing."

Pain crashed through her without warning. "You know Zach must have gone willingly, no matter what I want to think. The way he folded his pajamas… Rylan didn't drag him out."

"Those pajamas are the only evidence he went of his own volition. There is no evidence that he intended to be gone for any length of time. He didn't take anything of value to him."

Judith searched his face, longing to find certainty there, hungry to believe him. But she had to tell the truth. Not even to herself would she lie.

"That's…not true. He took Hercules. He…he didn't like sharing him. Especially with Sophie."

Ben didn't look impressed. "Did you have brothers or sisters?"

She frowned. "No. I'm an only child. Why?"

"I remember the way my brothers fought." He gave a grunt that might have been amusement. "Hell, one minute they were friends, the next Eddie would give John a black eye. Same thing with Nora. They'd let her tag along sometimes, no matter what their friends said, then the next day they'd torment her until she cried, and then laugh about it." His large hand cupped her cheek. "That's what siblings do. I've seen Zach be nice to his sister. They play together, don't they? Just because he says rotten things sometimes doesn't mean a hell of a lot."

Hardly aware she was doing it, Judith leaned her face against his hand. "You think I've been worrying too much."

"About that, yeah. Zach doesn't hate Sophie's guts. He's not running away because he won't share you with his sister. That's what you're afraid of, isn't it?"

The acute perception in Ben's brown eyes was unexpectedly comforting. He *knew* her. Right now she needed someone who did.

"Yes," she said on a sigh. "I'm afraid that I've given Sophie too much attention and left him out. I know I didn't realize how hurt he was because his dad took her and not him. I think even he knows how perverse that is—he didn't *want* to go, not then—but it hurt anyway. Does that make sense?"

"Hell, yes." Ben gave a grunt of frustration. "The damn phone's ringing again. I'll be back."

Sophie packed clean clothes and Susan left with the girls again, insisting that she didn't mind, that Judith needed to focus on Zach. As the station wagon drove away, Sophie turned her head and was still looking back when Judith couldn't make out her face anymore. Fresh guilt clutched at her; did Sophie feel abandoned anew? Should they be clinging together, proof that their family couldn't be torn apart? But she reminded herself of how cheerful Sophie had been. How happily she'd collected the Barbies she wanted to take with her. No. It was better this way. She was young and needed to be cushioned from her mother's anguish.

While Judith was seeing her daughter off, Ben had slapped together sandwiches for lunch. He watched like a hawk while she ate, only nodding with approval when she swallowed the last bite.

After lunch, she sat at the table watching him as he got on the phone again. He seemed to be nagging, cajoling, reminding.

"He's out there somewhere," she heard him say sharply. "Goddamn it, we're going to find the bastard!"

Might-have-seen reports came in, too. Some Ben dismissed easily. Others were possible, he admitted, though unlikely. On the map before him, Ben put small xs where the possible sightings placed either the car or the man and boy. They were too scattered to all be true. If Ben had been hoping for a clear trail, it had yet to appear.

She stopped listening to the conversations until Ben picked up the phone after it rang yet again.

One word penetrated. "Eddie?"

Wasn't that Ben's brother? The one he'd said wouldn't come to a family Christmas celebration if he knew Ben would be there? Ben's office staff must have told his brother where Ben could be reached.

"Anne's back?" Ben listened. "Yeah, she's probably right. Counseling can't hurt. I wish I'd learned to speak my mind twenty-five years ago. Listening to other people wouldn't have hurt, either.''

What did he mean? Judith wondered distantly.

Back still to her, Ben grunted. "Yeah, Christmas sounds good. I have horses.... Uh-huh, sure, the kids can ride.'' His shoulders hunched, as though the images of children astride his horses had punched through any momentary pleasure he'd felt in talking to his brother. "I can't stay on the phone, Eddie. Something's happened.''

When he started telling his brother about Zach, she hung on every word, reliving each agonizing moment of the past day and a half. She was gasping by the end, when he said quietly, "I'll get him back, Eddie,'' Ben said quietly. "You'll meet him at Christmas.''

Please let it be true, Judith prayed, jumping to her feet and rushing to the bedroom. Laundry. There must be dirty clothes. She had to occupy herself.

Behind her, she heard Ben say in a husky voice, "I've missed you, Eddie. Thanks for calling.''

He must have his family back. She was glad for him; she knew she would be—at another time—when her own pain hadn't worn her to numbness only thoughts of Zach could penetrate.

The afternoon stretched into forever. She ran out of things to do or the energy and purpose required to do them. Finally she sat on the porch swing, a magazine spread on her lap so that Ben would think she was still succeeding in distracting herself.

Zach and Rylan could be anywhere by now. What if they *had* left the country? It happened, she knew it did. Would it be possible to regain custody even if they were found?

The gray weight of despair settled over her. She stared unseeing at the barren lawn, the rutted lane, the dry grass in the pasture. The sun had disappeared behind the nearest ridge, and the night's chill crept along in the shadow of dusk.

Another night. Dear God, she couldn't bear another night. Or another, or another, or another. Yet she knew she must; she had done it before. But how? She didn't remember.

The phone was ringing again. She'd quit feeling a surge of hope every time it rang. It would be someone who remembered seeing a blue car in Bellevue or Boise or Reno. Places Rylan would probably never go.

The murmur of Ben's voice came through the screen door. She heard him thank someone. His footsteps approached; he came out onto the porch and sat beside her. She looked up dully, and her heart gave a bang, as if someone had shocked it into beating again.

The frustration and anger she'd become accustomed to seeing on Ben's lean, dark face were gone, replaced by something so intense, so triumphant, she could only whisper, ''What?''

''We've found him.'' He didn't smile, not yet. ''They're in Bend, Oregon. A resort near Mount Bachelor. Kane rented a cabin and parked behind it so the car couldn't be seen. But we got lucky. A state patrolman who'd been off duty the past two days remembered seeing the car pull in. The resort owner confirms the description, says the little boy didn't look very happy. They have a dog with them, a yellow lab, he thought."

"Oh, my God," she breathed. "It is them."

"Deschutes County officers have gone out to make the arrest. They'll call as soon as it's over."

She didn't know what she felt. Emotions swirled and erupted as if they were some dangerous chemical compound being experimentally mixed. Terror and exultation, hurt and longing... A whimper escaped her. "I'll go down there. I'll leave right away." She looked around blindly, knowing she needed to find her purse and car keys, not remembering where they were or even where she was.

Ben's firm grip stopped her from rising to her feet. "Not until they call and we know they have Zach safe. Then *we'll* drive down there. Do you really think I'd let you go alone?"

He might as well have thrown a spark to the volatile mix.

"Let me? He's *my* son, not yours! And I managed to drive across the country to get here!" she flared, then closed her eyes, realizing how ungrateful she sounded. More quietly, Judith said, "You've done so much. I can't tell you how thankful I am, but..." Her anger was doused as quickly as it had been aroused. Releasing a shaky breath, she looked at him pleadingly. "I want this to be for us. My children and me."

Ben's face twisted and he rose abruptly from his seat beside her. He went over to the railing and braced his hands on it, his back to her as he stood looking out at the yard. His shoulders and neck were rigid.

"Yeah," he said without expression, "I said I didn't want them, didn't I?"

Anxiety and hope swirled within her. But then she recalled that the worst part for her hadn't been his rejection of Zach and Sophie; it was knowing he'd denied his own child. If he could do that...

"Yes, you did. Why should you want mine when you didn't even want your own?" She took a breath. "But that's your business. I should never have assumed, just because you were friendly..."

Ben swung in a violent motion to face her, his mouth a thin line. "You had every reason to assume. Good God, I'd been hanging around here like a homeless dog begging to stay! And the kids..." His voice thickened. "I just didn't see what was happening."

Judith gripped the edge of the porch swing so tightly that the texture of the wood imprinted itself on her fingertips. "You were good to Zach and Sophie. That didn't give us any right to think you were ready for a walk up the aisle. It was my inexperience that let me think making love with you meant forever."

Ben scrubbed his hand over his face. In doing so, he stripped away every ounce of pretense and reserve. Everything that saved a man's pride. At the sight of his vulnerability, Judith's heart swelled painfully.

"I told you one thing and I felt another." Ben's voice no longer sounded like his. His throat worked. "I was scared. So damned scared."

"Scared?" she whispered. "Of what?"

"That if I let myself love you, I'd feel trapped someday, and then I'd fail you, and especially the kids." A raw sound came from him. Maybe he'd meant to laugh. "I always told myself I hated being around children. I'd spent enough years hemmed in by them. But lately, thanks to you, I've realized it was more complicated than that. I didn't do so great a job, especially with one of my brothers. I'd told myself I was sacrificing everything for them, that I'd done my best. Scary thought, when one of my brothers ended up hating my guts. Not a very good report card. I must have screwed up with them, and I didn't want that to happen again."

Something he'd said flashed into her mind. "It wasn't true that you're always invited for Christmas, was it?"

"Oh, yeah, I'm invited. Trouble is, if I go, my brother Eddie and his family won't. I know damn well which one of us the rest would rather have there."

"I don't believe it," Judith said fiercely. "You raised them! You gave up so much. They must see that!"

"Funny footnote." Ben massaged the back of his neck. "Just a while ago, Eddie pointed out that I was so busy playing martyr I hung around longer than I was needed. I gave up things I didn't have to, then hated everyone else for making me do it. Nice irony, isn't it?"

Judith stood, although her knees quaked. "We've needed you, and you haven't failed us. I don't believe you ever would. Look at these last two days! You promised you'd get Zach back, and you have."

His mouth twisted again. "*I* didn't get him back. I didn't do anything another cop wouldn't have done."

"That isn't true." Judith found the courage to step

forward, to flatten her hands on his chest. "Don't forget, I've been through this before. The other time—" she made herself remember "—the police went through the motions. They didn't care. They didn't hold me when I cried. They didn't stay all night or make me eat. There was no breakthrough, because they hadn't taught a boy headed for trouble that he could be somebody worthwhile."

"Tony's part in this was just luck," Ben argued.

But his hands reached up to grip hers, and he wasn't pushing her away, which emboldened her.

"It was luck that Tony went to the bathroom at the right time. But the rest wasn't. You didn't fail Tony. And because of that, you didn't fail Zach."

"I almost did." He squeezed his eyes shut. "When you told me he was gone…"

"What?" she whispered, scarcely able to breathe…to hope.

Ben opened his eyes. They were rimmed with red and wet with tears he couldn't hide. "I discovered that I didn't just love you—I loved your kids, too." His chest rose as he sucked in a huge breath. "But I guess I was a little late figuring that out."

"No. Oh, no." Judith wrapped her arms around him and hugged until he did the same to her. "Never too late, Ben…"

"Too late for my own daughter."

"Oh, Ben," she whispered, "I should have listened to you. Will you tell me about her?"

"Are you sure you want…" he began raggedly, then cocked his head. "Hell. The telephone."

"Yes." Now her heart did leap.

He let his arms drop with obvious reluctance, but his eyes never left hers as he opened the screen door. "Coming?"

"Are you kidding?" From somewhere deep within her, a smile dawned. It felt stiff and unfamiliar but, oh, so good. *Zach, you can come home now,* she thought. *This man will be the kind of father worth having.*

"Yeah?" Ben was saying into the phone. His dark eyes never wavered from Judith's. "You've got him." Some of the tension eased from his shoulders. "It went okay?" He listened again, then said, "The boy's mother is standing right here. Can she talk to him?"

Judith's heart threatened to break her rib cage. She reached out slowly and took the phone.

"Zach?"

For a moment she heard only the static of a cell phone. Then a small voice said, "Mom?"

"Zach." Her own voice broke. "You're all right?"

A distinct sniff came across the line. "I'm...I'm okay. Are you mad at me?"

"No. Oh, no!" Tears wet her cheeks. "I've been scared, and I've missed you terribly, but how could I be mad? I love you so much!"

Ben reached out and wrapped his hand around the back of her neck, massaging gently, letting her know without words that he was there for her.

"You never told Dad he could take me skiing, did you?" Zach asked bleakly.

"Skiing?" What on earth...?

"We were only going to breakfast." He spoke in a rush. "I just wanted to see him, and I knew you wouldn't let me. But then he drove all the way to Ellensburg before we stopped, and Dad made a phone call, and then he told me he had a surprise for me. He said he'd always wanted to learn how to ski, and that you'd given permission for me to go, too. He told me things you'd said, like making him promise to buy me a really warm parka, and saying to be careful, and it sounded like you, so I thought..." His voice died. "I was really dumb, wasn't I?"

"Zachary Kane," she said, putting all the love she could summon into her voice, "you're nine years old. You aren't supposed to be able to tell when an adult is lying. Especially when that adult is your own father."

"Yeah, but..."

"No buts. You shouldn't have sneaked out without telling me, but the rest of it wasn't your fault."

Zach sniffled again. "He didn't even really want to ski! He lied about that, too! It was just an excuse! I wouldn't have gone with him otherwise. I could tell he didn't like Hercules. He was just faking when he said he did!"

"I'm sorry," she said helplessly, wanting to hold him, feeling his tears even though she couldn't see them.

"It's okay, Mom."

"Was it scary seeing him arrested?" She'd imagined Sophie having to be physically wrenched from her father, sobbing, reaching out, seeing him handcuffed and led away.... Sophie was young enough that those memories were already blurring. Zach wouldn't forget so easily.

"He tried to get away." Zach let out a hiccuping sob. "He was really nervous and he kept looking out the window, so he saw them before they got all around the cabin. I told him I wouldn't go with him, but he dragged me out anyway. We went out the back door 'cuz the car was right there. But when he tried to push me in, I kicked and screamed, and Hercules bit him. Really hard. He let me go." Satisfaction sounded in his voice, despite the tears. "Dad was bleeding, and he's going to have to have stitches and everything."

"Hercules bit your father?" Judith echoed in astonishment.

Ben mimed disbelief.

"Yeah. He saved me." Zach blew his nose; somebody must have handed him a tissue. Either that, or he was using the hem of his T-shirt, which wouldn't be the first time. "Can we buy him a steak or something?"

"We can buy him a diamond-studded collar if you want." She smiled through her tears. "Kiss him for me, will you?"

"Sure." He sounded suddenly very young. "Mom, how am I going to get home?"

"We're coming to get you," she said firmly. "I'll bet somebody will take you home with them, just for tonight. But Sophie and Ben and I will be on our way as soon as we can. We'll be there sometime tomorrow."

Chief Bennett McKinsey gave her neck a last squeeze and backed up, leaning against the kitchen table, his eyes still lingering on her face.

"Ben, too?" her son questioned.

"Ben, too." She gave the subject of the conversation a saucy smile. "I think you'll be seeing quite a bit of him."

Sounding like his normal self, Zach demanded, "You're not going to marry him, are you?"

Her smile faded. "Would you mind?"

"Heck, no! That would be so cool!" He hesitated. "I mean, if he didn't mind Soph and me. He doesn't, does he?"

"What do you think?"

"He never acted like he did," Zach said doubtfully. "But sometimes he doesn't say what he means."

I told you one thing and I felt another. Had Zach known...? "What do you mean?" she asked cautiously.

"Like, he called Hercules a useless mutt and said he was good for nothing, but then he sneaked him a dog biscuit and scratched him right where Hercules likes it."

Judith smiled. "Ben just doesn't want to admit what a softie he is. I guess we can judge best by what somebody does, though, not what he says."

"Yeah, yeah." She knew he'd scrunched up his nose. "'Actions speak louder than words,'" he mimicked. "Ben doesn't say much, but sometimes I can tell he thinks I did good."

This was not the moment for a grammar lesson. "And it makes you just about burst with pride, doesn't it?"

"Yeah," he said thoughtfully. "I don't know why, but...yeah."

"Well—" she smiled at the man standing with his

arms crossed not three feet away ''—Ben's next action is going to be driving me all the way to central Oregon to pick up my son.'' Without warning, tears sprang to her eyes again. "Zachary Kane," she said fiercely, "I love you. Don't you ever doubt it!''

Then her son gave her a gift greater than pearls. "Why would I doubt it?'' he asked, obviously surprised.

Seeing her weeping, Ben handed her a paper towel. Her turn to blow her nose. He took the phone from her. "Hey, Zach, how do you like Oregon?'' A crooked smile softened his harsh face. "Yeah, okay. We'll see you tomorrow. Do you want to put Lieutenant Beck back on?''

As they talked, Judith sobbed a little more, but happily. She saw that Ben was writing down the addresses and phone numbers they needed to collect Zach tomorrow. Surely, surely, this time it would all be over. Rylan had truly lost his son now; he'd destroyed any chance of ever building a relationship between them. She would never understand the self-destructive choices he'd made. Despite their divorce, he could still have been a real father to his children. Now, please God, they were beyond his reach forever.

What's more, if Ben had meant what she hoped and prayed he had, Sophie and Zach would soon have the father they needed. The father they already loved.

And *she* would have the man she loved.

BEN HUNG UP THE PHONE and cautiously studied Judith. Though she was still mopping up her tears, he didn't miss the glow of happiness that shone from within her. It made him think of that night when she'd left all the house lights on to call him to her. To welcome him, she'd said. He couldn't believe she was really welcoming him now, not the way he wanted her to mean.

That disbelief lent a harshness to his voice. "We still have things to talk about."

"Nothing that can't wait." Her eyes were bright above her tear-stained cheeks. "Oh, Ben, is it really over?"

"You mean Zach's disappearance?" Hell, he was being selfish again. She wasn't happy because of him; it was the fact that her son had been found that had her beaming. "Yeah. It's over. He's safe."

Something in his tone brought a crinkle to her forehead. "You don't mind driving to Oregon?"

He snorted. "I was the one who wasn't going to let you go by yourself, remember? Hell, no, I don't mind. What I would mind is staying here worrying about you."

"I am capable..."

"I know you are." He moved his shoulders uneasily. "I'd go crazy if I had to stay here."

"Ben." Those clear eyes fastened on his, insisting on truth. "Do you love me?"

"God, yes! But there's something we haven't talked about yet."

Her eyes widened. "Something new?"

"Not something new, damn it!" he growled. "The fact that I walked away from a woman I'd made pregnant. The fact that, until a few weeks ago, I never even made any effort to find out whether the baby was a girl or a boy.''

Her voice softened. ''You need to tell me about it, don't you?''

''I need you to know the truth.'' He rubbed his hands over his thighs, scared to death now that the crunch had come. ''You think I'm going to have excuses that make it all right, don't you? But I don't have any. None. You need to decide whether you can live with a man who did something that ugly.''

The crinkles back on her forehead, Judith searched his face. ''Why did you?''

He swore. ''I don't know! I never even considered doing the right thing and marrying her. It just wasn't an option. I told her I didn't want to have children, and she said fine, and the next thing I know she's got tears in her eyes and she's telling me she's pregnant.'' Ben's chest heaved as if he'd run two miles and tackled a bad guy. Himself. He guessed in a way he was tackling himself. ''I...hell. I just panicked. And I really believed she'd done it on purpose. I saw the birth control pills in her bathroom, and a month later that package was still lying there without any more of those little pills punched out. But that's not an excuse,'' he added grimly. ''The little girl Kelly had shouldn't have to suffer because her mother figured wrong about a man.''

''Marrying her wasn't the only thing you could have done,'' Judith said tentatively, taking a step toward him. ''You could have taken responsibility in other ways.''

''I offered money.'' He despised himself for how

glad he was to be able to say that much. "I would have paid child support. Kelly wouldn't take it."

Concern still puckered Judith's forehead. "What did she do?"

"Married someone else. She tells me my daughter has a daddy, thank you very much."

"So maybe she's not suffering."

"No thanks to me," he said from between clenched teeth.

"You said you'd called this...Kelly. What did she say?"

He tried hard to see what Judith was thinking. She wasn't flinching, the way she had that night when he'd told her. On the other hand, she hadn't said, *It doesn't matter. I love you anyway.*

He wasn't even sure he wanted her to. Because it did matter.

"Same thing," Ben said tersely. "'We're doing fine. You didn't want her, so don't bother calling again.'"

She mulled that over, head cocked. She looked absurdly pretty, considering what she'd been through. A few blotches hadn't faded yet from her pale skin, and her hair was falling out of the cloth rubber-band thing that was supposed to be holding it, but the news that Zach was safe had returned the serenity to her face. Nothing he'd told her so far had shaken it.

A terrible thought came to him. Maybe he *couldn't* shake her serenity, because he didn't matter enough to her. Not the way her son did.

She was contemplating him again with an unnervingly thoughtful gaze. "So, what are you going to do?"

"I want to see her." The words were torn from him. "Just once, so I know what she looks like. And then…" He shook his head. "I did what I did. I can't storm into their lives insisting I get visitation rights or anything like that. For all I know, Kelly has gotten a court order terminating my rights. Maybe her husband has even adopted my daughter." He had to swallow at that one. *His* daughter, bearing someone else's name.

"That's true," Judith said, as if she were agreeing with a casual observation. But then she waited.

Ben swore and thrust his hands through his hair. "I figure all I can do is get Kelly to promise that if our daughter ever asks about me, she'll tell her that I want to meet her. We could go from there, but I want her to know that I wish I'd done things differently. That I'd still like to be a father to her, if she needs one."

Judith considered what he'd said, and she kept searching his face as if looking for…what? Insincerity? He endured her scrutiny, feeling as if she were performing open-heart surgery while he was yet conscious.

Finally Ben couldn't stand another minute. "Say something," he said hoarsely. "Tell me what you're thinking."

She pressed her lips together, then smiled tremulously. "I'm thinking that I love you so much it hurts. That I wish that little girl would someday call you 'Daddy.'"

He broke then. Crying like a baby, he took those

couple of steps to go into Judith's arms. And they closed around him with the kind of welcome and comfort and love a man could waste a lifetime wishing for. She cradled his head and kissed his cheek and told, him that a man who cared about any wrongs he'd done and tried to atone for them was one in a million.

When he finally got a grip on himself, Ben lifted his head and roughly wiped his face on his shirtsleeve. Judith smiled at him with such love she was luminous. She made him think of dawn, when the sun had just risen and painted the sky with colors he couldn't even name. There'd been times he'd been so awed by the sight of the sun rising he'd known that anything in the world was worth enduring for this.

She was his dawn.

"Will you marry me?" he asked, knowing he could make anything right if she only said yes. He could give her children what he hadn't known how to give when he was only a child himself.

She laughed softly, and tears shimmered in her eyes again. "Yes. Oh, yes, Ben McKinsey. I'll marry you."

He let free the breath he'd been holding. Cupping her face in his hands, he bent his head, but he didn't kiss her. He couldn't seem to quit feasting on the sight of her face. She was giving him heaven, no matter what kind of sinner he was. He swore then that he would never let her regret her decision.

"Did you mean it?" he asked abruptly. "When you said you'd like to have my baby?"

"More than anything." She tensed under his hands. "Which is lucky, because I'm a few days late. It might mean nothing, but..."

"You might be pregnant."

"Yes."

He had to grit his teeth against the most powerful stab of sexual hunger he'd ever felt. Pregnant. With his baby. Why did knowing her body might be ripening with his seed make him want to rip her clothes off and take her again, as if he had to claim her?

Later, he promised himself. Right now, she needed to get to her son.

"I love you," he said in a voice that couldn't be his. "Shall we head for Bend, Oregon?"

"Yes." Her lips touched his. "Soon," she whispered. "But not yet. We have...unfinished business."

Elation roared through him. The desire ripped free and he captured her mouth with desperate ferocity. "Soon," he agreed as he lifted her into his arms.

HARLEQUIN SUPERROMANCE®

Bestselling author
Ruth Jean Dale brings back

THE CAMERONS OF COLORADO

Cupid, Colorado...

This is ranch country, cowboy country. Land is important—family and neighbors are, too. And you really get to know your neighbors here. Like the Camerons, for instance...

Jason Cameron—ex-rodeo star and all-around ladies' man—has come home to Cupid. His friends and fellow bachelors aren't pleased because Jason is just too much competition on the romance front, charming all the women in the county, young and old. They figure Jason needs to fall for *one* woman and leave the rest alone.

And he does. He falls for Diana Kennedy and falls hard. She's a newcomer who's just bought the local honky-tonk bar. Sparks might fly between them, but Diana's not sure she wants them setting any fires.

Call it CUPID'S REVENGE! (#788)

Available May 1998 at your favorite retail outlet.

COMING NEXT MONTH

#790   THE WALLFLOWER • Jan Freed
Guaranteed Page Turner
Sarah Davidson is the lone witness to a brutal murder. She
has nowhere to run. And only one place to hide.
Masquerading as a high school senior, she tries to blend in
and not be noticed. But no one can ignore her. Especially not
Jack Morgan, her English teacher. Under ordinary
circumstances, he would be the perfect man for her. But he'll
never look at her as a woman unless she reveals her true
identity—and if she does *that* she just might wind up dead.

#791   LIKE FATHER, LIKE DAUGHTER • Judith Bowen
Men of Glory
Adam Garrick is an ex-rodeo cowboy, now divorced, and
owner of the Double O Ranch near Glory, Alberta.
Unexpectedly, he receives a letter from Caroline Carter, the
widow of his closest friend. He hasn't seen Caroline in years,
but she's coming to visit him, bringing her adopted daughter,
Rosie. The adoption was arranged by her husband, and
Caroline has never known the name of the biological father.
But Adam knows.... Can he keep this secret? *Should* he?

#792   BABE IN THE WOODS • Pamela Bauer
Brendan Millar's going to spend the summer in a cabin in the
woods to decide whether or not to become a priest. Along the
way, he'll meet a beautiful woman, help deliver a teenage
runaway's baby and fall in love. The question is: What will
he do when summer's over?

#793   WHEN SPARKS FLY • Lynnette Kent
Tess O'Connor knew when she transferred from the big city
to the Durham County Fire Department that she'd have to
prove herself all over again. What she didn't expect was
to be met with outright hostility. She was an experienced
firefighter—and a damn good one. Qualities team leader
Ray Minetti—who had no problem appreciating her as a
woman—seemed determined to ignore.